TRAGEDY OF POWER

Tragedy of Power

IAN WITHROW

Ink & Quill Press

The Tragedy Of Power

Republished by Ink And Quill Press, 2023

For more excellent works of fiction, visit Inkandquillpress.com

Edited by Hannah Brickey

Foreword

I've chosen to add this foreword in response to the success of the first edition of this novel. Many people approached me regarding the peculiar darkness of The Tragedy of Power. Some commented with concern that the book might be a reflection of my own illnesses.

In short, it is. I've struggled with depression myself for years. I've watched others fight and sometimes lose their battles with it as well. Depression, self-injury, and suicide are an oft-ignored daily reality for millions of people around the globe.

So why use my platform to write a dark, depressing novel? Because much like the story you'll find within these pages, depression often feels like a series of ever-mounting waves. It hangs like an invisible weight on your chest, pushing the air from your lungs so that you don't even think you can call for help.

I'm here to tell you that you can.

By purchasing this book, you're helping support the American Foundation for Suicide Prevention. I'm committed to sending part of all of my sales and subscriptions to AFSP, and I want you to know that I appreciate your assistance in that effort.

A single life lost to suicide is one too many. If you or a loved one is considering taking that drastic step I urge you reconsider, talk to someone.

Help is out there, and it absolutely gets better.

Acknowledgments

I can't properly express the gratitude I feel to all the people who helped make this pipe-dream of mine a reality.

To my beautiful wife, who took on the task of motivating me and providing guidance years before we said our vows, I couldn't have done this without you.

To The Wolfpack, especially Charlie, who stayed up with me long after duty hours for weeks and months on end, offering helpful advice and criticisms; I hope that through this book I can properly honor your help in some small way.

To the fighting men and women of the 139th MPAD; every one of you helped me accomplish this task while we were overseas and I owe the success of having written this novel in great part to all of you.

To the dozens of friends and family members who were interested enough to "pre-read" the manuscript and offer mountains of advice on everything from format to plot, thank you as well. This list of people to whom I owe so much could go on to become its own novel.

So without further ado, please enjoy.

Chapter 1

"Can't you drive any faster?"

As Allison squeezed the armrest of their Suburban with a herculean grip, the joint groaned in protest and seemed in danger of snapping.

"Yes, dear," her mousy, bespectacled husband said in the same tone one might take with a potential jumper at a bridge. He looked down at the speedometer of the vehicle.

55 miles per hour.

He looked back to the road just in time to see the 30 on the speed limit sign on the corner of Losey and Cherry St.

Usually, Allison loved seeing her hometown.

Galesburg was the kind of town that still had parks full of children and front doors that never locked. It had a main street that meant something. At the convergence of many of the major railways in Illinois, it often found itself passed through but rarely stopped in. Old brick roads mixed with newer asphalt and leftover hitching posts from the time when horses and carriages still dotted the streets.

She enjoyed driving slowly through it, taking in the sights of hundred-year-old houses and homey mom and pop shops and restaurants.

But today was different.

Blue and red lit up the rear-view mirror, and a police siren blared out from the squad-car behind them.

John resisted the deep-seated urge to pull over. Instead he

thought of his wife, of his soon to be born baby, and of just what the hell he was going to say to the police once they got to the hospital. This sort of thing always worked in movies, right?

Three blocks from St. Mary's John saw the parking lot, and the mess of traffic blocking the road to the entrance.

St. Mary's Hospital in Galesburg, Illinois is not what you would call a bustling place. Its sprawling halls seldom saw rare diseases or cases of any real importance. Rather, St. Mary's was simply "the hospital" for residents of the sleepy Midwestern town. So it was when Allison Corvidae had moved to Galesburg, and so it had stayed all the years between then and now.
"Dear, I think we may have to stop for the police now-" He began.

Allison, who was generally known for her quiet demeanor, was trying not to scream.
"Jonathan Corvidae, if you stop this car before we get to the door I will *murder* you!" Allison hissed through gritted teeth.
"Honey, it's just that-"
She glared at him.
"Yes, dear."

The bumper of the SUV shot sparks as it rolled across the concrete curb, jerking the occupants and causing Allison to wince in pain.
"Remember your breathing dear: two in, two out."

Jonathan wasn't really sure what he was supposed to be doing at this point, so he dug into all of the romantic comedies they had watched together while they were dating.

It didn't work.
The narrow-eyed stare that Allison gave him raised the hair on his neck, he knew he was lucky that looks could not in fact kill.

One last jolt from banging over the parking barrier at the edge of the parking lot and they were screeching to a halt in front of the emergency room doors. John stepped out and yelled.

"We need a doctor, my wife is giving birth!"

He was immediately tackled by a police officer.

As Allison was wheeled up to a hospital room on the third floor her husband was crammed into the back of a black and white.

"Where's my husband?" Allison kept asking, but the nurses only told her to relax and to breathe. Labor was hard, and complicated, and for the first several hours it seemed no progress was being made.

Late in the night, however, Allison heard a familiar voice calling through the halls of the hospital.

"Allie? Allie, baby, where are you?"

"John!" Allison croaked, and then stronger "Jonathan!" John burst into the room, his shirt un-tucked, his glasses askew, his breathing heavy, but his eyes bright with excitement.

"We're about to put her under, sir. There's some risk here to mom because the baby is not cooperating, so we're going to have to do a C-section. You should stay outside the room, so it's a sterile environment,"

John ignored her, moving instead to the bedside and taking Allison's hand.

"Baby I'm here, it's alright."

"Sir, did you hear me? It is best if you go outside," the nurse stated more forcefully.

John, at a whopping 5 foot 4, didn't tower over anyone, and his slightly doughy 160-pound frame was far from imposing, but the iron in his voice left no room for argument.

"No. I'm staying right here."

The nurse sighed with exasperation and snapped to. Within a few minutes a doctor had appeared, scrubbed in, and prepared for the surgery. John got squeamish at the sight of blood, so he stayed focused on his wife's beautiful blue eyes, her stark black hair, and her radiant smile.

"It's gonna be OK, I'm right here," he told Allison as she slipped off into a drug-induced sleep.

About twenty minutes into the procedure, when things seemed to be going well, John heard the doctor mumble in surprise.

"What the heck? How on earth did that get in there?"

"What is it? What's wrong," said John, turning to look towards the foot of the bed. The doctor was holding up a small but fully-formed feather; it was thoroughly soaked in blood, but definitely a feather. John saw the blood and watched his vision swim, then darken. The last thing he heard as he blacked out was a nurse's voice.

"Sir? Are you feeling ok?"

Then nothing.

"Jonathan," a soft voice spoke into the darkness through which John was swimming.

"John, there's someone you need to meet."

The voice was so warm, so soft, so familiar. Suddenly, as though someone had flicked a light switch, it hit him.

Allison!

Light started to slowly fill his vision from the edges, soon pictures were swimming before him and eventually the hospital room came into focus. Allison was looking over at him from a bed and there was a short woman in scrubs in front of him. He seemed to have been moved into a regular patient room, rather than the operating room.

"Hold still, darlin'," the plump little blonde chided when John tried to look around.

"You took a nasty spill and you got quite a gash on your forehead to show for it! But don't you worry we've got you and momma here all set up in a nice new room, ok?"

Just thinking about the sight of blood again made John queasy, so he shut his eyes tight and tried to stay very still. The woman was putting something cold on his forehead and he could feel her fingers working quickly and efficiently, a dab of some liquid, then covering his cut with some kind of cream.

Finally with a light pat she said, "All right! *I* think it's time you met the little angel, how about you?"

John snapped his eyes open, the thought of his newborn child pushing any lingering discomfort out of his mind.

"Yes! Where is he? I can't wait to meet him," John began to say excitedly.

"She," Allison lightly interjected.

"She?"

Allison chuckled at the stunned expression on her husband's face.

"The doctor said this kind of thing happens fairly often; the ultrasound seems to indicate one way and then the parents get a surprise instead."

Jonathan was lost in thought, though he must have been scowling slightly, because Allison looked at him with increasing worry and finally said, "John, you're not mad, are you?"

"What? No," John said "I just realized we painted her room all blue! What if she hates it? And we've hardly gotten any toys that a girl is likely to enjoy, and we don't even have a girl's name picked out!"

Allison laughed.

It was John's favorite laugh, the deep, belly-laugh that he associated with their most genuine and happy moments.
"Oh John, ever the *pragmatist*. Go and meet Lauren, already!"

"Lauren?" John said questioningly, testing the word for how it sounded in his head and of course teasing his wife with the delay.

"Yep, I love it, Lauren it is."

John stood up with a helping hand from the nurse.

"Are you feeling any dizziness or trouble with your vision," she asked.

John shook his head "no." He wouldn't say he felt great, as his head was pounding pretty hard, but he was definitely unwilling to wait to see his baby girl.

As the nurse walked John through the halls of St. Mary's, she introduced herself. Peggy had worked at the hospital for nearly 12 years, and she loved the maternity ward most of all. Something magical about the first time a parent got to see and hold their child really made her feel close to God. As for himself, John wasn't an overly religious fellow. In fact, the closest he came to regular prayer was when he got stuck behind a train on the way to work and was already running late.

Peggy continued to blather away while John's mind wandered.

John was naturally an introspective man. Apparently Allison had thought it endearing, because it was during one of his deep-thought sessions that she had approached him five years ago in the library of Knox College. Theoretically studying for his French final, he had been staring out the window of the first floor, a half-dozen opened textbooks on the table in front of him and a pen in his hand. The instrument was hovering scant inches over a blank notebook page when suddenly his table was occupied by a body.

A very pretty body.

Jonathan blushed with embarrassment as he remembered how the first thing he had noticed was Allison's short pencil skirt and shapely legs perched matter-of-factly upon his books. So intent had he been on her legs, in fact, that she had to cough lightly to get him to look up at her face.

"We're here, sir," Peggy said softly, in a voice barely over a whisper.

John snapped out of his reverie, he stood in a dimly lit hallway in a quieter section of the hospital. Before him was a large plate glass window and behind it several dozen small beds, most of them empty save five or so with tiny bundles of blue or pink cloth and tiny red-faced babies in various stages of sleep. His eyes scanned the group until he saw her. He didn't know how exactly he knew, but he knew it was his Lauren.

"C-can I go in and hold her?" he stammered softly, fearful his voice might wake the children.

"I'm sorry, sir, no one is allowed in there but hospital staff," the nurse began. "But I can bring her to you."

John waited as she softly opened the door and approached the crib. The nurse leaned down and picked up Lauren, tiny pink blanket and all, and gently brought her out.

All the parenting classes in the world couldn't have prepared John for that first moment he held her in his arms, or the soul-baring beauty of her golden eyes when she opened them.

With a tiny yawn, Lauren stretched, taking her father's breath away. Her small, pudgy fists reached out, and she brushed John's arm softly, instinctively grabbing onto it.

"Holy Mary," gasped Peggy.

The cut on John's forehead itched fiercely, but his attention was wholly on his daughter. He muttered a quiet response to the nurse's exclamation.

"I know, she's so beautiful, look at that blonde hair, and those eyes!"

He glanced up at the nurse, who was oddly silent, she was gawking at him as though he had sprouted a third eye.

"What? What's wrong with you?"

The nurse stared at him, shock in her eyes and said, "I-it's gone!"

"What the hell are you talking about?" John demanded, backing away slightly from the nurse. Lauren started to fidget in his arms and her perfect features broke into a tiny frown, and started to redden.

"Mr. Corvidae, your cut is gone, it's just gone!"

The woman was shaking like a leaf in the breeze. John shifted Lauren onto one arm, cradling her against his chest, he reached up to his forehead. Nothing. It was smooth, unbroken skin; no bump, not even a twinge of pain or tenderness. He felt his eyes grow wide.

"How?"

Lauren screamed. Demonstrating a powerful set of lungs her newborn cries echoed throughout the hall, startling both of the adults and causing the other babies to stir as well.

It was only two hours before the first reporter arrived.

"Kent Dailey, pleased to meet you," exclaimed the tall, well-dressed man as he burst into Allison's hospital room. Peggy followed him, red in the face and squeaking her displeasure.

"Sir, you can't just barge in here! This is a patient room! It is for families and friends! You're going to have to leave or I'll call security!"

Allison was irate. Not only was she unkempt, her hair a mess, no make-up, and wearing nothing but a thin robe, she was also breastfeeding when Kent barged in.

"Get out! I don't care who you are, get out!" shouted Allison, hurrying to cover herself. She looked at John and practically growled. "Who is this man and what the hell is he doing here?!"

John stammered as he began to tell off the intruder, but he was interrupted by the man's commanding baritone.

"Yes, Kent Daily, WGNTV," the man flashed what he certainly thought was a dashing smile and waited a beat, as though he ought to be recognized from his moniker alone. Seeing there would be no dawning revelations, he continued, slightly deflated.

"I'm a reporter," he said with a glint in his eye. "We've heard you were the subject of some kind of miracle. Care to tell us about it sir?"

Dailey accompanied his question, which was stated more like a command, with a blinking audio recorder and a fixed, plastic smile.

Allison exchanged a glance with John, who shifted his gaze nervously between Allison, Peggy, and the stranger. The man questioning them had all the trappings of a sleaze. His cheap suit and product-filled hair oozed smarm. He seemed harmless enough, though, considering. John took his cue, as ever, from Allison. Slowly she nodded, indicating her consent. "What exactly is it you want to know?" John asked slowly, in his manliest and most intimidating voice.

"Start from the beginning, and don't leave anything out. How were you injured?"

The interview lasted all of five minutes; it didn't take long for Kent to realize that the saps he was interviewing knew nothing. The "story" was probably made up anyway, as the man clearly had no head injury of any kind. As he walked down the hallway towards the front door of the hospital, he listened to the audio.

"I don't know, she was in my arms and starting to get fussy and she did this adorable yawn..."

He clicked the recorder off again. Garbage, nothing he could use, no good quotes, and the parents were barely religious, so he couldn't really play that angle either. He strolled past doors labeled as janitors closets and patient rooms when suddenly he came to a halt. The door next to him had a small, plastic sign that said "Security."

I wonder. He tried the handle, it turned, clicked, and the door swung open, revealing a cramped, dimly-lit room full of video monitors and empty soda cans. On top of a messy desk sat an archaic computer and the chair behind it was overfilled by a pudgy, acne-covered man who looked very, very surprised.

"Hey, you can't be in here, man," said the blob in front of him.

Kent scanned the man quickly and found a name tag on his wrinkled, mustard-stained shirt. Dave. Typical, banal sort of name.

"Dave, don't worry, buddy. I just have a quick couple of questions for you. The name is Kent, Kent Dailey."

A short while later Kent was rushing from the room, looking around surreptitiously. As he shut the door behind him, he clutched a USB drive like it was a fabled golden ticket. He had to fight the deep urge to skip down the hallway with glee. This was going to be good.

Allison was still lying in the hospital bed while John napped on the couch. As she flipped through channels on the old, box-style television that was sitting on the bureau across the room from her, she was barely paying attention, preoccupied with thoughts of her newborn baby girl and the mysterious events of the morning. In her left hand, she held the remote loosely and clicked through the channels absent-mindedly, but in her right she held a feather.

It was the strangest thing, a small, ivory feather; the doctor said it looked like a dove or sparrow feather. The real mystery on her mind was how it had gotten into the operating room to fall onto the table during her surgery. It was, after all, impossible that it had been inside her, right? *It wouldn't be the only impossible thing that had happened that morning,* she thought to herself, glancing at the unbroken forehead of her slumbering husband.

"... We bring you this special report, a woman has given birth to a miracle child at St. Mary's hospital in Galesburg, Illinois.."

The TV blared a familiar voice, her eyes snapped into focus just in time to catch the beaming, saccharine face of Kent Dailey.

"Let's roll the video."

A moment of static was followed by a security camera feed of the hallway outside of the newborn room. She saw John walk into the frame, the large cut on his head clearly visible, accompanied by the nurse, Peggy. They spoke quietly for a moment, and then Peggy went inside, returning a moment later with Lauren in hand. John gingerly took her from the nurse. Allison chuckled, he looked so nervous yet so at home with her in his arms. Suddenly she saw Lauren's tiny hand emerge from the blankets and touch John. A small shimmer of light shone from John's forehead and she watched as his cut rapidly faded away.

Allison's jaw popped open; their faces were plastered all over the news. She sat up quickly in bed, letting out an involuntary cry of pain as her stitches pulled tight. John woke instantly at the sound of his wife's pain and rushed to her side.

"What's wrong baby? Are you ok, do I call a doctor?"

Allison couldn't speak, the pain was incredible. All she could do was point at the television. The clip was replaying, with commentary from Dailey and his co-anchor, some ditzy brunette who usually did the weather and was likely chosen for her looks.

"...There you go, folks, you saw it here first. Our very own miracle, right here in Galesburg. More at eleven! For now, let's head over to sports, Mark?"

It took less than a day for the story to spread, and by the next morning reporters from several major news networks were outside the doors of the hospital, begging for interviews.

More startling were the dozens of sick and injured, alongside a small horde of other people who crowded the parking lot. Allison and John had spent the entire morning receiving visitors to their hospital room. It started with a few extra nurses showing up to make conversation, but by mid-morning there was a knock every few minutes.

"I'm tired of it, Allie," said John as yet another knock came to the door. "They shouldn't be pestering us, we're no different from anyone else in this damn hospital. We deserve some privacy!"

John walked to the door and yanked it open, fully intending to give the offending staff member a scathing rebuff. To his chagrin, however, the person at the door was a frail man, startled nearly to falling over by John's sudden and forceful opening of the door.

John gaped, with words stuck in his throat as he was totally off guard. The man before him looked to be in his early thirties. Rail thin and bald, he stood shakily in a hospital gown, one hand using his IV pole for support. A stiff breeze could well finish him off, it seemed.

"I'm very, very sorry, sir," began the man. "My name is Eric. I--I've been here a while and I heard about your daughter." Unsure how to proceed but feeling awkward for having scared the man, John let him continue.

"It's just that... I'm told I don't have much longer," Eric continued, emboldened slightly by John's silence.

"It's cancer, got my dad, too. But here I am, at the end of my rope, and the doctors say my best bet is to get doped up so as to have a 'peaceful transition.'"

He let out a scornful, barking laugh.

"As if that was supposed to make me feel more, I don't know, comfortable with it."

John was not a man who enjoyed awkward conversations, and for some reason, the cold, grim acceptance that he felt from this man as he callously discussed his imminent death put him even less at ease than usual.

"I'm, ah, very sorry for you," he said, kicking himself immediately for how flat and forced it must have sounded.

"Don't be," said Eric. "I brought it on myself, I smoked my first cigarette at eleven years old, I drank myself to sleep every night since I was nineteen. I've wasted my life, what little of it there was, anyway. I'm not even sure why I came up here, I just... I always wanted kids, and when my girlfriend left after I got sick..."

He trailed off a bit, the last bit of light in his eyes dulled as he spoke of his misfortune.

"I," he paused, "I don't suppose you'd like to come in for a moment," John offered, motioning to the room behind him.

"Do you suppose it would be ok?" Eric asked quietly. "It's just that I've never been a part of anything, never seen anything big. I never saw the states, I never traveled overseas or met nobody famous. I guess, maybe I thought if I could just see her, maybe it might give me a sense of having done something before I go."

"John. Let him in, come on over here, Eric, it's a pleasure to meet you," Allison spoke from the bed, Lauren bundled in her arms.

Always the kindest woman, John thought. How could he not be in love with her, with a heart so warm?

Eric gingerly approached the bed, his steps unsteady and slow. As he got near, Lauren let out a coo and reached out with both hands in the air, causing the three adults to chuckle unanimously at her antics.

"She truly is beautiful," Eric began, "may I?"

He slowly reached a finger out towards Lauren's out-stretched hand when Allison nodded her approval.

Eric felt Lauren's tiny hand wrap around his outstretched finger. She was warm and had a surprising strength to her. When she opened her eyes, they were like fresh-forged gold, with a depth beyond her age. As she held his finger, he felt renewed, at peace. His cares and worries slipped away and he felt strengthened. He didn't know what it was he had been searching for, whether something to hope for or a way out, but he knew he had found it. She had given it to him.

John watched carefully.

From a few feet away he could see the change overcome Eric as Lauren gripped his hand. His complexion regained a healthier flush of pink, his back was less bowed, and his eyes seemed brighter.

"Thank you, I'm sorry to have bothered you. I don't even know what I came here to find," stammered Eric. "I'll leave you two alone, they'll be wondering where I ran off to."
John nodded, his mouth slightly agape. He was mystified at the change that had overcome the stranger.

As Eric left, he said, "The doctors say I have a couple of weeks left, if... if you wanted to drop by. I don't have any family or friends really, I'm in 116..."

He was clearly embarrassed as he ducked out of the room. John noticed that his steps had more energy, the pole was less for support than it had been, and he seemed to move with a new purpose.

"Did you see that," breathed Allison, her eyes wide.

She spoke to her husband in a voice barely above a whisper. The two stared at their young child, in awe of the effect she'd had on the man.

The Corvidaes spent the next week shut in at the hospital, hoping to wait out the storm of media outside. Eric stopped by several more times during their stay. Miraculously, he had been declared cancer free just four days after his first meeting with the family. He claimed Lauren was the reason, given the circumstances Allison and John had no doubt he was right. He came in to share the news with them, bringing with him a bottle of champagne, for which they were scolded by an irate Peggy. He was so grateful in fact, he had tried to offer the family money, but they declined. He swore to pay them back somehow, someday.

Finally though, Allison was healthy and whole and they could find no further excuses to stay inside. Far from having abated, the crowd had swelled as rumors flew from nurses who had handled Lauren.

As they stood in the waiting room, staring out the large plate-glass windows at the crowd, Allison snaked her hand out and gripped John's.

"What have we gotten ourselves into here, John," she said, her voice laced with worry.

"How can we raise a child like this?"

John felt the concern in her voice tighten around his heart with vice-grip. He felt the same. Outwardly though, he stayed strong, flashing a smile at his wife, he said in as comforting a voice as he could muster, "One day at a time, dear, one day at a time."

Chapter 2

The last few years had been a whirlwind. It was hard to believe Lauren had just turned eight years old a month ago. In her short life, she had probably traveled more of the United States than anyone her age. Her popularity was higher than ever, and why shouldn't it be? She was received with fervor everywhere she went, providing hope in a dark world, as the tabloids said.

Her abilities hadn't diminished, and over the last few years there wasn't a malady she'd run into that her touch couldn't heal. She had led a charmed life, like something out of a fairy tale. She had never broken a bone, never even gotten so much as a paper cut or a bruise without it healing almost instantly.

There had been a learning curve, certainly--raising a child as...unusual as Lauren hadn't been easy. They had been thrust into the limelight instantly: meeting visiting heads of state, local and national religious leaders, making the news every time they turned around.

Allison scowled slightly. The news hadn't always been kind to them, often passing judgment on their lives from afar. John had to quit his job within a year. Thankfully, Lauren's gifts, and the kind donations of her supporters, had more than covered their bills. Allison and John had refused to charge the desperate people that sought their daughter's gift. Somehow it hadn't seemed right, like they would be taking advantage.

If it wasn't for the difficulty they had with traditional employment, they wouldn't have accepted anything at all.

For their part, they had tried to ensure that Lauren was raised in as normal an environment as possible. They'd met with mixed results. Especially since the public relentlessly sought her gift, which the Corvidae's did their best to share as best they could.

"We're on in five, Mrs. Corvidae."
Allison snapped out of her reverie, looking down at Lauren, who was quietly reading a book on the carpeted floor of the waiting room. She had grown more beautiful with every passing day. Short for her age, she retained a very young appearance, and her face beamed innocent joy and brought smiles to everyone who beheld her. Her blonde hair fell like spun gold, though on this occasion it lay down her back in a neat little braid.

"You ready, sweetie?"
Lauren looked up, nodding at her mother. She looked back to her book almost immediately.

Am I ready? Allison asked herself silently. She reached into her purse, feeling the smooth glass of the tiny bottle within. She glanced again at her daughter. *I have time.*

Three minutes later, she emerged from the bathroom backstage, her lips and throat tingling with the slow burn of bourbon. The drink did the trick: she could feel her nerves ease almost immediately.

Lauren approached her, towed by a stage-hand. The no-nonsense woman in her dark blue skirt and blouse spoke quickly and curtly.
"Ok, remember you'll have about fifteen minutes with Mr. Dailey. he'll give you the signal and then it's off stage left." Allison hoped this was a good idea. The family agent had been adamant about it.

Allison had her doubts. She remembered, none too fondly, first meeting Kent. His rise had been meteoric. After breaking the story about Lauren, he had been catapulted into the national news anchor scene. By continuously covering her exploits, not always to Lauren's benefit, he had secured himself a late night talk show less than a year later. So a reunion was unavoidable, at least according to their agent.

"Ok, showtime folks," the bossy stagehand said.

Allison put on her best smile and gripped Lauren's hand. They strode out into the blinding lights of the stage together. The stage was massive, dominated by a large wooden desk and tall halogen light fixtures. Kent met them on the floor. His arms wide, he went in for a hug, wrapping his arms affectionately around Allison. She resisted the urge to flinch at his unexpected gesture, but as soon as she began to awkwardly hug him back, he let go, turning his attention to Lauren. "Hello, young lady! You likely don't remember me, but I certainly remember the day we first met." He used a slow, "kid-friendly" tone, and flashed a conspiratorial wink at Lauren.

"Actually, I do," Lauren said in even, friendly tones, like a diplomat might. "You haven't aged a day." She returned his wink and he seemed shocked at her precociousness. "We'll, aren't you precious!"

The audience laughed appreciatively at the unexpected charm of the girl. Kent led the two to a pair of oversized, leather-clad chairs next to his desk. After they took their seats he took his own.

"So, let's get down to brass tacks," he began, leaning forward slightly as he spoke. Something in his voice, some latent aggression caused Allison's neck hairs to stand on end. But she knew she was trapped.

"There's been a lot of arguing, these past few years." Kent indicated a large screen behind him. It displayed video footage of religious protests around the world, including several that had turned violent.

"Almost every major religion has claimed that you are a sign, specifically, that their religion is true and that all others are false."

Kent ended the statement in a questioning tone, and looked expectantly at the pair. Lauren looked up at her mother, who usually handled the hard-ball questions. The family had always been very careful not to speak about religion during interviews.

Allison shifted in her seat, her lips set in a thin frown. The silence lengthened and Kent finally broke in again, saying, "Well, maybe we can't say that, but at least we ought to be able to say what religion you follow, Mrs. Corvidae?"

Allison hesitated a moment before giving as diplomatic a reply as she could manage.

"I--I'm, uh, well I was raised Catholic--"

"Catholic!"

"Yes, but-"

Kent's loud voice drowned Allison out.

"We'll have to call the Pope and congratulate him. Sorry, folks, if you didn't choose Catholicism it might be time to reconsider!"

The crowd laughed appreciatively, and Kent smiled his biggest smile.

Allison's and Lauren's discomfort deepened.

"Seriously, though," his tone changed once more."I think there are a lot of people out there who have some real questions that I think it's about time we answer."

Lauren sensed her mother's worry, and sought to put her at ease, answering before her mother had a chance.

"Well, Mr. Dailey, I don't have all the answers, but shoot." She tried to smile as big and as friendly as she could.

"That's the spirit." He made a show of checking some papers on his desk before addressing Lauren. "Can you tell us your favorite place you've visited and helped people?"

"I think my favorite was the Grand Canyon. It was beautiful at sunset, and sunrise, especially."

Kent nodded. "And did you heal lots of people there?" "Well, there were a few yes, but I think in some ways the Grand Canyon heals people, too. Getting that close to nature has to be good for you."

Kent smiled and exclaimed to the crowd, looking directly into one of the cameras. "Well, I don't usually take health advice from kids, but in this case I might make an exception!"

His remark was met once again with dutiful studio laughter.

"And have you encountered anything you couldn't fix? Any person you can't cure?"

Lauren nodded, a hint of sadness in her face as she replied.

"I can't heal my mom, or her daddy, my grandpa. Those are the only two people that have gotten sick I haven't been able to help."

"And why do you suppose that is?"

Lauren shrugged and looked at her mother, who took this question for herself.

"Well," began Allison, "as far as any doctors have been able to tell us, it's impossible to heal anyone the way Lauren does, so we're just grateful that it works on most folks."

Kent nodded again, but he seemed more to be waiting for another opportunity to speak, rather than truly listening.

"So, if you can heal anyone, uh excuse me almost anyone," he led into the question softly, but his tone sharpened like a blade as he finished. "Will you be travelling overseas at some point?"

"What do you mean?" asked a surprised Lauren.

"Well, with your incredible gift, you've done no work out-side of the United States, arguably the place that needs your gift least of all in the world."

Allison was taken aback, it wasn't really something the family had avoided *intentionally*. She racked her brain for a good answer, and Kent caught scent of her indecision immedi-ately.

"I guess the question is, why haven't you and your daugh-ter spent time in Southwest Asia or Africa? Certainly funding isn't an issue, I understand you've done quite well for your-selves utilizing your daughter's talent?"

As Kent spoke, the large television screens hanging above them changed to short clips of humanitarian aid workers and doctors treating masses of the sick and dying in some of the most impoverished nations. The atmosphere in the room darkened, and grumbling began amidst the studio audience.

"I--I'm sorry, I've been trying real hard, and I think I'm helping people--"
Lauren was stammering, her face red with embarrassment.

"Of course, no one blames you, young lady, it *is* an awfully big burden." Kent said, looking pointedly at Allison.

"She's just a child, Mr. Dailey."
Allison broke her relative silence.

"She's *my* child, and frankly, I wish she could live a normal life. It's bad enough she's spent almost her entire life so far be-ing carted around the country, she doesn't need to be paraded around the world every waking moment!"

With her outburst concluded, Allison stood swiftly, taking Lauren by the hand she marched offstage.

Kent's response was drowned out by the pounding in Allison's ears as her blood boiled with rage. It wasn't until they got to the parking lot of the studio that she began to calm down.
"Mommy, can you not squeeze so hard, it hurts," Lauren's

small voice broke through her anger and she let go of her daughters thin wrist immediately. For a brief moment there was a red mark where Allison had clearly been gripping like a vice, but before their eyes it faded and returned to her soft pink skin once more.

Appalled, Allison reached out to Lauren and wrapped her in a bear hug.

"I'm so sorry, baby, mommy is just...very frustrated with that mean man."

"But mom, why did he say that stuff? We *do* help people, don't we?"

Allison chewed on her lip.

"Honey, you're doing great. That bad man was trying to make you feel bad. He wants to hurt us because... well, I don't know why to be honest baby. I guess because he thinks putting other people down makes him look better somehow."

She searched her daughter's face for understanding, but couldn't shake the feeling she was botching her little pep talk.

"Let's get in the car, ok? We're going home."

The car ride from Chicago was awkward for a long while, as minutes turned into hours.

The silence was finally broken by Lauren.

"Mom, was he right?"

Allison felt her heart leap into her throat. The pain in Lauren's voice was palpable.

"No, baby, you don't owe anyone anything. You help so many people because you're kind and good. Don't let him make you believe otherwise."

Lauren nodded her understanding, but as she stared at the increasingly rural landscape outside the window, Allison could tell that she still had doubts.

Allison barely remembered the car ride. Her racing mind had her body on autopilot. By the time she pulled into the driveway of their quaint, single-story family home on the outskirts of Galesburg, she was awash in emotion. She could barely contain the tears threatening to slip from her eyes. She was a horrible mother. She had let her baby be humiliated and made to feel awful for things out of her control, and in front of millions of people around the world.

The neighborhood was quiet and dark, being mostly filled with the elderly or families with school-age children like hers. It tended to settle down by 9:00 p.m. The lights were on in the house, so Allison knew John must still be up, waiting for them.

The thought of facing him, of what he might say about her failure, was frightening. As her thoughts swirled, her anxiety took on a tinge of anger. She deflected her self-loathing, finding reasons to direct her rekindling wrath at her husband.

If he had been there he could have done something. It wasn't fair to leave her alone to chaperon such an important interview. He could have stepped in and said something to prevent Dailey from running over them the way he did. By the time she gathered the nerve to shut the vehicle off and face him, the flames of her anger had grown, fanned by guilt and shame.

While her mother put the car in park, Lauren slipped out of her seat-belt and trudged slowly to the house. She felt like she had failed today. No one had ever suggested she should be doing more before. Or had they? Had her parents simply shielded her from the reality that there were horrors beyond her knowledge? Should she have been doing more?

She thought about her journeys, of the crowds of people she usually met. She didn't know what AIDS was, or how someone caught malaria, but the way the man at the studio had said those words, they sounded bad. Lauren realized she rarely knew what was 'wrong' with the people she helped. Crowds usually met her when they traveled, and people liked to touch her hands, and her parents simply told her that they would feel better afterward.

Lauren trailed behind her mother as they approached the door. Allison fumbled for a moment with her keys, and when she finally got the door to unlock she threw it open with a frustrated shove, causing it to bang loudly against the wall of the living room.

John, who was standing in the room with two glasses of wine in one hand and an opened bottle in the other, was startled to the point of spilling some of the deep red liquid onto the floor. He swore as the red began to soak into the hardwood.

"Dammit, Allie, you scared the hell out of me," he began, only to be cut off by his wife.
"Dammit Allie? Dammit Allie! How dare you!"

John attempted to placate her as he approached and tried to give her a hug.

"Baby, come here. I'm sorry"

Allison's already loud voice instantly rose higher.
"Where the hell were you! We needed you today and you stayed in this fucking house! Didn't you see what they did to our little girl?"

She slapped the glasses out of John's hand, causing them to shatter and unintentionally slicing a thin line into her palm. Pieces of glass flew across the room, tinkling across the worn cherry-wood floors as she shouted.

Blood welled up from her wound, sprinkling across the floor.
Lauren let out a startled peep, her eyes wide with fright.
"Dammit, John." Allison's tears finally broke through her self control and began to flow down her face. She clutched her hand, crimson slipping out between her fingers as she turned to Lauren.

"It's ok, baby, go to your room. Mommy and Daddy just need to talk."
Lauren retreated to her bedroom, but the door did little to

stifle the ever-increasing volume of her parents fighting. The screaming match seemed to last forever as Lauren huddled beneath the blankets of her small bed. She must have fallen asleep eventually, because she woke to a slowly brightening sky outside her window.

Cautiously Lauren walked out from her bedroom. She went first to her parents' room, but found it empty, the bed still made from the day before. She continued on to the common area of the house, where she found her father sleeping on the brown leather couch in their living room. He looked cold and uncomfortable, wrapped in a spare blanket and without a pillow. The only evidence of the fight the night before was a somber red stain in the wood grain of the room. It stood out sharply amidst the cream-colored walls and the warm tones of the other floorboards.

Lauren returned to her room where she took the blanket from her bed and brought it out, placing it gently over her father's sleeping form. She brushed his face gently, and his expression softened from a scowl to that of peaceful slumber.

Unsure of what to do, Lauren thought of what she might like if she were unhappy, and came to what she thought was a good conclusion: pancakes.

John was walking through a grassy field, wide and green, with gentle, rolling hills. The landscape was well lit, though there was no sun in the bright blue sky. The air smelled sweet, like maple trees in the fall. Before him, the only standout in the otherwise fairly featureless plain, stood a tall tree. From a distance it seemed to shine, a mix of silvers and coppers, and as he got closer he could see why. Where leaves would be expected, instead the tree was covered in every kind of dish he could think of. Dozens of skillets and pans--even a tea kettle--clinked gently alongside forks, knives and spoons in the slight breeze. Aside from the chiming cutlery there perched a large white dove on the uppermost branch, singing softly. The tune was familiar but he couldn't place it. He must have scared the bird as he approached, because it suddenly sprang to life. Flinging itself upward into the sky, it set the whole tree shaking.

John awoke with a start to a crash of clattering pans and the faint smell of smoke. He bolted upright, nearly falling from the couch as he did so.

"Allie," he called as he stumbled to his feet and rushed to the kitchen, where the smoke seemed to be coming from.

He had to stop and laugh at the scene before him, so un-expected that he could hardly process it in his newly awakened state.

An oblivious Lauren danced precariously on the top step of a black and white stepping stool. Her earbuds were in and her iPod clearly cranked to max volume. She was singing shrilly along to Amazing Grace, though to hear her sing it, you might expect it was a rock ballad rather than a hymn. Flour covered at least a quarter of the kitchen, counters, table, and floor included. She was mixing something that looked like paper mache in a large bowl with the biggest serving spoon the family owned. The stove in front of her had two skillets and a large saucepan on the burners, all three turned to high heat. To her left, atop the counter, was a plate piled high with various roundish flat objects ranging in color from tan to black and in size from palm sized to plate sized. The only part of the room that didn't look like a disaster was the kitchen table, upon which sat table settings for three.

Lauren, for her part, seemed to have recovered emotionally from the night before, and John could only assume that she had determined pancakes would be the solution to their problems. If only that were true.

Before John's thoughts could darken further, he heard the front door open behind him. Turning, he saw Allison, her hair mussed and her eyes tired, still wearing the button-down white blouse and black skirt she had on for the interview yesterday. Her matching blazer was slung over her forearm and her heels were held in one hand by their back-straps. She gave John a tired look. Her eyes were bloodshot and he could see she hadn't gotten much sleep.

He put a finger to his lips as she opened her mouth to speak, eliciting a confused look from her. He motioned her to come over and she did so, as he approached he held an arm out to her. She embraced him, burying her head in his shoulder and clinging tightly to him. John noticed that she reeked of cheap liquor but he said nothing. After a moment of holding her as she silently sobbed against him, he reached a hand up to her cheek, brushed a tear from below her eye and kissed her gently on the forehead.

John turned his eyes back to the kitchen, and Allison followed his gaze to the sight of their little girl, unknowingly reminding them of the good they had done, the reasons they fell in love, and giving them hope.

As if on cue, Lauren turned slightly while belting out a particularly heartfelt chorus. Upon seeing her parents in the doorway, she froze. The spoon she held to her mouth like a microphone dripped lumpy batter to the floor and the bowl in her other hand tilted dangerously, threatening to empty its contents at any moment.

"Mommy!"

Lauren's delight could have melted the coldest of hearts, and to her parents it was a warm blanket of peace.

Gifted, miraculous, endearing, were all traits of their darling angel. Good cooking, however, was not yet counted among her talents. Nonetheless, Allison and John dutifully choked down several pancakes each, trying not to cough when their chewing uncovered clumps of flour.

After breakfast, Lauren scooted off to take a bath at her mother's insistence. John and Allison began the monumental task of tackling the chaos their kitchen had become. Content for a time simply to be in each other's presence, they didn't speak for several minutes.

"Allie, I'm sorry," John began, prompting Allison to halt her efforts to scrub dried batter from the counter. "I...should have been there."

"Don't, John. Don't blame yourself. It's our fault, both of us. We should never have done this to her. Or to us."

Allison's eyes welled up with tears. She was desperately unhappy, and John could see it clearly.

"Allie, I've been thinking." John hesitated; he tried to gauge his wife's mood, unwilling to repeat last night. "We could stop. We could leave and just disappear."

Allison opened her mouth to speak but John cut her off, determined to speak his mind while he still had the nerve.

"Hear me out. There's a place for sale down south, near Cobden. I've been setting aside money every month since this circus started and we could buy it outright, no paper trail. We'll go, we won't tell anyone. We can start over, we can work on...work on us for a while."

Allison was swept away to another time and place when John spoke of Cobden. It seemed like a lifetime ago that they had spent their honeymoon there, in an off-the-beaten-path cabin in Southern Illinois. Cobden was a town of a few hundred, nestled in the heart of the Shawnee National Forest, welcoming to strangers, with the sort of small town charm that brought out the kindness out in anyone.

Doubt, however, did not let her linger in the land of what could be for long. She returned to cold reality, to her bare feet on the rough wood of the floor and the lukewarm rag in her hand.

"How, though? How can we just up and leave?"

"It's a wooded lot with a cabin on it, about 30 acres. There's an old mobile home on the property that just needs a little patching up..." John trailed off near the end, losing nerve when Allison didn't seem convinced.

She looked around the room, her eyes stopping on many of the dozens of knick-knacks that made it home. Family portraits hung on the walls, drawings and finger-paintings on the fridge.

Allison started to speak, but before she could, John cut her off.

"Allie, we can't keep doing this. I can't keep doing this." He spoke with desperation, making a last-ditch attempt to convince her. "We'll use a fake name, we can live off our accounts until things die down, and...and I can find something when we get there if we get low on money."

It was Lauren's reappearance that made up Allison's mind. She re-entered the room, hair still wet and wrapped in a pink, unicorn-covered beach towel that covered her tiny frame and dragged behind her like the train of an over-large dress.

Her eyes were filled with hope, her heart calmed from the storm the night before and mended with the promise that her parents were still here, her family still together.

The rest of the day was spent in a flurry of activity. The Corvidae house was a sea of barely contained chaos as the accumulated lives of its three residents were systematically boxed, labeled, and crammed into the shrinking cargo space of the family van.

By nightfall, the house was in disarray. It wasn't empty, but it no longer looked like a home. Of course, they couldn't fit everything in the vehicle, but they would manage with what they had. The constant tour of talk shows and television appearances had been a considerable windfall for the family, and being frugal by nature, they had plenty of money saved up. As the van pulled out of the driveway Lauren took one last look at her home, illuminated softly by a streetlight and fading fast into the night. It was the only home she had ever known, but she wasn't too worried about leaving it behind. Lauren had never been to a normal school, having been home-schooled, and she had little contact with kids her own age because of her celebrity status. With fresh optimism, she looked to the future.

Chapter 3

The smell of wet grass and wildflowers filled the evening air. It was Lauren's favorite smell: nature. Something about lying in tall grass, smelling the dew, and feeling the gentle silence of the earth truly centered her. She was resting from a long day of romping in the woods around her house. Woods that over the past six summers had become an extension of her home.

Especially when things got bad.

Lauren shook her head, clearing away the thunderclouds of worry before they could fully form in her mind, turning her thoughts to the very real storm clouds on the horizon instead. The breeze picked up and lightning flashed, the scent of rain now mixed with the fragrances of the Shawnee forest. There was a tinge of ozone to the air, accentuating the faint feeling of desperation in the late August evening warmth.

Tomorrow she would begin her first day of public high school. So far she'd remained in homeschooling, mostly for fear of being recognized from the non-stop news coverage following her disappearance. But the girl who had run away six years ago had been replaced by a young woman.

Lauren's hair had changed from childish curls to flowing, gentle waves that inspired jealousy from her peers. She was taller as well, having sprouted to almost five and a half feet. She was self-conscious, however, as she still looked awfully boyish to her own eyes. She had no curves whatsoever. She remained rail-thin to the point of looking fragile.

"Elegant," her father always chided her when she was being self-deprecating. Her golden eyes, like bottomless pools of amber, were the only thing that hadn't changed. No, she mused, it was very unlikely that anyone would recognize her now.

The sun slowly settled over the horizon, blazing glorious oranges and reds across the thunderstorm as it rolled in slowly from the west. She waited until fat summer raindrops began to sprinkle the grass around her before she rolled to her feet and began the trek home.

She was only three miles or so away, and her long, tawny legs chewed up the distance with smooth grace. Lauren loved to run these trails: the thrill of the scenery rushing past, the adrenaline filling her muscles, and the slow burn settling into her lungs and legs as she ran. One blessing of her longer legs, as well as her trim body, was that she could run like the wind. Her father took great pride in her ability to run, and talked at great length with her about joining the track team when she finally started public school. It was one of the only things she wasn't worried about.

With more than a mile yet to go before reaching her yard, Lauren realized the storm was a bit worse than she had judged. The rain was coming down in sheets now, so thick she could barely see. Water pooled everywhere in the low-lying southern Illinois hills. Lightning arced across the skies and peals of thunder shook the trees around her as she ran. Wind whipped the rain nearly sideways with such force that it stung like hail.

It's a good thing I know this area so well, Lauren worried to herself, *I'd hate to be lost out here in this.* Know it well, she did. Lauren could navigate these paths blindfolded if she had to, but the path was still treacherous.

Lauren's muddy sneaker slipped across a rain-slick rock, rolling her ankle and sending her tumbling and scrambling into the brush beside the trail. She felt branches whip across her, and catch her hair as she crashed into the underbrush, and she gasped in pain as a particularly sharp twig lashed across her cheek. Her arms windmilled as she tried to halt her momentum, and finally she managed a tenuous hold on the trunk of a passing oak tree.

Deep breath, take stock, she thought to herself. Her ankle was twisted and swelling, and she felt a warmth running down her cheek in contrast to the chilly raindrops. Reaching up she wiped her face. Pulling her hand away she could see it was speckled with blood.

"Dammit," she swore as crimson dripped onto her gray tank top. Lauren fought back the urge to cry and waited impatiently for her gift to kick in.

Within moments her ankle let out a popping noise and she winced as it reset to its proper position. Similarly, she felt a familiar tingle as the cut across her cheek closed up.

Lauren, a tomboy, was no stranger to the kinds of injuries most outdoorsy children sustain. Bruised shins, cut fingers, poison ivy, and the like. Of course, Lauren didn't experience these exactly as other children might. She learned early on that these would, for her, be passing issues, destined to last no longer than a few moments.

That didn't change how uncomfortable they were, though.

She still felt pain. She felt it twice over, in fact. For every injury she sustained she also felt the discomfort of her instant healing. For minor cuts it was a tingle, the kind of pins and needles you might experience from having your foot fall asleep. More significant injuries caused a more severe reaction. When she broke her arm at a public playground at ten years old, her parents had to carry her back to the car and leave, for fear her screaming would cause someone to call the police.

Lauren looked down at herself, checking her clothes for damage. Sure enough, there were several small tears in the soft jersey material of her shirt. It was one of her favorites.

Her evening soured, Lauren set off for home once again, albeit at a more reasonable pace.

Night had fully fallen when she at last entered her yard. Yard was a bit of a misnomer. It was more like a clearing in the woods, a few acres of empty grass surrounded by a low barbwire fence. In the middle sat the family home, a pair of double-wide trailers that had been connected together. They wouldn't look like much to a casual observer, but to her they represented sanctuary.

Yelling emanated from the house as she walked the last few dozen yards to the door.

"What the hell does it matter if she gets back in by dark, John?" her mother's voice. "It's not like literally anything could happen to her, for god's sakes!"

"That's not the point. She's our daughter and it's our job to make sure she's--"

Her father's voice cut off sharply, accompanied by the sound of breaking glass.

Lauren hesitated, her hand inches from the door handle and she debated staying out longer.

Sanctuary indeed.

The decision was made for her. Allison yanked open the door.

"I'm going for a drive," she said acidly, looking over her shoulder at John. When she turned back to the door she saw Lauren standing there uncertainly.
"Um, hi, sweetie," stuttered her mother. "I'm going out for a quick drive. Don't wait up."

Allison gave her daughter a quick peck on the cheek, and Lauren tried to ignore the smell of wine on her breath.

Lauren reluctantly moved aside as her mother walked past, one hand on her pregnant belly and the other on the railing beside the back steps.

"Mom," Lauren began to say, her voice meek with doubt. "Maybe you shouldn't... y'know..."
Her voice trailed near the end as Allison didn't even turn around while replying.

"Baby, don't worry, I just...don't like being cooped up in the house, that's all. Besides, I've still got four months before your brother is due, anyway!"

Allison slid into the driver's seat of their old pickup truck, another new addition to the family since the move. The SUV had been well suited for the conditions of the back-country roads, but it was also expensive. John had pointed out that it was going to be important to have a durable-and-cheap, vehicle when Lauren finally learned to drive. The twenty-year-old Ranger certainly fit the bill. Lauren wasn't even sure if plastic had been invented back then.

Lauren stood in the rain a few moments longer, watching her mother turn the vehicle down the long driveway towards the road and set out. Eventually though, the rain pouring down her face and soaking her clothes chilled her to the bone and forced her inside the house.

Her father was still standing where he had been when Allison walked out, his eyes glazed and his gaze distant. He was hunched over slightly and had the posture of a man defeated. He shook himself as Lauren entered and tried to put on a brave face but Lauren could tell he was hurting inside.

They hugged. The long deep hug you give a friend whom you cannot help, but can only hope to support.

"So," he began a little lamely. "Are you, um, ready for school tomorrow?"

She had never felt less ready. Her worries flooded in, now that she was away from the peace of the woods. Would she be able to make friends? What if someone recognized her? What if her gift was revealed and the torturous reality that was her early childhood returned? Would she do well in school? Was she going to be behind her peers? These and more bogged her down, filling her with dread. Not to mention the fears she had for her parents and for her unborn brother. But her father had enough to deal with.

"Yep," she said in a cheery tone, smiling reassuringly at her dad. "I'm thinking tomorrow will be a great day."

He smiled, a genuine smile this time. She knew she was his pride and joy, and to see him happy she would endure anything.

"I'm really tired, though, so I'm gonna hit the hay, OK, Dad?"

He nodded and tousled her hair gently.
"You might consider a shower first, Lolo."

She hated that nickname, and was going to remind him of that when suddenly he froze.

"What happened?" he exclaimed in a worried tone, touching her shoulder where the blood had stained her shirt.

Damn it. She had hoped the rain would wash it all out.

"Oh, I took a tumble on the trail running home," she said lightly, hoping to avoid a scene. But her father was intensely protective of "his little girl."

"You were running in the rain? You could have broken your neck," he scolded. But his words had no bite of anger, only the fearful tone of paternal concern.

Lauren refrained from mentioning that as far as they knew, it wouldn't have mattered if she did. She doubted he would appreciate the cynicism. She opted to nod her understanding and simply reply with what she knew she needed to hear.
"I know, Daddy. I'll be more careful," she gave him another hug

and walked past him to her room. As soon as the door was shut, she breathed a deep sigh.

Her room was dark, except for the faint glow of the stick-on, glow-in-the-dark stars still clinging to her ceiling, relics from an older time. In many ways she enjoyed the darkness as much as the light. Where a bright sunny day could lift her spirits and encourage her, the cover of darkness lent her a feeling of true privacy, a comforting blanket of anonymity and unfeeling. In the darkness there could be no expectations of her: she was truly safe in her solitude.

Tears came unbidden to her eyes, suppressed these past few months and brought out by the stress of the evening.

For a while things had been good again. The family had been using a pseudonym, Corbeau, since they'd arrived down here. It was her father's idea. He'd been studying French when he first met Allison, and it was the translated version of their family name. The change of scenery brought a wave of relief from the stresses and pressures of the celebrity lifestyle she had grown up in. Not once did she miss the attention or the fame, the endless hours of talk-shows and the media circus. Homeschooling allowed her to spend time with her parents, and being an introvert, she didn't really miss the company of others her age. Even when they had started going to town more regularly in recent years, she hadn't felt the need to make very many friends.

But the rosy glow of a new home in a new place couldn't cover the fact that her mother's drinking hadn't stopped. It couldn't repair her father's heart every time she left to "take a drive." They still tried to hide it from her, and deep down, Lauren was fairly certain that if it weren't for her they likely would have split years ago.

Or they would still be happy with each other, like they were before she came along. The thought came unsolicited, as it always did when she started to dwell on the broken nature of her home.

For a while, when they found out Allison was expecting again, the family had felt whole, unbroken. The drinking had stopped for a few weeks, the fighting was at an all-time low, and Lauren felt less need to escape to the wilderness to de-compress. But within a month her mother was reminding them that, "Some doctors say you can have a glass of wine each night through the second trimester..."

Lauren slipped out of her sopping wet clothes. One advan-tage to the home was that she had her own bathroom, com-plete with a shower and a gigantic cast-iron bathtub. The heat of the water stood in stark contrast to the chill she had felt before, and it did wonders to help her relax.

As she rinsed the suds from her long hair she contem-plated the morning to come, running through mental check-lists of the items she would need to bring to school.

By the time she was toweling herself dry, she was con-sumed with the lists in her mind. Did she have enough note-books? Was one going to be enough for each class? What if her classes were across the school from each other and she didn't have time to go to her locker? Maybe it would be smarter to have a larger notebook and split it between two classes that were back to back?

It wasn't until she started pulling on jeans that she realized she hadn't gone to bed yet. She put a palm to her forehead, feeling foolish. Lauren, you're a ditz, she thought to herself. She took the jeans back off, opting for fuzzy pajama pants and a light tank-top instead.

Lauren's bed was huge, a king size. It was one of the few material possessions she truly treasured. It had cost a fortune, she was sure, but as she rarely asked for things, her parents had been happy to oblige. Snuggled beneath a mountain of blankets, Lauren was in the lap of luxury, but sleep still eluded her. Minutes ticked by, turning to hours as she lay still, her mind restlessly wandering from one worry to the next. Sometime around 3:00 a.m. she heard her mother come home. She could finally let go of the tension she didn't even realize she had, and drifted fitfully off to sleep.

Lauren awoke with a start to the blaring klaxon of her cell phone alarm. Bleary-eyed, she reached out, smacking the cell phone repeatedly until, finally, it was silent again. Grabbing hold of the offending device, she pulled it to her face.

7:35.

Panic overcame her. Class started in 25 minutes and she lived half an hour from the school. Lauren leapt from the bed, tripping over her mess of tangled blankets and banging her shin against the side table as she did so.

Cussing was frowned upon in the Corvidae home, at least officially, but the creativity with which Lauren was currently swearing would make most men blush.

John looked at his watch. It was getting fairly late and Lauren still hadn't come out of her room this morning. He couldn't be certain but he thought he could hear her talking to herself in there. Suddenly, a loud bang rang out through the house from her direction. Cautiously he approached the door, aware that disturbing a teenage girl was akin to poking a lioness with a stick. He knocked softly.

No answer.

Slowly, ever so slowly, he eased the door open. Lauren was hopping around on one foot struggling to jam her other one into a sneaker. A rapidly fading bruise adorned her forehead, and he couldn't help but notice she was haphazardly dressed. Her cargo shorts were hardly a match for her mid-calf striped socks and sneakers, still muddy from the night before. She was wearing a hot pink cami she usually slept in, and seemed to be trying to throw on a dark gray hoodie while simultane-ously tying her shoe. It wasn't going well.

"Dad," she screamed at him as though everything were his fault, and he barely dodged the black and white converse sneaker that sailed past his head. "I'm trying to change!" John ducked out, feeling lucky to survive.

"Oh, ok, honey. Um. I'll get the car ready. You know school starts in twenty minutes, right?"

Lauren's reply was caustic. "Yes, I am aware, thank you!" Exactly three minutes later, Lauren was running from the house, her hair unbrushed and her backpack flapping behind her. She tossed her bag into the bed of the truck and ran for the door. Midway to the cab she froze. She looked in the bed to see over an inch of standing water soaking into her backpack.

Lauren made a sound like steam escaping a teapot mixed with a growling animal, her face conveyed such apocalyptic rage that her father didn't even look her in the eye.

It was a very quiet and uncomfortable car ride to the school, and when they finally pulled up at 8:12, she wordlessly exited the truck with a defeated sigh.

"Hey," John spoke to her as she began to plod away, "Chin up, Lolo, you're gonna do great."

Lauren almost didn't turn around, she was so consumed by worry, but she knew it would matter to her dad. Turning and waving she forced a smile.

"I know, Dad, thanks for the ride."

She faced the school once more. It was a squat, single-story affair of red brick and black window frames. Sighing to herself, she covered the distance to the entrance and pulled the big glass double door open.

To be fair, the lobby was considerably friendlier in appearance than the dull exterior. It had a nice white and red checkered tile floor, and the walls were covered with murals and plaques. Off to the right was a desk, where an elderly woman sat behind it reading a newspaper.

Unsure of how to proceed, Lauren approached her.
"Excuse me, ma'am, I'm--"
"Late, and on the first day, no less. Not the right impression, young lady."
The woman's tone was sharp, like a librarian who had just caught you writing in a book. Her piercing blue eyes bored into Lauren's from over the classified ads.
"Yes, ma'am, I'm really sorry. I-I've never been to a public school before. I don't, um, I don't really know how this works."
Lauren was foundering, and something in the woman seemed to sense that, because her tone softened considerably. She introduced herself as Margaret the receptionist, and after looking over Lauren's paperwork, she directed her to her first class. Room 117.
Lauren looked at her cellphone. The bright digital display read 8:19. The door before her was covered in a mirror finish, and had the words "Smile! You're our brightest treasure!" written across it in childlike block letters. She stared at her reflection. The girl looking back at her was too skinny, her socks were both striped and colored, but an unmatched pair. Her shoes were filthy. Her hair was a mess, though untangled at least. She silently thanked her parents for giving her hair that tended to behave.
Another minute ticked by before she finally got the courage to reach out to the door. With one hand she tucked a strand of loose hair behind her ear as the other struck out to grab the handle.
She squeaked in surprise when the door opened on its own. A tall, handsome man in dark slacks and a hunter green button-up was looking at her expectantly.
"Are you coming in?"
She looked like a fish out of water, taken entirely aback. From where he had pushed the door open, she could see it was a one-way mirror, and the class had been able to observe her

uncertainty the entire time. She was mortified.
The class erupted in laughter behind the man, obviously her teacher, until he glared back and scolded them.
"Guys! That's no way to treat a new student!"
Turning back to Lauren, he spoke warmly.
"Welcome to Biology, the reason you're blushing!"
Clearly he thought his joke would make her feel more comfortable. It didn't. With yet another imperfection to obsess over, Lauren felt her face grow hotter and hotter, and she was afraid if she blushed any harder her cheeks would combust.
"Yes-thank-you," Lauren's words were rushed and she moved past the man into the classroom. The only open seat was in the front row, close to the middle of the room. Of course, she thought to herself. She took her seat as quietly and unobtrusively as she could, an impossible task given its location.

"Everyone, this is Lauren Corbeau, she's joining us this year from out of town! I trust everyone will make her feel welcome."

Lauren read the blackboard. It was covered in horribly penned chalk writing. The most legible section was the top right: "Mr. Harrison's BIO 107 – Rm 117."

Mr. Harrison was still talking, but Lauren was in a fog. She was clumsily getting out a notebook and fishing around in her soggy bookbag for a pen when he broke through her daze.
"Lauren? Hello?"

"Y-Yes, sir." Lauren knew he had been speaking to her, but was shamefully unaware of what he had been saying.

"I was just saying we're going to be starting the year with a discussion about birds." He looked at her as though this should hold some special relevance or meaning to her.
She was clueless.
"I, uh, thought that might interest you, given that your name-- Corbeau, that is--is the French word for crow?"
Lauren was at the same time interested in hearing more and

desperate that he should turn his attention, well-meaning or otherwise, to literally anyone or anything but her.

Perhaps sensing her discomfort, he did return to the lesson, and spent most of it discussing the Corvidae family of birds. Lauren felt her ears burning well into the class, and couldn't help but suspect that the fervent whispering from the rest of the students were about her.

The rest of class was interesting enough for her to forget some of her embarrassment. Apparently the crow family included rooks and ravens as well. If her name had to be a group of birds, it figured she would get the ugly, carrion eating ones.

The bell at the end of class was piercing, and it made Lauren jump, eliciting snickers from the back of the class. Scooping up her bag, Lauren looked at her schedule. English was next.

Lauren enjoyed books. The solitude of a steaming cup of cocoa and a good romance novel was, in her opinion, a fantastic use of time.

"Hey." A female voice from beside Lauren. "You're the girl from out of town, right? Moved into the old Miller place a few years back?"
The girl speaking looked about Lauren's age, though considerably more developed. She had mature curves, and an exotic, Latin countenance. Luxurious, midnight-black hair framed dark brown eyes that perfectly suited her bronzed skin.

Lauren nodded shyly. "Yea, my mom and my dad and I moved from up North."

The girl nodded appreciatively.

"You're a city girl, huh? Lemme guess, Chicago, right?"

Lauren sensed a hint of derision in the way she said the name. The hairs on the back of her neck pricked up a bit.

"Yep, we lived in the suburbs since I was a little kid," Lauren began in a cheery tone, hoping to win the girl over. As she spoke, several other girls their age approached, arranging themselves behind the young woman.

"C'mon, Lita," another girl said in a disinterested tone as she approached the group. "Oh my god, you're a girl?". She barked out a laugh, looking Lauren up and down, disdain clear on her face.

"Ay Dios Mio, Lita, she looks like a homeless person."

Lauren was a little taken aback by the tone and severity of the girl's words. She knew she looked silly, her dirty, mismatched clothes were a raw nerve that the girls words found easily. Anger bubbled up within her. How dare this girl speak to her like that?

"Well, screw you, too." The words slipped from Lauren's lips before she could stop herself. The stress of her morning had turned her normally patient demeanor sour.

Lita punched Lauren in the middle of her stomach, hard. The unexpected blow left her breathless and her eyes opened wide in shock. She had never been struck by another person before.

"You're gonna have to learn your place around here, bitch," Lita whispered threateningly.."

Lauren's cheeks flushed with embarrassment and pain, and her eyes were wide with shock.

Lita raised a finger to brush a strand of loose hair out of Lauren's face, but she flinched away.

"Shame, you're almost pretty."

Lita followed her words with a hard shove, sending Lauren sprawling to the floor.

Mr. Harrison seemed to appear from nowhere. Suddenly Lauren couldn't understand why she had ever disliked him. He helped her to her feet as Lita took on a simpering, innocent tone and looked down at her with mock concern.

"Oh my gosh, Lauren! Are you ok? You must have slipped on

all that mud on your shoes," condescension slipped into her tone as she ended her sentence.

The girls left, cackling to themselves as they did so. Mr. Harrison moved to help Lauren to her feet but she recoiled, unwilling to make physical contact.
"Don't worry" he said, hands still outstretched awkwardly.
"The first day of class is always the hardest, right!"
She certainly hoped so.

The hallways were starting to clear and Lauren got the distinct impression that she was about to be late, again. She thanked her teacher and rushed off to her next class.
When she got to the door of the classroom, she saw most of the other students were still milling about in the hallway, catching up on their summer vacations. Lauren took the opportunity to slip into the room and look for a seat near the back.

When she got into the room she paused to take stock. The walls were lined with bookcases, each over-stuffed with books of every size and color. There seemed to be only one other student. At least, she thought they were a student. A charcoal hoodie and a pair of jet black jeans seemed to be occupying the far corner of the room. The person wearing them had his, or her, head down on the desk and seemed to be dozing.

Lauren felt the urge to sit as far from the door as possible, so she took the seat adjacent to the mysterious figure in the back row.

After taking her seat, Lauren occupied her mind by scan-ning the titles of the books nearest to her. Weiss, Hickman, Seuss, Bronte, Lackey, Salvatore, Heinlein. There seemed no rhyme or reason to where a particular title or author might be found. They weren't grouped by genre, nor were they in alphabetical order. As she sat trying to discern the system she knew had to exist, she heard a muffled voice from the hoodie speak to her.

"Your socks don't match."

Exasperated, and already on the defensive, Lauren replied sharply, "What's it to you?"

The figure sat up, curly red hair falling from below the hood as a pale, freckled face revealed itself.

"Sorry, I tend not to think before I speak, I didn't mean to offend you." The girl had a small but beautiful voice. Her face was childlike, with slightly chubby cheeks, and small features, aside from her huge green eyes.

Lauren apologized, feeling like an ass for having snapped at the girl, and introduced herself.

"Erin Engle, nice to meet you." The girl stuck out a hand. She wore black nail polish, and a wide black cloth band on her wrist. The tail end of a half-healed cut poked out the end of the wristband.

Lauren caught herself staring at the girls hand, unsure what to do.

"I'm sorry, I, um, I'm germaphobic," Lauren stuttered out, terrified that if she shook Erin's hand her cut would heal, and she would be discovered. Erin looked a little hurt, and largely unconvinced, she began to return her head to the desk.

"I'm sorry, I know it's weird," Lauren began, desperate not to ruin what might be her only good encounter of the day. "I just have a thing about touching people, that's all. It really is good to meet you."

With the petite redhead to talk to, English class was considerably easier than Biology had been, and with Erin as a guide, the rest of the day was fairly tolerable as well. She showed Lauren to her classes, and sat next to her in the ones they shared. Erin filled Lauren in on the local politics of the student body. It was a dizzying nest of intrigue and drama.

The two hit it off nicely, with Erin's particular brand of introversion meshing well with Lauren's. It seemed Erin was given wide berth by Lita and her gang, though snide remarks followed the two of them throughout the day.

Aside from lunch, when Lita and several of her girlfriends started pretending to trip over imaginary obstacles and making birdlike cawing noises any time Lauren walked past, the day progressed more and more smoothly as time went on.

Chapter 4

Lauren hated driving in the snow, it made her nervous. She knew she had no reason to fear for herself, but the idea of losing control of the two tons of metal she was driving and potentially hurting someone else was terrifying. Despite the massive snowfall of the night before, school had not been canceled, so she was on her way to Erin's house to pick her up.

Over the last year and a half their friendship had blossomed into the single greatest facet of her high school experience. Lauren was still the butt of most jokes at the school, highlighting the insular nature of the small town she resided in, but Erin was always nearby to cheer her up.

Erin had a deadpan, sarcastic sense of humor that caught most people off guard, and a nihilistic outlook that ostracized her to everyone but Lauren, who found it fascinating.

The truck hit a pothole in the frozen dirt and snow of the winding forest road, lifting Lauren out of her seat and yanking her from her musing. White-knuckled, she determined to pay closer attention as she drove.

Before long, she was navigating the small, half-plowed roads of Cobden. Pulling up in front of Erin's house, a low single-story home with blacked out windows and a broken gate set into the faded, white-picket fence surrounding the yard, normally overgrown but currently blanketed in pristine snow.

Right on cue, Erin exited the house. Locking the door behind her, she waved at Lauren and navigated the snow drifts to the truck, clambering inside as quickly as she could.

The old truck had one hell of a heater, and Erin was holding her hands to the vents, cursing the cold. Her expletives were well-chosen and flew with a natural, practiced ease, causing Lauren to laugh at her friend's frustration. It never ceased to amuse; Erin's high, childlike voice slinging swear words like a sailor.

As Lauren pulled the truck back into the street, she glanced once more at the house her friend had emerged from. It was like a faded vision of the American Dream: the driveway was, as ever, empty. In all the time she had known Erin she had never been inside her house, and had never met her parents. It seemed they were always working, out of town, or both. To be fair, she considered, perhaps she was just being nosy. Nonetheless, she never missed an opportunity to scour the windows for some hint of...what? She didn't even know.

As she wondered to herself she cruised the slowly rolling hills of the town, making her way towards the high-school in unusual silence.

"Isn't it a bit early to be lost in thought?" Erin chided her, poking Lauren in the ribs and causing her to jump with a start.

Unfortunately, Lauren had in fact been lost in thought and her knee-jerk reaction to the surprise of being disturbed was to plant her foot firmly on the brake pedal. The truck's ancient frame began to slide as the wheels locked and the tires failed to grip the icy pavement. As it slid, the truck began to list slightly, rotating to the left and drifting into the oncoming lane of traffic.

The boxy frame of a 4x4 filled Lauren's vision and she heard Erin let out a strangled scream.

Thankfully, the vehicle in front of them was much newer than her old truck, and its anti-lock brakes pulled it to a sharp stop. Lauren and Erin coasted closer and closer until finally the tires caught a rougher patch of road and jerked the truck to a stop. The sudden halt jarred the passengers, knocking them about the cab.

"Erin," Lauren turned instinctively to her friend. "Erin, are you ok, are you hurt?"

Erin was sitting rigidly, her eyes glassed over and a look of abject terror on her face. Both of Erin's arms were braced against the dashboard in front of her as though she were readying for an impact with a train.

"Erin, Erin!"

Lauren grabbed her friend's arm, her gloved fingers wrapping around Erin's wrist. Erin jerked back to reality, tears coming to her eyes as she began to shake.

The man in the SUV in front of them honked angrily, but Lauren ignored him.

"Hey, are you ok? Are you hurt?" Lauren felt Erin's wrist for signs of swelling though it was hard to tell beneath the thick winter coat she had on. Old habits surfaced and she started to slide Erin's sleeve up her arm as she reached with her left hand, putting the tip of her gloved finger between her teeth and pulling the glove off.

As her sleeve pushed up onto her forearm, Erin pulled back, taking her arm back with surprising force. Lauren got a good look at several deep purple scars, thick ones, that laced across her arm before Erin yanked her sleeve back down. Another of Erin's mysteries, another set of questions left un-asked.

"I'm ok," Erin said through her tears. "C-can you take me home, please?"

She had never skipped school, or even been intentionally late, but Lauren had also never seen such emotion from her normally withdrawn companion. Erin was never exactly a ray of sunshine, but in this moment she was so visibly shaken that Lauren couldn't find the words to respond immediately.

Instead, Lauren nodded her head, she pulled a sloppy u-turn in the street, eliciting even more frustration from the man across from her.

Minutes passed in silence, much deeper and less comfortable than before. Eventually Lauren pulled up in front of the home. She prepared to put the truck in park, but Erin broke her silence.

"Go, um, go ahead and park in the driveway."

Lauren was surprised. Erin had always told her that her parents came home from working third shift shortly after they went to school.

Instead of arguing, Lauren did as she was instructed and parked the truck. It wasn't until the engine stopped that Erin began to calm down, but her breathing was still erratic and her complexion paler than usual.

Erin reached for the handle of the door, hesitating a moment as she grabbed hold of it.

"Do you want to come in?" She spoke so softly, Lauren wasn't sure she had heard her correctly.

"Do I want to come in..." Lauren confirmed, "Like in your house?"

Erin's cheeks flushed as she responded.

"I'm-sorry-it's-fine-never-mind," she gushed, clearly mistaking Lauren's clarification for a lack of interest.

"Wait," Lauren reached again, grabbing Erin's wrist before she could escape the truck. "Yes, please."

As they crunched through the snow to the door, Lauren couldn't tell who was more nervous, herself or her friend.

"I'm, uh, sorry about the mess," Erin said meekly as she unlocked and pushed open the front door, revealing a dimly lit living room.

The girls piled in, stamping the snow from their boots. Erin took Lauren's coat from her, hanging it on a hook behind the door before beginning to remove her own.

Lauren looked around. The room was loaded with stacks of books, giving it a slightly cramped appearance, but was otherwise quite neat.

How to Balance a Checkbook.

Household Finances For the Totally Unprepared.

With Hard Work – Success!

Lauren scanned the titles as she waited. It seemed over half of the books were some kind of self-help manual, everything from keeping track of finances and managing a mortgage, to furnace and plumbing repair books. The rest ranged from literary classics like Shakespeare to the latest trashy teen romance novellas.

She wasn't sure what she was expecting, but a book-filled, otherwise totally normal-looking living room wasn't it.

The floors were bare wood, and a small green sofa, a dull brown recliner, and a small coffee table with an old lamp on it were the room's only furnishings besides a pair of overloaded bookshelves and the mountains of writing everywhere. There were, however, three doorways leading from the room, one on each wall. As Lauren peered down the hall, her gaze met with Erin's.

Erin was standing sheepishly, looking at her, one arm hanging down in front of her, the other nervously across her body, her hand gripping the opposite shoulder. Her black leggings, knee-length plaid skirt, and dark gray long-sleeved shirt made her stand out from the cream colored walls. A little storm cloud with puffy red eyes amidst the clutter of the house.

Erin seemed supremely uncomfortable, clearly not used to having company.

An awkward silence grew between the friends as Erin foundered socially. Lauren's stomach chose that precise moment to growl in protest of her lack of breakfast.

The tension flowed out of the room and Erin started giggling, her laughter had a tinge of hysteria to it, but the edge had been taken off the atmosphere in the room.

"I've got frozen waffles, pop-tarts," Erin listed off breakfast options with all the authority of a worried mother.

"I'm ok with cereal if you are," Lauren replied, happy that the mood had brightened.

Erin motioned for Lauren to follow her and walked through one of the doorways into a small but well-lit kitchen. The room couldn't have been more than 15 feet to a side, with an old gas stove, warm brown wooden counters and, surprisingly, a full half-dozen bright, uncovered windows. Sunlight streamed onto the worn linoleum and gave the room a bright and inviting disposition that wasn't hinted at by the dull exterior of the building.

Erin fetched a pair of bowls and spoons, as well as a box of generic bran flakes from the cabinets, and set them on the small round table in the center of the room.

"I hope you don't mind 2%," she said as she retrieved a jug from the fridge. She was visibly calmer, but there was a light quake still in her voice.

The girls chatted over their bowls of cereal for nearly an hour, and their topic of conversation roamed wildly, but never did it stray to discussion of their near-wreck. Eventually though, Lauren plucked up the courage to say something about it.

"So, are you ok?" she began, treading carefully and looking for the right words. "You seemed really...upset."

Erin's expression turned stony, and she lapsed into silence, staring down into her cereal as though looking for answers.

"I'm sorry, forget I mentioned it. I just want to be sure you are ok."

Erin raised her head. Unlike earlier, she was able to keep her tears in check, but only barely.

"No, I'm not," she stated rather matter-of-factly, with a piercing sadness that struck Lauren to her core.

"Lauren, have you ever hid something from someone? Something big, but something that you wanted to share with them but couldn't?"

Lauren froze, unsure exactly what was coming next.

"We've been friends now for a while, honestly I think you're the best friend I've ever had and I trust you but I just, just-" Her words came quicker and quicker, running together until she cut herself off.

Erin stood, pushing her chair back slightly as she did so. Her tone and the abrupt shift of position took Lauren off-guard, who sat there with her spoon halfway between her mouth and bowl.

Erin paused for a moment, took a slow, deliberate breath, and grabbed the bottom of her shirt. Quickly, as though she were afraid she might lose her nerve, she slid the thin fabric up over her head and shoulders, revealing a black sports bra and her alabaster skin.

Thick, ragged scars of purple traced across Erin's chest and arms. They ranged from pencil-thin to thicker than Lauren's finger. Most of them were old, faded, but a few fresher, angry red lines ran along her wrists and forearms.

Erin's crimson hair stood in stark, beautiful contrast to her ivory skin. She had the look of a porcelain doll that had been broken and repaired. The scars did nothing to hide her beauty, though, at least not in Lauren's widened, startled eyes.

Lauren couldn't help but feel a tinge of jealousy at the gentle, sloping curves before her.

Erin was twisting her shirt into knots as she wrung her hands. She eyed Lauren nervously, staring intently for what her reaction might be.

"How," Lauren began, her voice barely above a whisper.

"It was four years ago," Erin cut her off. "It was late, my mother was asleep in the back seat, my dad was driving. We were on the way home from St. Louis."

As she spoke, Erin's voice took on a distant tone, as though she was detached from the memory.

"The guy that hit us, the cops said he had been drinking. I didn't find out until a month later when I woke up. He hit us head on, I went through the windshield of our jeep and they had to cut me out of the back seat of the other vehicle."

Lauren's jaw dropped. She was amazed that her friend and her family had survived, and her reaction in the truck was suddenly made clear.

As they spoke, Erin sheepishly put her shirt back on.

"I'm sorry," Lauren said lamely, wishing she knew what else to say. "How did...are your parents...that is, do they also have...?"

Lauren couldn't think of a way to phrase her question, so she simply nodded at the scars.

"No, they don't have scars," Erin replied simply.

Slowly it dawned on Lauren.

"My mother died instantly, dad lasted a few days..."

Erin's voice trailed off, and Lauren felt an incredible desire to give her a hug, some kind of embrace to let her know she wasn't alone.

But she couldn't.

The pair spent the morning talking intensely. It was as though the floodgates had been opened and Erin poured her heart out. For nearly four years, Erin had been living here virtually alone. She was supposedly in the custody of her aunt, Veronica, but she had rarely seen the woman since the accident. Apparently, she would swing through a few times every month, borrow money from Erin's life insurance check for drugs, spend a night, and usually be gone by morning. Erin had little love for the woman, and it seemed it was mutual.

Well, that explained the self-help books: Erin had to be an adult, to pay bills, to balance a budget all on her own, starting at the tender age of 12.

Lauren couldn't imagine the pain Erin must have felt, must continue to feel every day. She tried to imagine losing her mother or her father, even just one of them, but the thought brought chills to her heart.

As noon rolled around, the mood had continued to improve, and the bond between them had deepened. They were discussing the finer points of online bill paying when Erin interrupted abruptly.

"Do you want to see the rest of the house?" asked Erin, suddenly standing. "I wouldn't mind changing, and you must be baking all bundled up like that."

Erin motioned at Lauren's thick winter turtleneck and jeans. Not waiting for a response she continued.
"You're a little thinner than I am, obviously, but some of my stuff should fit you."
Lauren opened her mouth to say she was fine, but Erin was already on the move.
Erin set off down a different hallway, shorter this time. At the end was a large wooden door, which she opened. Upon entering, it was clear that this was the master bedroom.

Again Lauren was surprised by the furnishings of the room. A huge four poster bed dominated the center of the room, several framed pictures hung on the walls, though most of them were covered with black cloth. A door to the side seemed to lead to a bathroom, and a large walk-in closet dominated the other side of the room. More books were piled in the corners, and the furniture all seemed to be the same

warm, brown wooden variety of the rest of the house.
"Go ahead and make yourself comfortable, sorry again for the clutter," said Erin, as she walked into the closet, stripping her shirt off again as she did so and tossing it into a small pile of laundry in the corner of the room. As she disappeared around the corner, Lauren looked around for a place to sit. There weren't really any options besides the bed, so that's where she sat.

A few minutes later Erin returned wearing a black pair of shorts and t-shirt. Her pale, shapely legs were covered in the same deep scars as well, a harsh tapestry of the past. She was putting her unruly curls up in a ponytail as she walked, something Lauren had never seen her do.

In fact, Lauren thought to herself, it may have been the girliest thing she had ever done. The way she expertly bundled and restrained her hair made her look as though she would be at home on any volleyball court in the country.

A grin must have broken out across Lauren's face, because Erin froze.

"What?"
Lauren tried to stifle a laugh but couldn't.
"You try dealing with this mess." Erin's voice was laced with frustration. "It's a nightmare! I dream of having hair as straight as yours!"

Erin nodded her head back to the closet.
"Go ahead and change if you want, you can wear anything you like. I have a bunch of pajamas on the left."
Lauren was reluctant, but the house was warm and her clothes were stifling. Furthermore, she didn't want to seem ungrateful, she knew her friend was in a delicate state.

The closet was full, but Lauren could probably count the number of items that weren't black, red, or dark gray on a single hand. She slipped out of her heavy garments, holding various items up to guess their fit.

She must have been taking a while to decide, because Erin poked her head around the corner and gave out a low, teasing whistle.

Lauren jumped in surprise and covered herself up, blushing in her underwear.

"Hey!" she laughed, "No peeking!"

Erin had a huge grin on her face.

"Serves you right for making fun of my hair! I just wanted to make sure you didn't get lost back here."

"Well I am doing fine thank you!"

Lauren pulled a pair of sweatpants off a shelf and threw them at her friend, who ducked back around the corner with a chuckle.

Alone again, Lauren couldn't stop blushing at the thought of her friend's gaze. Her senses oddly heightened, she rushed to find an outfit while ignoring the sudden heat she felt.

Finally, Lauren settled on a pair of plaid pajama pants and a black shirt.

The pants were loose, and the shirt had plenty of room left in it, too. Lauren looked at herself in the floor-length mirror she found in the closet and picked her appearance apart.

Walking back into the room, Lauren found Erin curled up on the bed, watching a small television set and absentmindedly toying with the remote.

"...been nearly eight years since her disappearance, but people across America, and in fact across the world, have not yet given up hope..."

Lauren stepped into the room and the hair on the back of her neck rose. The voice coming from the television belonged to a man who still featured prominently in her nightmares: Kent Dailey.

"...Today we're going to be speaking with Cardinal Giordano Bruno. I hope I'm saying that correctly." Kent spoke with boundless enthusiasm and as Lauren approached the bed, his beaming face came into view on the screen. "Now, Mr. Bruno, you're from the Vatican. Can you remind us where the Pope weighs in on all of this?"

He hadn't changed much, except that his perfectly positioned hair now had a touch of gray to it. He still looked young, a camera-friendly sort of charming. Except the eyes. The eyes still spoke malice to Lauren's heart.

"This guy is such a tool," Erin said with obvious disdain, surprising Lauren. "He totally abused the story of that girl to get where he is, and he just can't let that shit go."
In that moment, Lauren loved Erin. She beamed at her friend, speechless with joy that someone else saw Dailey for the jackal he was.

Erin looked over, having expected a response to her comment. What she saw instead was Lauren's big, goofy grin looking back at her.

"What?" she said, confused but grinning as well. Lauren's smile was infectious.

"Nothing," said Lauren, who quickly tried to hide her expression. Discussing Dailey wasn't something she wanted to do.

Suddenly suspicious, Erin pressed for information.

"What do you mean it's nothing? You've got a huge dumb grin on your face for something."

Scrambling for a distraction, Lauren picked up a pillow and whacked Erin with it.
Erin lay there, eyes wide in shock at the unexpected attack. For a brief moment Lauren thought perhaps she had crossed a line. Erin really wasn't much of a physical contact sort of person, and Lauren had definitely gone to great lengths to avoid it their entire relationship. But, swiftly enough, Erin's surprise turned to an impish grin and she retaliated with a pillow of her own.

The fight only lasted a few minutes before both girls were tuckered out, their hair mussed and their cheeks red.

Lauren was sitting on a stack of books beside the bed, brushing her hair out of her eyes while Erin sat on the floor, leaning her back against the mattress.

As she tucked a stray lock behind her ear, Lauren noticed a small streak of red on her pillow.

"Oh my god," she said a little too loudly, "Is that blood?"

As she snapped her eyes up to look at Erin their gaze met. One of the freshest cuts on Erin's arm seemed to have split in their excitement, and a tiny stream of blood was working its way quickly towards her elbow.

"Shit," Erin said, standing quickly and walking to the bathroom, hand pressed against the wound.

Lauren followed her, her unclad feet making no noise as she padded across the hardwood and onto the slate gray tile of the bathroom. Erin was examining her arm in a mirror, applying pressure with a cotton swab from a jar next to a deep sink set into a gorgeous green marble counter. A huge tub set into the floor dominated the master bathroom. It seemed extravagant in the otherwise fairly normal home, an impression that was further magnified by a separate, mid-sized walk-in shower.

Tiny red droplets led a trail to Erin, who was swearing softly under her breath.
Lauren was far, far outside her comfort zone. Obviously this injury wasn't from a years-old car accident, but how does one broach the topic of...whatever this was?

Erin met eyes with Lauren's reflection in the mirror.
"It's, um, less crazy than it looks."
It was a statement, a question, more. It was the beginning or the end of a conversation, and Lauren wasn't sure which.

Lauren opened her mouth to speak, thought better of it, and closed it again, prompting a response from Erin nonetheless.

"I know what people say about me in the hallways," she began. "I know people notice the cuts, I know you notice them. I don't want people to notice them. It's not for them, it's for me."
Lauren nodded, trying to understand, as Erin turned around to face her.

"This is going to sound crazy, and I don't really want to talk about it--"
"You don't have to," Lauren interrupted, frightened by the direction she thought the conversation might take, frightened it would somehow hurt their friendship.
"I do. I do, Lauren, I can't talk to anyone else, I don't have anyone else. Somebody has to know, maybe that's part of it."
Erin had a desperate look in her eyes as she spoke those last words. So Lauren again became quiet, and let her friend speak her mind.

"It's, um, it's like this right? I don't really know how to start. The scars from the accident, they let me know it was real, I mean I know it was real because here they are, all over me."
Erin traced a finger across a particularly deep scar on her left arm.

"When I got into that car, I had my parents, I had a life, and hopes, and dreams. When I woke up they were all gone, replaced by these scars. I didn't understand, I still don't understand. There are times I wonder if I am still in that bed, and that this is all some twisted fucking dream, and I look at these scars and I think, 'No, this is real, look at these scars, feel this ugly roadmap of your history carved into your body.' I know it was real because I can feel that it was real. Most of the time it helps. It grounds me. Sometimes it doesn't."

Erin's finger crossed from the old to the new, dragging a line of fresh, cherry-red blood as she traced the open cut. Ice wrapped around Lauren's heart as she did so.

"I do this, um, to myself. I do it when I have a really bad day, when I have trouble telling what's real or what isn't. I can, um, cut myself and see the blood, feel the pain, and I know that it has to be real. What's more, I can look back the next day, or the next week, and say yes, this is fresh, the others are old, they must be different, it can't be from the accident. Sometimes I can go without it a while, when the pain is low and the memories stay distant. Sometimes the pain's inside, though, sometimes the doubt and the anger in my heart is...more."

By now both girls were crying again.

Lauren wished again that she could embrace her friend, that she could give her that simple comfort. But it was impossible. She thought about their conversation earlier in the morning, about Erin's bravery.

Maybe someday she'd be brave enough to share her secret too.

Chapter 5

Gabriel was sleeping. His jet black hair was a mess and his ruddy face was scrunched up in reaction to whatever he was dreaming about, but he was finally sleeping.

Lauren had been trying anything and everything she could think of for the last two hours trying to comfort him.

The lithe seventeen-year-old was sprawled across the couch in the living room, with Gabriel in a net-walled crib beside her. Her shoulders ached from holding the fussy toddler, and the time-worn cushions felt fantastic. Lauren sighed deeply, relishing the silence,

Aside from her little brother, she had the house to herself. Her parents were out on a date trying to, how had her dad put it? 'Recapture the spark.' Lauren tried to remain hopeful, but things had been getting worse lately, a lot worse.

Gabriel had been delivered almost two months early, and mom had been so drunk at the time that they couldn't even give her pain medication for fear her heart would stop. The memory of that night still gave her nightmares; waiting outside the hospital room, the yelling of doctors, nurses. Police running in and out of the room.

Yes, Gabriel had been born with a host of problems, in a broken home. It must seem such a dark and scary world to him.

Every day Lauren woke up staring at the ceiling and wondering how two people could fall desperately in love with each other, get married, and then suddenly stop.

The only conclusion was that something had changed. Lauren tried every morning to convince herself she hadn't been that change. Every day she put on the unfailing, smiling facade she knew her father needed to see, and tried to run from the question that haunted her.

Pestered by her subconscious, Lauren stood and paced softly around the room. Her tan legs drawing the same tight circles as her thoughts.

Lauren wasn't sure how she would have gotten through it without Erin, since that day in the truck their friendship had been unshakable. They spent time together most every day; walking through the woods around Lauren's home; babysitting Gabriel, who seemed to bring a special, joyous light to Erin's eyes; or simply doing homework and taking turns bitching about their treatment at school. In all honesty, the bullying was preferable some days to the stormy atmosphere at home. Better the enemy you can hate, instead of the painful knowledge that the ones you love will hurt you.

The time she spent at Erin's house was by far the most enjoyable though, often times they would simply read, both absorbed in a book, music blaring over the radio, sharing chocolates or popcorn and ignoring the world outside the door.

What Lauren felt in the woods while running, Erin felt within the sanctuary of her house wrapped in a blanket and lost in the written word. To share that time with her was a valued treasure. Despite her own love for the freedom of the outdoors, she was surprised at how familiar Erin's home felt too.

Like she was where she needed to be.

Lauren smiled to herself at the thought, and her pace slowed as the tension left her mind. Their conversations together ranged far and wide during those quiet, lazy afternoons; from school to politics and beyond. They were the types of talks that stretched the mind and bonded the heart.

Eventually the low rumble of an engine pulled Lauren back to the present. It was definitely the truck. She glanced nervously at Gabriel, she didn't know how long she had been in her own little world but with his condition she felt guilty for her lapse.

He was fine though, his little feet kicking at his blanket as he slowly rolled over in his sleep.

Lauren strained to listen to the tone of her parent's voices as they approached the house, but they were speaking quietly so it was hard to tell their mood. Then again, if they weren't yelling at each other, maybe things had gone smoothly.

The lock turned and the front door opened, Lauren's smile was firmly painted onto her face as her mother and father entered the room.

"Hi guys," she said cheerily. "How was the *date*?"

She winked playfully at the pair, hoping she sounded sincere.

Allison looked at her daughter, managed a weak smile, and then walked off towards her bedroom. John stayed behind, a troubled look on his face.

"Sweetie," he began, his tone sad and defeated. "I think your mom and I might need you to take Gabriel to his doctor's appointment tomorrow. We uh, are gonna go to a meeting."

Meeting? He couldn't be talking about a divorce, surely things weren't that bad? She had considered it of course, but still clung to the hope that somehow it would all work itself out.

John sensed Lauren's worry.

"These past couple years have been... We're gonna go and talk to someone, a professional, about what's going wrong so maybe we can fix it."

There was a determination in his voice, and she knew he had not yet given up on his marriage.

Lauren breathed a small, barely audible sigh of relief.

"Like a counselor or something."

"Yes. Lauren, I know you've noticed this but things aren't really uh, going... well. Between your mother and I. Gabriel was kind of a wake-up call for her. He has to be. I can't do this without her, I don't want to. But... something has to give."

Lauren's discomfort grew, her father's voice was deeply laced with emotion. She could hear his voice crack as he finally opened up to her about the worries that must have plagued him since Gabriel was born. Maybe before. She wasn't used to seeing him this vulnerable, it was frightening. Her father had always been her rock, a grounded place in an uncertain world.

"I'll do it, dad, don't worry. I'll watch him." she replied, hoping to stem the tide of emotion.

Gabriel had to be seen regularly, especially when he was this young. The doctors at St. Mary's told them fetal alcohol syndrome could cause all kinds of unexpected issues, and that close monitoring was the best prevention.

John smiled at her.

It wasn't the weak, forced smile of his wife, but one filled with genuine pride in his 'little girl.' He reached out for a hug, and they embraced.

Once again he was her rock, and some of her anxiety was laid to rest.

Lauren helped her father move Gabriel and his crib back into her parents' room and then headed to bed herself.

Sleep eluded her.

She pulled out her phone and shot a quick text to Erin, an expert at putting Lauren more at ease.

Hey.

Erin knew her well enough to respond quickly to the single word message. A tiny bubble popped up immediately telling her that "Er-bear" was typing.

Hey, everything ok?

Yes/No. Dad's taking mom to see a counselor tomorrow. I won't be at school, taking Gabriel to the doctor about 1.

Unsurprisingly, Erin jumped at Lauren's unspoken invitation.

Want company?

Gonna skip? Just for me? :p

Course I will, wanna bring him over in the am? Can hang here a while...?

Deal, see you at 8?

Psh, I love you, but I'm sleeping in. See you at 10..30? ;)

Love it, ok sleeping beauty.

Just what I needed, Lauren thought to herself as she snuggled deep into her blanket and drifted off. Erin lifted her spirits every time.

Lauren woke with a start, unsure of what had roused her from her sleep. Her bedroom was dark, lit only by the dim, silvery light of the moon. A gentle tapping at her window startled her further, eliciting a startled squeak.

Erin's shadowy form was outlined against the glass. She waved before quickly tucking her hands under her armpits, clearly chilled.

Lauren slipped out of bed, goosebumps raising on her bare legs in the cool air as she walked to the the window and slid it open as quietly as she could.

"What are you doing here?"

"Working on my tan."

Lauren stifled her laughter. It certainly wasn't the first time erin had visited her in the dead of night, though their midnight walks usually took place in warmer weather.

"Get out here you tart, I'm freezing my ass off."

Lauren looked down at herself, her boyshorts and tanktop were hardly warm enough to brave the cold.

"Let me throw some pants on, one sec."

Erin let out a dramatic sigh, rolling her eyes.

"If you must."

Minutes later the two were crossing Lauren's yard. A comfortable quiet followed the young women into the woods. They walked close together, warding off the weather as they strolled beneath the branches. This first twenty minutes or so were spent in a cozy silence, but as Lauren's mind woke up, her brow creased.

"So, you're worried that your parents are gonna split huh?" Lauren was no longer surprised at how well Erin could read her mood, and pick out what she was thinking. A simple nod was all she needed as confirmation.

"Look, Lauren," Erin paused along the path, her face bright with the moon's light. "I'm always going to be here for you, ok? No matter what happen. Besides, you're tough. You're going to be ok."

Lauren paused as well.

"I know, I'm just. I can't help but feel like..."

"Like maybe it's your fault?"

"Yeah."

Lauren turned to continue down the path with a defeated hunch in her shoulders, but Erin stopped her with a hand on her shoulder. Lauren turned back to her and was surprised by a swift, firm hug from her normally reserved companion.

After a moment of shock, Lauren returned the embrace. She was acutely aware of the heat of her friend's body, even through the fabric of their jackets. Lauren knew the danger, it was an electric hum in her mind. Erin's bouncing curls, only a few inches from Lauren's face, smelled of sweet flowers and spices.

Every rustling leaf, every gently creaking branch, stood out sharply in Lauren's mind. She was just about to speak when Erin pulled away and turned back down the path.

"Thanks," Lauren said simply, striding quickly to catch up after a brief pause.

"For what?"

Erin's smile was beautifully infectious, it lit up her whole face.

"For the hug," Lauren said with an exaggerated eye roll. She took a risk and nudged her friend playfully.
"Oh no, that was all for me," Erin laughed at Lauren's look of confusion and nudged her back.
"You walk too damn fast! You're like a gazelle when you worry, I just needed a break."
"Ah, is that so!"

Their banter continued as the two pushed deeper into the woods. Lauren found herself hoping that her friend was only kidding, and thanked the darkness for covering the red in her face.

The next morning dawned cool and foggy. The late summer heat had started to give way to chilly nights and cooler days these past few weeks, but the humidity remained. They were left with thick fog banks that floated like ghosts in the early hours before the sun burned them away.

Lauren loved it, they way the fog blanketed the landscape and created a deafening silence. She glanced down at her watch, it was only 7:04, she was two miles into her morning run and still felt energetic, so she decided to push past her usual turnaround point. Her feet carried her deeper into the woods than she usually went, and she embraced the peaceful solitude. In her mind she was running through a primordial forest that had never seen a footprint. It was easy enough to believe in the silent, magical landscape of misty trees. At 7:25 her alarm beeped and reluctantly she turned and headed for home. Her footfalls were nearly silent as she padded back towards her house, more at peace than she had in a very long time.

Lauren peeled out of her sweat-slick clothes and tossed them to the floor as she stepped into the shower. Her muscles burned from the abuse of eight long miles. Steaming hot water soon soothed her tight calves and her breathing and heart rate returned to their normal levels, leaving her only the endorphins of a runner's high.

Her spirits were soaring, a welcome change from the gloom she had felt lately. As she tried to put a finger on exactly what had changed, her thoughts turned to Erin. To their moonlit escapade. To the warmth of her embrace, a risk she'd only dreamed of taking a few short years ago. Her cheeks flushed at the unbidden thought, and she felt a shy smile cross her lips. Shaking her head in the steamy haze, she turned the water cooler to clear her mind.

She was whistling as she emerged from the bathroom, eliciting a look of surprise followed by raised eyebrows from her father as he sipped his morning coffee.

He was wearing a tie, highly unusual. Lauren snorted with laughter as she walked dripping across the room, wrapped in a towel and putting her hair up into a makeshift turban with another.

"Just what are you laughing about young lady," he chided jokingly.

Good, he was in a good mood too.

"Nothing father dearest," she replied, adopting a silly British accent.

"Very good, carry on," he followed suit. "Pip pip!"

"Pip pip, yes indeed," she dropped her tone, holding an imaginary pipe to her lips.

The pair of them burst into gales of laughter as she stepped into her room, still smiling.

Lauren slipped into a pair of dark blue leggings and a bright green tank top to go with her lime colored sneakers. She was, after all, still working on expanding Erin's color palette.

Lauren practically danced her way into the living room. Swooping down and picking up Gabriel, she lifted him from his crib and spun in slow gentle circles for a moment, causing him to erupt into youthful squeals of delight.

Gabriel hadn't started to talk yet.

The doctors tried to be positive about it but at two and a half years old Lauren and her parents were long past starting to worry.

Lauren loved to pick him up, to play with him and tickle him, to simply hold him. Secretly, in her heart of hearts, she prayed that someday her gift might help him. That she might rid him of the terrible curse that Allison's negligence had wrought. But it didn't. Like her mother, and her mother's side of the family, her power seemed to have no effect on Gabriel.

It was odd, the way she thought of her mother since Gabriel's birth. More and more it was *Allison*, instead of *mom*.

Was that cruel?

Guilt clouded her mind as she justified the change within herself.

Lauren shoved her gloomy thoughts away, unwilling to sacrifice her good mood. Forcing another big smile she stopped spinning and held Gabriel against one hip as she wandered into the family kitchen.

Settling Gabriel into his high-chair was almost always a struggle, but today he cooperated and Lauren had no trouble getting him situated before making them each a bowl of cereal.

Breakfast was busy, loud, and warm. The whole family gathered around the table, reminding Lauren of happier times. They spent nearly an hour talking, laughing, being a family again. Lauren hadn't seen her parents so comfortable with each other in a long time. Eventually though, the time came for their appointment and they got ready to leave. Lauren picked up Gabriel and walked them to the door.

"Have a good day sweetie," Allison said, giving her daughter a gentle hug. Lauren smelled only faint perfume, and she dared to hope that maybe, just maybe things could turn around.

"Take care of the little guy," her father began, giving them each a kiss on the cheek. "And, young lady."

His stern but loving look pulled her distracted attention from her brother.

"Don't get too used to skipping school, ok?"

"Aye aye captain," Lauren gave a joking salute as she replied. She and Gabriel waved as their parents pulled out of the drive, watching until they rounded the bend in the narrow drive.

"Well now, mommy and daddy are gone, what shall we do, huh?"

Gabriel cooed back as Lauren took him for another spin above her head.

Her watch said it was barely past 9, so she had time to kill.

The pair made their way into the living room, Lauren holding him expertly as he energetically tried to escape. Lauren pulled out an old battered box of wooden blocks, an heirloom from her own childhood, and plopped her brother down in front of them. She clicked on the television. The family had only recently gotten cable, mostly for the educational programming that Gabriel might benefit from.

A panel of commentators greeted her as the screen flickered to life. Five thirty-something women discussing gossip and news. A skinny blonde with big hair was in the middle of a rant of sorts.

"Well, Bonnie, if you must know then yes. Yes it is important to believers that the eighteenth anniversary of the Rebirth is in a few weeks!"

As she spoke she clutched a small necklace in one hand, visibly angered at whatever her colleague had said moments before.

"Casey, now you know I didn't mean anything by it, it's just that not everybody believes the same things you do, ok? We can all just agree to disagree?"

A stout brunette was backpedaling, while the other three fixed nervous smiles and glanced back and forth from the cameras to their comrades.

Casey, the blonde, had a too-wide look in her eyes and clearly wanted to continue, but she calmed down and collected herself.

"So, as I was saying, believers in the Reborn Immaculate Child will be turning out in droves in the coming weeks as they celebrate the birth of the girl they believe to be the reborn savior. This year will mark the tenth since the disappearance of the Immaculate Child, but believers have still planned demonstrations and events around the world."

Lauren watched with morbid curiosity. It seemed that there was to be a parade in her honor in her hometown of Galesburg, and that one of the churches there would be renamed to the Corvidae Place of Healing Worship. She snorted, unsure whether to be amused or terrified at the idea of people still obsessing over her.

The program droned on for a while about her life, the eight years of her youth she had spent touring the country, and what her followers were doing now. They replayed footage of her meeting the Dalai Lama when she was six, as well as various other interviews with important people. It was, admittedly, somewhat interesting, Lauren thought. At least until they played a clip of her final interview with Dailey.

She clicked the TV off with disgust, Gabriel started to cry. "Aww baby bear, don't worry. That's a very bad man. Lolo is here to make you smile."

She picked him up and blew a raspberry on his tummy, immediately sending him into a fit of giggles. She glanced at her watch, 10 on the dot.

Screw it, Erin will deal with us being early.

Lauren, still carrying her little brother, collected his things and made ready to depart. Her dad had already set aside a bag with toys, diapers, extra clothes, and his favorite snacks so it was a simple matter of slinging the strap over one shoulder and she was almost ready to go.

As a finishing touch, Lauren slipped on a long, thin, wrist-length pair of gloves. A present from Erin for her birthday last year, the gloves made Lauren feel more secure in public and meant more to her than Erin could possibly have known. The gloves themselves were of supple, ultra-thin leather in a neutral brown. Lauren loved them.

When Lauren arrived at Erin's house, she pulled into the drive. She reminisced for a moment on the first time she had done so. She put the truck in park behind Erin's beat up moped, a dangerously unstable machine in Lauren's opinion, which she had bought a few months back. A loud banging noise startled her, ringing out in the clear morning air. It seemed to be coming from Erin's fenced-in backyard.

Lauren and Gabriel shared a confused look. The sound seemed to excite him though because he smiled widely and clapped his little hands.

Grinning back, Lauren exited the truck. She walked over to his side and hoisted him out. She grabbed the diaper bag from the truck bed and approached the house, the door was unlocked and had a bright pink sticky note on it.

A/C is broke. I'm out back, help!

Love,

Erbear

Lauren was puzzled. Erin was perhaps the least mechanically inclined person she knew, despite of her hoard of instructional manuals and guidebooks.

The banging came again, this time persisting for nearly a minute. The noise prompted Lauren to enter, calling out for Erin as she did so. No answer.

Lauren headed for the back door and upon exiting she found her friend. Erin was standing in a pair of shorts and a camisole, headphones in and a mp3 player tucked under her left shoulder strap. In one hand she held a hefty, wood-handled hammer and in the other a collection of time-worn diagrams.

Erin was smashing the hammer repeatedly into an ancient air conditioning unit that protruded from one of the house's windows.

Somehow, Lauren doubted the manual specified that particular course of action.

A few years ago, when they had first met, it would have been a cold day in hell before Erin showed this much skin outside. Even within the privacy-fence lined confines of her yard. But as her friendship with Lauren had deepened so too had her confidence grown.

Now here she stood, her arms and legs exposed to the bright rays of the sun, her scars open to the world. Lauren had to concentrate to see the scars these days. She had grown so used to them, they were so much a part of who Erin was, that they didn't stand out anymore.

Instead, she saw her friend as she truly was; beautiful.

"Fuck," Erin shouted with frustration, giving the machine one last whack with the hammer. She turned around, freezing when she saw she had an audience. Her breathing was heavy, her cheeks and chest flushed with exertion. She yanked out her headphones, managing to look sheepish and peeved at the same time.

"You uh, look a little crazy, hon," Lauren said with laughter in her voice.

"Watch it," Erin growled in response, pointing the hammer at the pair. Wiping her sweaty brow and tucking a strand of hair behind her ear, Erin cast a last, angry look at the morning sun, as though its brightness and heat had personally offended her.

It was quarter-past ten and already the day was shaping up to be a muggy one.

Erin couldn't pretend to be mad for long though, because Gabriel immediately captured her attention.

"Well hello young man," she cooed at him. "Your big sister is a making fun of me isn't she? Yes she is!"
Gabriel giggled at her tone and the attention he was being paid. He babbled a nonsense reply.

"What's that? She's a pain in your ass too?"
Erin followed her words by sticking her tongue out at Lauren as she walked past, back towards the door.

"Hey," Lauren said, irked. "Don't say stuff like that in front of him, he might pick up on it..."

Her words trailed off at the end, and the two shared a more serious look, they both knew that Gabriel wasn't likely to be speaking anytime soon, and why.
"Sorry," Erin paused and gave her a sad, understanding look. "I know. You're right."

She cast around for something to ease the tension and settled for tickling Gabriel's feet.
"Your big sister is usually right, you know that little guy?"

The awkward moment of silence passed, and the group headed inside. They made their way to the living room, where Lauren placed Gabriel in the large playpen set up there. Shortly after Erin had met Gabriel, she had insisted on spending some of her monthly life insurance check on the playpen. It was huge, took up most of the living room, and it had taken them hours to figure out how to set it up, but Lauren admitted that it was incredibly convenient at times like this. Lauren pulled out a few of Gabriel's favorite toys, a pair of bulky plastic dinosaurs, for him to play with.

With Gabriel safely stowed, Lauren followed her companion to her bedroom. To Lauren, who spent much of her time outdoors, the house felt comfortable. Erin was a different story. Before she even entered the room she could hear Erin loudly lamenting the heat, her griping ranged from actual words to the loudest and most pathetic sighing that Lauren had ever heard.

When Lauren crossed the threshold she saw the room was empty. Erin must be in the walk-in, presumably changing clothes. Lauren flopped herself down on the bed, kicking out of her shoes. Erin must have heard her come in, because she called out from the closet.

"Seriously, who the fuck invented bras? They're hot, and constricting, and sweaty, and *dumb*; obviously invented by a man!"
Lauren laughed out loud, Erin's reaction to the would-be tragedy of having no air conditioning was hilarious.

Erin poked her head back into the room, glaring from the doorway. Wordlessly she returned to rummaging around through her wardrobe. Lauren threw up her hands, feigning innocence.

Finally, with an exaggerated sigh, Erin re-entered the room. She was wearing a tiny pair of dark blue shorts, smaller than anything Lauren had seen her wear before. Lauren couldn't help but follow the path of Erin's swaying hips across the room from her vantage point. The shorts left very, very little to the imagination as Erin's curves pushed the fabric to the limit. She didn't have a shirt on, instead she wore a black, front-zippered, heavy duty sports bra which was doing its best to suppress Erin's well-developed chest, but wasn't really up to the task.

Meeting her friend's gaze, Lauren blushed a little and averted her eyes. Mostly. She chided herself internally on peeking. Well, for getting caught at least. One of the few things she had yet to get fully used to was Erin's unabashed nature at home, which was so opposite her demeanor outside the house.

Erin held in her hand a bunched up ball of fabric, which she carried across the room to the nightstand. She yanked open a drawer, pulled out a long, orange-handled pair of scissors and savagely chopped the ball in half. Setting the scissors back down she held up the newly modified item, it was a shirt, although realistically it was more of a crop-top at this point. She nodded as though satisfied and pulled the shirt over her head, it left a fair amount of her midsection exposed. With her new garment in place she reached up, undid the zipper of her bra and pulled it off her shoulders, throwing it into the closet and then collapsing down onto the bed with a huge, drawn-out sigh of relaxation.

"So," Lauren began, holding in laughter. "That's a pretty bold fashion statement you've got going on there."

"Listen, the further into the alphabet you get, the more amazing it feels to finally set your ta-tas free," Erin replied, stretching out on the bed but being careful to leave a space between herself and Lauren.

Lauren looked down at herself, her own chest had yet to develop as far as Erin's and frankly at this point she had given up on ever having more than she'd already grown. Erin had considerably more to deal with, though Lauren didn't know exactly how 'far into the alphabet' she was. She was jealous of Erin's shorter, curvier stature, preferring it to her own tomboy-ish looks. Though she would never admit those feelings to her friend.

It wasn't that she was ashamed, not really anyway. But the idea of physical contact with another person was still too mortifying to really contemplate.

"Seriously, I think I'm going to melt," Erin whined, oblivious to the envy her friend was feeling. "And my ass barely fits in these damn shorts anymore, I look like a hoochie and I'm too hot to care."

"You're not going to melt, drama-queen," Lauren said, exasperated. "But yes, you look ridiculous, where did you even get those shorts? I mean, I love that they're something other than black, but they look like they were made for a 10-year-old kid."

A brief pause followed before Erin spoke.
"They are made for a 14-year-old, if you must know, and I'm not *thrilled* about the color."

"You stuffed your ass into shorts from four years ago," Lauren asked, lifting her head from the bed and looking at her friend incredulously. "Why would you even do that to yourself? Why did you keep the dang things?"

"I was hot," cried Erin. "I can't be held accountable for the desperate measures I was forced to take! Besides, I resent the phrasing 'stuffed my ass into' being applied to anything."

The haughty, indignant tone that Erin took on was too much for Lauren, who laughed even harder.

"We can't all be bean-poles you hussy. I bet you fit into clothes from when you were six!"

Their banter was interrupted by Gabriel, who chose that moment to start screaming bloody murder. His piercing wails were easily heard across the small house. Lauren slipped gracefully from the bed, her long strides carrying her from the room in just a few steps. Erin attempted to do the same but snagged a foot on her bedding, crashing to the floor instead.

"Ouch, fuck," Erin said, causing Lauren to pause briefly. "No I'm fine go ahead."

Lauren didn't miss a beat, she sprinted down the hallway, her socks skidding on the hardwood. Gabriel was laying on the ground near the center of his pen, his face reddish purple and covered in tears and snot.

Lauren let out the breath she was holding, he was fine, just upset. She stepped over the low wall of the enclosure and picked her brother up. Gabriel was shaking in her arms, Lauren looked around for the cause of his distress but could see nothing.

"What is it, what's wrong," Erin asked, stumbling into the room.

"I don't know, I don't think he fell or anything," came Lauren's worried reply.

Lauren began rocking Gabriel gently in her arms, and when that failed to quiet him she instead put him on her chest and patted and rubbed his back. Gabriel screamed and screamed until he ran out of breath, and then continued to cry noiselessly, his mouth open in silent howls. Lauren grew increasingly worried, though she tried not to show it, and Erin sat on the couch, nervously biting her fingernails and staring intently at the pair.

Lauren felt Gabriel stiffen in her arms, then go limp. Alarmed, she held him back a moment to see him better. His eyes were half-closed, and drool was dripping from his mouth. He stiffened again, his tiny body going rigid and quivering. Lauren's eyes widened in fright.

"Erin!"

Erin stood up, hands over her mouth.

"What's happening, why does he look like that," Erin cried, her voice high with fright.

Gabriel finally went limp again, but his complexion was patchy, ranging from red to deep purple to almost gray.

Lauren had never seen a seizure before, but as her baby brother stiffened once more she knew that's what this must be. All clarity of thought left her, and without a word she tore across the room, yanking the door open so hard it smashed into the wall as it swung.

In an instant Lauren was out of the house, her strides eating up ground as she crossed the front yard. She halted her sprint by banging into the door of the truck, fumbling in her pocket for the keys as she opened the unlocked door.

With Gabriel's small form still held tightly to her chest she fumbled to start the ignition and violently shifted the vehicle into reverse as it fired up.

Erin was barely past the doorway as Lauren spun the truck, tires barking on the asphalt and then stomped hard on the gas, leaving smoke and rubber on the road in her wake.

Cobden had no hospital.

The nearest one was in Anna, the next town over. Lauren prayed as hard as she could, begging someone, anyone to help her. To help Gabriel. The roar of the engine couldn't drown out Gabriel's strangled cries as he bounced back and forth between rigid silence and limp screaming. The scenery outside the truck blurred as Lauren accelerated faster and faster.

Gabriel's cries grew weaker and weaker. Lauren tried to ignore it, to deny it within herself. She held her tears in, biting her lip so hard it bled. The thin red needle of her speedometer had gone beyond the numbers listed on the dashboard, and still she stamped her foot as hard as she could on the pedal. The check engine light came on, she ignored it. Smoke began to billow from under the hood, she ignored it. Gabriel's cries grew weaker still, and then shuddered to a raspy halt. He stopped tensing.

She couldn't ignore it.

The truck began to make a high pitched, shrill keening noise as the rural landscape between the towns gave way to the larger, more developed streets of Anna. Cars honked and swerved away from Lauren as she whipped through the town. Lauren was nearly there, she could see Union County Hospital. In front of the hospital was a large, well maintained expanse of grass. Rather than drive around, Lauren cruised right off the road and onto the grass, the tires of the truck kicking up dirt and tufts of grass as she did so. The truck sputtered, jerking violently, and died at the edge of the lawn.

The hospital was still a few hundred feet away, she hadn't even made it to the parking lot. Lauren rocketed from the cab, Gabriel clenched in her arms, and ran with all her might towards the door. She didn't know what she was saying, but she was screaming for help from anyone who could hear her as she blew into the waiting room like a tornado. A woman in blue scrubs ran up to her, taking Gabriel from her arms.

The woman was speaking, yelling even, but Lauren couldn't hear her. All she heard was silence, Gabriel's silence.

"...Happened! How long has he been unresponsive?"

Sound returned with a rush, a deafening roar of noise erupted as Lauren tuned back in. The woman was looking at her, desperate for an explanation. Gabriel was being taken down a hallway, surrounded by nurses and a pair of doctors.

Lauren moved to follow, but the woman held up a hand as if to stop her.

"Don't touch me," Lauren screamed at the top of her lungs, she shoved the nurse with both gloved hands, causing her to stumble backwards. She ran after her brother, following until she was stopped by a large security guard. The man restraining her was like a mountain. She couldn't see the sadness in his eyes as he held her gloved wrist, all she saw was her own rage and despair. He didn't flinch as she exhausted herself pummeling her free hand into his arm.

Finally, panting, she sank to her knees sobbing. Immediately the man let go, allowing her arms to fall to her side. He stood silently beside her, as if unsure what to do.

She didn't know how much time had passed, every moment felt like an eternity to her, but the nurse came back to her. She asked the same questions as before; what happened, when, how, where. Lauren answered softly, her voice robotic, distant.

After a time the nurse left.

Lauren stayed where she was, silently detached from the chaos around her. A million thoughts crossed her mind, a thousand doubts and countless worries. What did she miss? What if he had permanent damage? How could she forgive herself if she had made his life harder than it already was?

As though summoned by her thoughts, the pair of doctors re-entered the hallway, they'd been crying.

No.

The doctors saw her, still kneeling on the floor, and one began to cry again.

No-no-no.

Lauren sat, horrified. She knew what those looks meant. One of the doctors opened his mouth to speak. At the same time, the security guard reached out to place a comforting hand on her shoulder.

Something within her snapped, ice flowed through her veins and her heart stopped as surely as her brother's had. She slapped away the guard's outstretched hand, rising to her feet. Turning on her heel she ran. Out of the lobby. Out of the hospital. Across the lawn. Past her smoldering truck. Lauren ran down the city streets of Anna, out into the wilderness between it and Cobden.

Her socks were tattered, stained dark red with the blood of a dozen blisters and cuts that had formed and healed as she ran. Her shirt was dotted with crimson from a nosebleed she had developed a few miles ago, it had only lasted a moment, her gift had seen to that.

Her body ached, but it was nothing compared to the shards of glass inside her heart. Night had fallen over an hour ago, and still she ran.

Headlights on the highway did not slow her pace, it wasn't until she heard Erin screaming her name that she finally slowed and stopped.

Erin came screeching up on her moped, slamming hard on her brakes, stepping away from it and ignoring it as it fell over in her haste to reach her friend. Erin had been crying, she wore long black jeans and a thick hoodie. Without hesitation she wrapped Lauren in a hug, the thick fabric of the hoodie warmed Lauren as she wrapped her arms around her. Lauren noticed the growing chill of the night air for the first time. Slowly, Lauren wrapped her arms around Erin.

They stood that way for several minutes, silently embracing.

Lauren had never felt so small.

Chapter 6

Lauren looked at herself in the mirror. She'd lost weight. Unsurprising.

Everything she ate, even old favorites, tasted like ashes in her mouth. The woman looking back at her had also lost much of her healthy glow- the tan she had cultivated all summer had faded in the thin winter sunlight.

She had the house to herself, again. Her father was at work and her mother had been gone for more than five months now. When Gabriel died, Allison had left. She didn't say where she was going, she didn't say if she'd be back, she'd just... left.

"Another gift from the girl who just keeps on giving," Lauren whispered solemnly.

The woman in the mirror said nothing, she simply stared back. The stare haunted her, she looked into her own soul and she saw the blood of her brother on her heart.

Epilepsy, the doctors had said. Rare, but not unheard of in children with fetal alcohol syndrome.

"There was nothing you could have done. No way to predict it."

The words did nothing to comfort her.

They were a jagged pill for the girl who could cure anyone. Anyone but the people she loved, it seemed. Her thoughts turned, as they always did, to Gabriel's face. It wasn't the face she wanted to remember, not the smiling, laughing, joy-filled angel she missed every day. No, it was the blue-gray face. The lifeless, agonized little face she had carried into the hospital.

Lauren played the scenes over and over again in her mind. Should she have called an ambulance instead of driving? Maybe if she had left sooner, when he first started crying. Doubts piled onto doubts, building until they threatened to overwhelm her. Again her anger flared, higher than before. She had been angry for weeks, always simmering and threatening to boil over. At first, Erin had been the solution. She was the only person who could possibly understand the pain. But she wasn't here, not now. Another problem she had created for herself; Lauren had been pushing away the only person she could truly confide in, and she didn't even know why.

Lauren pounded a fist against the mirror once, twice, again. She lashed out at her reflection. She hit it harder than she intended, shattering it into dozens of large, razor sharp fragments. She gasped in pain as falling pieces of the mirror sliced open her hand, wrist, and forearm. She stood shocked while blood splattered everywhere as the cuts spread wide, dousing the white porcelain of the sink.
All other thoughts left her, the fire in her arm drove them away. She watched as her wounds stitched themselves back together, leaving just one mid-sized piece embedded in her palm. Slowly, excruciatingly, it was pushed out by her healing flesh, landing with a clatter in the sink before her.

As the last traces of the cuts disappeared, Lauren examined her arm closely, not even the faintest hint of her injury remained. What's more, the pain had been so distracting, so intoxicating in the way it had wiped her mind clean of Gabriel. Even now, after the fact, it stood fresh in her mind, forcing out other, darker thoughts.

Her cellphone rang. It was the soft, beautiful violin solo that she had chosen for Erin's ringtone.

"Hey... haven't seen you since school on Monday.. You ok?"

Erin was worried. She could hear it in her voice.

"Yea, of course I am," she tried to control her tone, unwilling to worry her friend further. She tried to remember what day it was. "I, um, just woke up from a nap, so I'm a little fuzzy. It's, um, Wednesday right?"

"Lauren it's Thursday. Night. Like eight o'clock at night."

Shit.

"Lauren?"

"Yeah, I'm here," Lauren replied. Could it really be Thursday? Where had the time gone? Did it matter?

"I'm coming over," Erin said forcefully.

"No, no, it's alright I'm ok. I think I might just be uh, getting a cold or something, it's got me out of it," Lauren lied.

"No, you misunderstood, it isn't optional," Erin said. "I meant to say I'm in your driveway and walking towards the door."

Lauren panicked, she stared at the pool of red in front of her and tried to think of a way to get rid of it, or explain it away. Hastily she turned on the hot water in the sink, full force.

"What is that racket? Did you turn on the shower," Erin questioned her suspiciously over the phone.

"No, I'm washing my hands," Lauren was stumbling over her words, making it up as she went along. "I was, um, I had to pee."

"Well-"

"I'll see you at the door, gimme three minutes, Okay bye," Lauren interrupted her friend and hurriedly ended the conversation. She ran to her room and grabbed a sock from the floor. Dashing back towards the bathroom she began scrubbing at the sink and counters, hoping to hide the evidence of her injury.

A knock on the door. Damn, that was fast.

"Coming," Lauren shouted.

The sink had a stubborn pinkish tinge to it, but it would have to do. She ran back into the living room, tossing the sock through her bedroom on the way.

When Lauren opened the door she could tell her friend was displeased. Erin had the look of an irritated mother. Like a woman whose child had been misbehaving.

"I take it we stayed in again today," Erin spoke with a scolding tone, casting a meaningful look at Lauren's attire.

Shit.

Lauren was wearing her favorite 'nightgown,' it was actually a sleek, ivory button-up shirt that had been her mother's. The shirt clung suggestively to her, and it was the only garment she had on, a fact she was suddenly much more aware of. The shirt extended to her mid-thigh, much shorter than just about anything she would consider wearing out, and it wasn't even buttoned up all the way, leaving a lot more of her chest out than she was comfortable with. She realized with alarm that she must look like the cover of one of Erin's trashy romance novels.

Lauren felt her face grow flushed. Embarrassed, she half-crossed her legs and crossed her arms in front of her chest.

"Lauren," Erin's voice was heavy with worry, and as Lauren's eyes refocused, pulling her from her discomfort, she could see that Erin was very clearly near to tears.

She wanted to say she was okay again, she wanted to lie to her friend to keep those tears at bay, but she couldn't. On the phone, or in a text message, but not to her face, not into the eyes of her truest friend. Instead, Lauren broke their gaze, looking down at the floor instead.

Erin took a tentative step forward, putting her arms out for a hug, but Lauren balked, taking a rapid half-step backwards. The pain in Erin's eyes was evident, and she awkwardly lowered her arms. After a silent moment Erin turned back towards the door, but Lauren stopped her.

"Wait. Please don't g-go," she stumbled a little over the last word, tears springing to her own eyes as a lump formed in her throat.

Erin didn't turn around, but her head perked up and she stopped moving.

"Why," she said dejectedly.

"Because it hurts, and I'm alone, and I need you," Lauren was breathing shallowly now, the memories and the heartache were pushing back towards the surface again.

She wanted so badly to tell her friend, so desperately to unburden herself. But after so long, she wasn't sure she knew how.

Erin turned back to see Lauren's face streaming with silent tears and her shoulders shaking with raw, unfiltered pain.

Again the silence lengthened between the two of them, until Lauren felt certain that she would turn away again.

Erin looked around the living room. It was one she had seen many times before, the couch, the bookshelves, it was all familiar, but it had grown cold since last she'd seen it. Gone was the warmth, the feeling of home that used to fill the Corvidae house.

Lauren watched her friend's gaze wander, and she tried to figure out what she was thinking. At the same time she fought within herself, she raged against the high walls of secrecy she had built. She raged against the fear that spoiled the love she had for Erin, the fear that her gift, her past, would destroy it all. She opened her mouth to speak at least a dozen times, but nothing came out.

Erin seemed tense, like she was angry as well, but when she lashed out at Lauren it was still unexpected.

"What the hell are you thinking!"
Lauren trembled, it was the first time she'd ever heard Erin shout in anger.

"You 'need me'? Then where the fuck do you get off pushing me away? You ignore me, you ignore most of my calls, my texts, but you 'need me' right? On whose terms? I'm not a yo-yo to get yanked around, Lauren!"
Erin was livid, her own pent-up emotions spilled out through her words.

Lauren tried to speak, but was interrupted before she could begin.

"No, don't you say a word! Look Lauren, I know you're hurt right now, I get it, I know the pain you're feeling. I know it better than I want to, better than anyone should."
By now Erin was choking on her words, stuttering through her own tears as she laid her heart out before her friend.

"Lauren, I've *been* where you are, I *know* the pain you're feeling and I know the darkness you're walking through. I d-don't have a f-family, you're all I have and you're p-pushing me away. I loved Gabriel, we both lost him, we don't have to lose him alone. I need you, I don't want to lose you both."
Lauren felt suddenly ashamed.

"I'm sorry."

Lauren's voice was meek, quiet, but in the tense silence between the pair it carried well.

Lauren could feel the tension building between them as Erin visibly contemplated her simple apology.

"I don't want you to be sorry! Dammit Lauren I want my friend back!"

Erin grabbed a pillow from the couch and with a frustrated half-shout half-growl threw it across the room. She missed, but in doing so she slipped and landed squarely on her bottom.

Immediately, Lauren's hands flew to her mouth. She tried not to, but burst out laughing. It broke the spell, ripping through the ugly atmosphere of the room. Lauren was so stunned she couldn't help but laugh. She let out a half-hiccup half-snort, eliciting a giggle from Erin as well. The tension flowed out of the room like a refreshing wind that stoked the glowing ember of their bond.

"So, what now?"
Erin answered Lauren's question with a sniffle and a mischievous glance.
"Put some pants on, I've got to introduce you to the greatest catch-all solution mankind has ever made; alcohol."
Lauren had never had alcohol before, she knew that Erin occasionally got liquor from her aunt, but she'd never had any herself.

"I don't know Erin... It's late...".
"Lauren, please. You have to get out of this house. You need air. You need change. You need to live."

Nodding, Lauren walked off towards her room, with Erin right behind her. As she walked through her door, she spotted the blood-soaked sock she had hastily thrown there. There was no way that Erin would miss it.

"Um, hang on," she muttered, spinning around and blocking the doorway. Erin nearly bumped into her, pulling up an inch or two short.
"What? What're we stopping for we've got bad decisions to make!"

Lauren looked for an excuse to keep Erin away.
"I'm uh, naked under my shirt," Lauren blushed furiously, both because of her admission and for the fact that it was true.

"This may come as a surprise to you, Lauren," Erin said sarcastically. "but everyone is naked under their clothes."
Lauren didn't think it was possible to blush harder, but she felt as though her cheeks would burst into flame.

"No," her voice was tiny with embarrassment. "I mean I'm not wearing any underwear!"

It finally clicked in Erin's mind, and she blushed a little as well.

"Well I hardly see how your panties can be in a bunch about it if you're running around commando," Erin attempted to use her trademark wit to cover her embarrassment. "I'll um, I'll wait out here I guess, but slap a hurry on it!"

Lauren nodded, and dipped into her room, closing the door behind her. First order of business was to hide the sock, which she did by stuffing it deep into her clothes hamper.

Next, Lauren turned to her dresser. She paused. For once she was actually stumped as to what to wear.

"What do you wear when you're going to get tanked," she wondered aloud to herself.

"Something cute! Dress up for once," Erin's voice carried through the thin wooden door, her unsolicited advice startling Lauren.

Hmm, a dress. Lauren decided to break from convention and run with it.

She pulled a sensible pair of red underwear from her dresser, slipped them on, and then turned to her closet. A few minutes of rummaging around revealed a smooth, dark brown satin dress that she'd received from her grandfather for her sixteenth birthday, but had never had occasion to wear. The dress was slim and form fitting down to the hips, where it flared slightly into a flowing skirt that reached to her knees. It had a long, revealing split on the left, up to the middle of her thigh.

As she removed her shirt she wondered if she ought to bother with a bra, opting against it since the dress was strapless.

With the dress in place she gave a spin in front of her mirror, wondering if her spur of the moment decision was a mistake. She shook her head and moved to take the dress back off.

An impatient knock on her bedroom door reminded her that Erin was unlikely to appreciate a lengthy fashion decision. The knock also solidified her dedication to her silly prank. Lauren slipped on her gloves and pulled open the door, waltzing past her stunned comrade as though nothing were out of sorts.

"Oh, now she's speechless," Lauren teased, full of bravado.

Erin was just as sharp as ever, quickly composing herself and sauntering past to the front door.
"Well, I suppose if you feel that's appropriate attire to leave the house in..."

She let her sentence end in a tone that suggested Lauren had thrown on sweatpants and a hoodie.
"Oh, so you want me to change then?"

Lauren turned back to the doorway of her bedroom.

"Not what I said lovey, you look gorgeous. But if we wait any longer it'll be *legal* for us to drink. Now text your dad that you'll be sleeping over and get your fine ass in the truck. If you ride with me on the moped in this weather and that slinky getup you'll catch your death."
Oh, right. Lauren had forgotten for a moment that it was early January. Time had lost much of its importance to her these past five months.

"Well, I could drive us both in the truck y'know," Lauren said, realizing that Erin must have already braved the weather once to get here.

Erin didn't hesitate.
"Good idea, it's freaking cold out."
After donning a pair of fur-lined boots and a warm jacket, Lauren led the way out into the snowy landscape of the yard. The girls locked up the house and rushed as quickly as they could to the ancient machine in the driveway. The trucks discolored paint job was hidden beneath the snow, but Lauren knew it bore the scars of the abuse she had put it through the

day she had lost Gabriel. She had insisted that her father fix the broken truck, rather than get a new vehicle. She clung to it like she clung to every memory of her brother, with desperate obsession.

Erin sensed the storm clouds brewing in Lauren's mind and nudged her.

"Come on thundercloud," she said softly, reassuringly. Lauren smiled weakly, but did as she was told, putting the truck in gear and heading off to Erin's.

Lauren hadn't visited much these past months, less and less as time had gone by in fact. Not because she didn't want to, but because she had been slowly sinking deeper and deeper within herself. She didn't realized how much she'd missed it until she stood there again.

Here was a place that still felt like home.

"Alright dove, pick out a movie," Erin said, tossing her jacket aside and kicking off her boots. "I'll get the booze and we'll make this a proper slumber party."

Lauren kicked out of her own boots and headed for the DVD shelf in the bedroom. They'd watched most every movie Erin owned, many of them more than once, but they had a few particular favorites. Usually sappy romances from the golden age of cinema.

Erin's collection spanned a vast breadth of genres, from gritty horror films, which she enjoyed considerably more than Lauren, all the way to the feel-good redemption stories and tear-jerker romances that Lauren preferred.

Lauren thumbed through the titles, reminiscing on the many nights they had spent together eating popcorn and pining after the kind of love that seemed only to exist on screen, or huddled in terror at some new and horrific slasher film. Eventually she settled on one of their favorites, 'The Breakfast Club.'

She was just popping it into the tray of the dvd player when Erin reappeared, she held a frost-covered bottle of pale yellow liquid and a pair of shot glasses. She also had a small grocery bag, but its contents were impossible to determine through the dark plastic.

Smiling, Erin shook the nearly full bottle, sloshing its contents.

"You're in for a treat," Erin said in a sarcastic tone. "My aunt seems to have purchased the cheapest, shittiest bottle of tequila she could find. Probably why she didn't finish it."

Lauren grimaced, "Fantastic. Y'know maybe we shouldn't drink it? We could wait till we get something better..."

"Did you pick out the Breakfast Club? Oh honey no, that's not a tequila movie," Erin set her supplies down amidst the blankets of the bed and began to search through the film selection for herself.

Less than a minute later she paused.

"Hey Lolo, have we watched 'Wild things' together yet?" Erin looked back over her shoulder at her friend on the bed, who was peeking inside the grocery bag.

The movie didn't ring a bell, so Lauren shook her head no.

"Are we doing the thing with the limes and the salt?" Lauren asked hesitantly. She knew that there was some special way you were supposed to take a tequila shot, but she certainly didn't know how to do it properly.

"Yep, if you're gonna do it, do it right," Erin said playfully. She paused, giving Lauren a funny look before continuing. "So whaddya think... try something new?"

She waved the case at Lauren, who shrugged and nodded her consent.

As the dvd played previews for other movies Erin began to explain the process of correctly shooting tequila.

"Honestly, this might be easier with your gloves off?"

Lauren hesitated, but shook her head no. Erin shrugged, she was long-used to Lauren's peculiar hang-up regarding touch.

"Alright then, first, lick your hand, right there between your thumb and index finger."
Erin laughed at Lauren's obvious confusion, and demonstrated. Lauren followed suit,
"Next, you pour some salt on your hand, right on the same spot," she said, taking Lauren's gloved hand and pouring salt on it from a shaker she got from the bag.
"Next, you take a slice of lime," she pulled a small tupperware container of freshly sliced limes from the bag as well, taking a single slice out and handing it to her companion. "No no, in the same hand as the salt."
Lauren could tell that Erin was having a blast enlightening her, so she patiently followed her instructions to the letter.
"Ok," Erin continued, after setting herself up as well and pouring each of them a shot. "So the order is this; Breathe out, lick the salt, pound the shot, shove the lime in your mouth and bite down on it, got it?"
Lauren looked unconvinced. "I'm going to bite into a lime. Like straight into it?"
"Trust me, it'll be better than leaving nothing but tequila in your mouth," Erin replied, laughing at her friend's lack of experience.

"Ready? We'll do it together."
Lauren took a deep breath and nodded.

Erin nodded as well, raising her shot to cue Lauren in.

They began simultaneously. Lauren thought the salt was bad until she got to the tequila. It tasted like death. Stale death. Immediately, she regretted her decision as her body tried to decide whether to gag or simply stop breathing. She scrunched her eyes shut as they watered, then forced them back open, waving her hand in front of her open mouth hoping to fan out the gasoline she had just filled it with.

Erin was mumbling something from around the lime wedge in her mouth, pointing at Lauren and clearly trying not to laugh.

Lauren coughed, sputtering until Erin reached out and shoved the lime in her hand up to her mouth. Surprisingly, it helped. A lot, actually.

After a moment Erin took out her own lime wedge. she was holding her sides and howling with laughter. Eventually Lauren followed suit, spitting out her lime and scowling at her friend.

"I'm sorry, but that was adorable. How do you feel?"

Lauren felt a little lightheaded already, but that was likely from the horrible aftertaste of the tequila. She was, however, unwilling to admit defeat to her more experienced friend and so instead she did her best to act nonchalant.

"Nothing to it," she lied.

"Oh, I'm sure, all that coughing was because it went down the wrong pipe right," Erin replied winking.

The video was finally at its main menu. It featured a pair of sultry, scantily clad women and a rugged looking man. Her cheeks flushed a bit while her mind raced.

"What is this movie about," Lauren inquired, her curiosity piqued at the risqué menu screen.

"Well, it's kind of a thriller. A drama. With um, with a bit of dark romance, I guess you'd say?" Erin stumbled a bit over the words, which was unusual.

"You'll like it. Oh, and we can play a drinking game with it too!"

Lauren was certain that Erin's sudden excitement spelled trouble.

Maybe it was the tequila, maybe it was the funk she had been in lately, but Lauren decided to throw caution to the wind.

"Fuck it. What's the game?"

Erin's confidence was infectious, and before she had even explained the game Lauren caught herself grinning as well.

"Well, this movie has a ton of... surprises in it, but you're also pretty smart," Erin began innocently. "So I propose that every time you are taken by surprise - anytime something really, *truly* unexpected happens - we take a shot?"

Lauren's eyes narrowed.

"And I alone will decide when I am surprised? That seems overly sporting of you. What's the catch?"
Erin feigned offense.

"Lauren! I'm hurt. Yes of course you alone decide if you're surprised... or if you're gonna chicken out."

There it was.

Erin knew her well, and knew that she would be honest to a fault, and likely too proud to turn down a drink.

"Deal."
The movie had been on for less than an hour, and Lauren's head was swimming. The girls were six shots in, and giggling madly at the drop of a hat. The room was spinning suspiciously in the corners of Lauren's vision and it felt like someone had turned up the heat in the house by at least 10 degrees.

Erin was pouring another shot as the two women on-screen went from trying to kill each other in a swimming pool to passionately making love.

"I didn't say I was surprised," Lauren protested, failing horribly at keeping a straight face.

Erin spilled liquor on her long-sleeved shirt in response. "Dammit, don-don-don't you try to deny it. There's no way you saw that coming!"

Erin was stumbling over her words and mumbling through a mouthful of sleeve as she tried to lick the freshly spilled tequila off her arm before it hit the bed.

The shots were going down a lot easier, for both of them, and Lauren's mind was delightfully clouded. All thoughts erased except the here and the now.

She really was enjoying herself.

"Ok f-fine, pour it up sishter," Lauren's words were slurring noticeably and both women erupted in laughter again.

Salt, tequila, and a little bit of lime later and Lauren was shaking her head to clear it of tequila fumes. Erin swore, she seemed to be caught in her shirt as she tried to remove it. "Hold still," Lauren admonished her.

Erin obeyed, one arm out of her sleeve, the dark shirt was pulled up and covering her face and left arm. Her stomach and ample chest were left exposed but for a deep purple, lace-covered bra. It was lingerie really, and nothing Lauren had seen before. The scars across her body, almost the same purple, carried Lauren's attention across her sweeping, graceful curves.

"C-come here you drunk," Lauren stuttered, distracted by the sudden heat she felt.

Lauren tentatively reached out and helped her friend get herself unstuck, handing her the shirt after she did so. Erin tossed it over her shoulder and it landed on the floor behind her. Sighing drunkenly, Erin fanned her flushed cheeks. "Thanks," Erin's tone was lower, different in some way that Lauren couldn't quite nail down. In her intoxicated state it felts velvety and warm.

Erin reached up to brush a loose lock of crimson hair out of her face, the motion drew Lauren's eyes down to her elegant neckline, and lower. The lingerie she wore teased Lauren with tasteful coyness.

She was staring.

Lauren snapped her eyes back up to Erin's face, incredibly conscious of her actions. Her cheeks blazed and the room felt hot. She looked to the television. She was hoping to find something to distract herself from her own embarrassment, but the women on screen were even more intimate than before. Her eyes immediately darted back from the screen to her friend's face. She was terrified but excited. Her whole body craved what the two women on screen had, but she forced herself to remember it was beyond her grasp. Her mind insisted she see Erin's facial expression to read her mood.

Whatever she expected, she didn't find it.
Erin was looking at Lauren with a curious expression, she was leaning slightly forward and her cheeks were flushed a deep scarlet that almost matched her hair.

Their eyes locked for several quiet moments, the only noises were the sounds of passion from the film, underscoring the tension in the room.

Both girls opened their mouths to speak at the same time, their jumbled words yielding two sheepish grins and another pause.

"G-go ahead," Lauren's voice was barely above a whisper, her posture mirroring Erin's. Her heart was beating out of her chest and she gripped the bedspread beneath her tightly, hoping Erin didn't notice.

"I was, um, just going to ask you if," Erin paused, took a deep breath and continued. "If we were still playing our game…"
"Game," Lauren said questioningly, her mind raced, what game?
Erin nodded, she put her hands on the bed, leaning even closer to her friend. A few strands of hair fell across her face again, adding a messy grace to her looks that Lauren found incredibly distracting.

"The one where we um, take a shot whenever something… unexpected happens," Erin's voice was melted chocolate, sweet and rich.

"Oh," Lauren almost breathed the word, her chest was tight and her gaze was locked with Erin's.

Erin crawled closer, her hands on the bed just outside Lauren's lap and her body only a few inches away. Her chest rose and fell with her deep, heavy breathing and Lauren caught the smell of her perfume. It was the same intoxicating combination of midnight rain and roses, at once familiar and exotic.

"So, are you surprised," Erin looked deeply into her eyes, the question was heavy with meaning.

"By the movie?" Lauren's reply was meek, timid.

Erin shook her head, "No."

Lauren's breath caught, she couldn't speak so she nodded instead. She felt heat growing in her cheeks, her chest, and elsewhere. Erin's full, cherry-red lips seemed only a heartbeat away from her own, and Lauren caught herself lost in her emerald green eyes.

Erin seemed to hesitate, then she sat up, they were so close that her chest brushed lightly against Lauren's, sending an electric fire through her entire body.

"Give me your hand," each word dripped honey as Erin spoke, and Lauren timidly reached a single gloved hand out to her.

Erin took her hand, holding it gently in her own. She kissed it softly, right where Lauren's thumb met her index finger. The heat of her lips warmed Lauren through the thin leather of her gloves, she lingered a moment before pulling back.

"To help the salt stick," again Erin's voice sent a shiver through Lauren, who half-closed her eyes at the unfamiliar sensation.

Sure enough, Erin lightly poured a small portion of salt onto Lauren's hand where it half melted on the glove. Next, she poured a shot from the half empty bottle and put it gently into Lauren's hand, the cool glass standing in stark contrast to the heat pulsing through her.

"Ready?"

Erin's question was stated with quiet confidence, it swept Lauren's mind clear of everything outside that moment.

"Erin wait, I need to, um" Lauren's mind was clouded, she was drunk on Erin's presence as much as the tequila, she couldn't seem to put words together or decide what she needed to say. Obediently, Erin waited a moment. She reached behind herself, but Lauren didn't see because she was so enthralled by her closeness.

"I-I," Lauren's mind raced with sudden doubts, a thousand things that could go wrong, but she couldn't get the words out.

"Lauren," Erin's voice was husky, it melted into Lauren's mind in a way that settled her fears. "Tell me, what, what do you want?"

The question hung heavy in the air, and Lauren had no idea what the answer was. Synapses fired throughout her body, betraying her desire and making it impossible to concentrate.

"I-I don't have a, um, a lime," Lauren whispered timidly.

Erin nodded, half-smiling in a way that caused Lauren's lips to part as her breath was taken away again.

"Go ahead, I'll get you one."

Maybe it was Erin's instruction, maybe it was her need for courage, but Lauren did as she was told. Shyly, aware of Erin's steady gaze, she licked the salt from her hand and, closing her eyes for a moment, drank the harsh liquor. She barely noticed it. Opening her eyes she looked for the lime, and saw it.

Erin was holding it between her full, perfect lips. The juicy center was pointed at her, and their lips were only centimeters apart. It was a suggestion. It was an offer. It was insane.

Lauren accepted.

Erin moved forward as Lauren did, their lips pressing firmly together as Lauren bit into the lime wedge. The tartness of the lime in combination with the warm, wet embrace drove Lauren over the moon. After a brief moment of hesitation, Erin reached up, wrapping her arms around Lauren and twisting her fingers into her long blonde hair. They pushed closer together as the kiss deepened, Erin's chest pressing against Lauren's.

Lauren felt weak, her body responded to Erin's advances with a mind of its own. She allowed herself to fall backwards onto the bed and felt a thrill of electricity as Erin followed her forward. Erin's hair gently tickled her face and neck as it fell around them.

Every detail felt raw and clear. The softness of the sheets, the heat between them, the cool droplet of lime juice that made its way down her cheek.

Erin pulled back for a brief second, taking the lime from her mouth before returning to Lauren and kissing her once more.

Erin kissed her way down Lauren's jawline to her neck and across her shoulder, causing her to instinctively reach up and wrap Erin in her arms. Lauren's fingers traced the deep scars across Erin's back only to feel them disappearing beneath her hands.

Clarity struck Lauren like a lightning bolt. Terrified, she grabbed Erin's shoulders and pushed her roughly away.

"Erin, we can't!"

Erin looked shocked at the panic in Lauren's eyes and voice. Her shock quickly turned to anger and Lauren could see that she was incredibly hurt by the apparent rebuff.

"What, Lauren? I--"

Lauren was hysterical, her eyes wide with shock as she took in the sight of Erin's pristine, flawless skin. The dulling effects of the alcohol were offset by stark terror as Lauren looked at what she had done.

Erin backed away, creating a space where she had been on Lauren's lap a moment ago.

"I don't understand..." her eyes started to swell with tears. She reached timidly to touch Lauren's face but sharply pulled back when Lauren recoiled.

"Don't!" Lauren said, too forcefully. "Don't, you can't, you can't *touch* me!"

At her words, Erin looked at her hand as though it had done something wrong. Her confusion grew when she saw the blank, featureless skin of her arm. Suddenly panicking herself, she stood.

"No, no, no, no!"

She stared in abject terror at her arms, holding them in front of herself and turning them over and over again. Her scars were gone, all of them. She leapt from the bed, stumbling drunkenly as she left the mattress and ran to her bathroom.

Lauren followed. She sprinted after her friend, hurrying around the corner.

Erin stood before the bathroom mirror, toiletries scattered about the small room. As Lauren watched, she ripped her bra off, clawing desperately at her chest for the scars that Lauren had taken from her. She spun, looking in shock over her shoulders and seeing her back was clear as well.

They locked eyes, a haunting look of betrayal on Erin's face. "Why?"

Erin's simple plea wasn't what Lauren expected. She expected how, or what, but not why.

Lauren tried to answer her, but the words were caught in her throat. Erin quickly drew her own conclusions.

"Why, Lauren?"

Erin was screaming.

"Why would you do this to me? You should have told me!"

Erin was sobbing, holding herself close as though suddenly ashamed to be seen.

"You took them away from me," she leaned forward on the sink, her knees weak. "You took all of my memories, you took my past. I would have given you everything I had, and you took more."

Erin's pain broke Lauren's heart as well, and she found the will to speak at last.

"Erin, I'm so, so sorry. I didn't-"

"Get out." Erin's interruption was quieter, very matter of fact.

"But, Erin," Lauren tried to continue.

"Get. Out." Erin said with more force. "Get out!"

Lauren flinched as Erin ripped the mirror from the wall, smashing it to the floor. She dodged a hairbrush, and then a bottle of soap as Erin flew into a rage. Finally she was forced to retreat behind the bathroom door, which Erin slammed behind her.

Lauren tried for nearly an hour to get Erin to respond to her, but she would only sob and scream that she never wanted to see her again. Defeated, she stumbled to the front door, pausing only to grab the tequila on her way. She pulled it open and stepped into the ice-cold winds of winter. She made her way to the truck, tripping and skinning her knee badly on the gravel as she did so. She swore, watching blood pour from the scrapes until it slowly stitched itself up again. She took a long pull from the bottle, as much as she could stand before her weak constitution forced her to stop.

Lauren climbed into the truck, swearing drunkenly as she put it in reverse and rumbled backwards into the street.

Her drive was short-lived. She crashed into a telephone pole less than a hundred yards from Erin's house.

When she regained consciousness her vision swam as she tried to clear her head. She didn't know if she had been out for a moment or an hour but the horn was blaring and broken glass littered the cab. A sharp pain in her chest caused Lauren to look down. A long, splintered piece of the pole had pierced her flesh just above her left breast. She absentmindedly wondered if it had pierced her heart, or if the pain she felt was from Erin alone.

Lauren pulled the splinter from her chest, amazed at how deep it had been. Thick red blood welled up from the wound and ran in streams down her chest.

"Just like Erin's," she wondered aloud, examining her arms and finding dozens of pieces of glass embedded there as well.

As she brushed the glass from her skin, she watched the cuts fade as Erin's scars had done.

At least she can make more, she thought bitterly. She felt guilty for her thoughts and then suddenly terrified. Lauren slammed into the door, it refused to budge, so she climbed out of the now empty windshield instead, slicing open her palms as she did so.

Lauren half-ran, half-stumbled back to the house, finding the front door unlocked as she had left it. She burst in, screaming Erin's name. The house was quiet, with only the loud, intrusive sounds of the dvd menu playing in the background.

"Erin? Erin!"

Lauren rushed to the bathroom door, jiggling the handle. It was locked. She screamed herself hoarse calling Erin's name and smashed her shoulder into the door again and again, trying to force it open.

But there was no answer.

Chapter 7

With a crack and a bang, the frame of the bathroom door
finally gave, sending the door flying open forcefully. Lauren
fell into the room, jarring her wrist painfully. Her hands
slipped on the slick floor as she tried to stand and she stared
horrified at the flood of crimson covering the tile. She
couldn't see Erin right away, from her vantage point she could
only see her pale, lily-white arm hanging over the side of the
deep, cast iron bathtub. Her wrist was laid open as far she
could see. Unable to stand, she crawled to the edge of the tub
and grabbed Erin's hand. It was still warm.

With renewed hope, she braced herself and managed to
stand. Her knees immediately weakened, however, when she
saw what Erin had done to herself. Thick, wide gashes were
carved across her body, everywhere that Lauren could see. Her
body was familiar, beautiful, and Lauren knew every cut
intimately, every ragged line. Erin had retraced the wounds of
her past from memory.

Erin was terribly still, her eyes open and her pallid lips
parted slightly, as if she were about to speak.

Gingerly, Lauren reached out to touch her cheek, it was
cooler than it should have been. Lauren felt cracks form in her
very soul.

She couldn't be gone, she refused to accept it.

She ripped off her gloves and reached out. Gripping Erin's shoulders, she shook her violently. The voice that had been stolen from her by shock and horror returned with a vengeance. She screamed at her friend to wake up, to say something, anything.

Erin's body was limp, her head rolling like a doll and her arms dangling freely.

Lauren felt every detail of the room burning itself into her heart. the dark, blood-soaked floor, cherry-red against the ivory tiles. Erin's beautiful body, carved by the butcher of her inner demons. The pool of blood she lay in. The unforgettable sadness in her eyes.
Someone must have heard the screaming, because the sound of sirens rose in the distance, but they fell on deaf ears within this private hell.

Lauren stopped shaking her friend, but couldn't let go. She held her close, wrapping her in a fierce hug. Her tears splashed against Erin's face as she poured out her heart, begging for a second chance.

Erin's perfume still clung to her, its sweet aroma burdened by a sickly tinge of death.

She screwed her eyes shut, feeling suddenly sick, and held on tighter.

When the police arrived, they found her still clinging desperately to her fallen friend.

They were speaking, shouting at her, even. They were trying to separate her from Erin, but their voices sounded like the buzzing of distant bees. Lauren was sinking into darkness and she didn't care if she ever came out.

The harder they pulled, the more desperately she held on. Erin's body was her tether, the thin line that tied her to reality, and they were trying to take it away from her.

Eventually the strong arms of the policemen and EMTs pried her away. It was only then that Lauren realized she was still screaming.

When Lauren was finally pulled from Erin, she felt as though all light was pulled away as well. She fought the men holding her with the ferocity of a tiger, clawing at them, kicking and biting, trying to get back to Erin. But they were too strong. Several times she felt her fingernails dig deeply into flesh, and deep within her mind she registered the sounds of pain she caused. But she was an animal, reacting only to the deep pain within herself.

Eventually she was dragged from the house, the cold air hitting her blood-covered clothing and chilling her to the bone. A young man was shining a flashlight in her eyes and two larger men in dark blue police uniforms were holding her arms behind her back and half dragging half-carrying her down across the yard towards a wailing ambulance. The flashing lights and piercing sirens were disorienting against the darkness of the night, and Lauren's stomach turned.

With little warning she emptied the contents of her gut, it reeked of tequila. The two officers dropped her, jumping back to avoid being splashed.

"She's probably got alcohol poisoning, get her to the ambulance," the voice of the young man, it was distant sounding and her vision swam and flickered in and out of blackness as he spoke.

Retching again, Lauren landed on all fours. The officers seemed unwilling to take hold of her now that she was making such a mess.

Another medic joined the first and they lifted her to her feet, with an arm over each of their shoulders they made their way to the ambulance, seating her on the back of it.

"Can you tell me your name?"

The concern in the man's voice was clear, and he stared intently into her eyes.

She couldn't seem to keep focus on anything, nothing kept her gaze for longer than a moment.

She threw up again.

"Go back inside, I can take care of this one," the second man ran off again, heading back across the yard.

"Honey, hey, I need to know your name," the man's voice was meant to be soothing.

"L'ren," she managed to mumble in response, her head hanging low between her knees. She was staring down at the asphalt, sounds and sights coming and going as the world spun violently around her.

The sound of squeaky wheels rumbling across the pavement temporarily pulled Lauren's gaze from the ground between her feet. Paramedics were rushing to load a gurney into the second ambulance, on it was Erin's broken form, her porcelain skin covered by a red-stained sheet. The cloth clung to her, stuck to her skin by the blood that covered her body.

Lauren's mouth was dry, it tasted of bile and her eyes burned because they had no more tears to shed. The sheet did nothing to hide Erin from her. She could see her blank, hollow eyes clearly in her mind. She could smell the blood and, perhaps worse, still feel her lips and hands.

Lauren tried closing her eyes, but it only made the visions clearer. There was an incredible pain in her chest, like a titan was gripping her heart and crushing it within his hands. The pain bloomed across her chest and she tensed her back muscles until she literally shook with pain.

The electric whine of a defibrillator built and then discharged, one of the paramedics yelling 'clear' as it did so. Lauren scrunched her eyes harder, wishing she hadn't seen her friend's body flopping on the gurney.

Lauren couldn't take it anymore, she stumbled dizzily from the tailgate of the ambulance, wobbling unsteadily on her bare feet.

"Hey now, you need to sit back down so we can take-" the paramedic was speaking to her in a calm, even tone, but Lauren ignored him.
She bolted.

The man made a move to grab her but she slipped his grasp and took off over the pavement and into the woodline across the street. There was shouting behind her, and she could hear the man chasing her, but her instincts took over. Her strides lengthened and her arms picked up a steady rhythm. She could hear him swearing as he fell behind, the wind whipping her hair behind her.
She ran for a long time. She was trying to run from the pain but it seemed the harder she ran the more it hurt.

The pain in her chest filled her lungs. It gripped her heart and tightened around her throat. By the time she reached the edge of town she was literally gasping for air. The tension in her back mounted, the muscles felt like they were going to rip her chest open or peel back from the bones, whichever gave first. She stumbled, falling to the cracked, dead grass that lined the highway.

She began to grow fearful, could you truly die of a broken heart? It certainly felt like it. It seemed when she breathed that there was no place for the air to go, her chest was full and getting fuller, as though filled with stone.

Her breath grew shallower and shallower. As she began to hyperventilate she clawed at her own throat, looking down she saw ugly purple bruising beginning above her breasts and spreading across her chest. Her eyes widened with terror. She tore open the deep v-neck of the strapless dress, watching the ugly purple spread to the middle of her rib-cage.

She started to black out, wondering if Erin had felt this helplessness and pain when she died as well.

With a sickening crunch and searing pain, she felt the skin on her shoulder blades split wide and felt rivers of blood running down her back. The pain was too much, and she finally slipped into unconsciousness beside the road.

The dull rumble of a powerful engine and the gentle sway of a large vehicle rocked Lauren awake. She was confused, she was laying on an unfamiliar bed, it smelled of stale cigarette smoke and cheap wine. She seemed to be wrapped in some strange fluffy blanket.

Stranger still, the clothing she had on felt all wrong, it was scratchy and overlarge.

Still groggy, she cracked open her eyes, her vision was blurry and the room was dark.

"Erbear? I think we fell asleep," Lauren mumbled and reached out a hand, searching for her friend. Instead, her hand dipped into a mysterious container of ice-cold liquid. She jerked it back, suddenly wide awake. Her eyes snapped open and she frantically examined the small, cramped room she was in. She was laying on a tiny bed, beside it, in a cup-holder like you might find in an automobile, was a glass of ice water. The small space was decorated sparsely, a wooden crucifix here, an old portable television there, and a tiny door directly opposite her.

"Erin? Erin!" She called again, still confused. Then she saw the dress, it was on a hanger at the foot of the bed. Still torn. Still covered in blood.

Lauren scrambled to get out of the bed, trying to shove off the funny blankets, but they seemed caught on her somehow. As she stood up she banged her head on the low ceiling. "Dammit," she swore loudly, punching the ceiling in anger and stepping from the bed. She put her weight down on a piece of the blanket and pain shot through her back, unfamiliar nerves cried out in protest and she immediately pulled her foot back.

"Ahh!" she let out a startled exclamation at the unexpected pain. What was happening to her?

Lauren felt the vehicle stop swaying, slow down, and finally stop, but she was absorbed in the blanket. It seemed to be covered in big fluffy white feathers, and she was having trouble finding the ends of it, it seemed to shuffle and move when she did.

The engine settled into a steady idle and she heard movement from the other side of the door.

Lauren looked for something to protect herself with, only now realizing how bare she was. She was wearing oversized flannel pants that were clearly made for someone much shorter and wider than her, they were cinched at the waist with what looked like the belt to a bathrobe. She had no shirt on, only a massive brassiere, it was almost comically too large for her, the shoulder straps being the only thing keeping it on her chest.

Her self examination halted as the door swung open.

It was a woman. A plump, older woman with too much makeup and a pair of wild, horn-rimmed glasses.

"Hey now youngin', jus' calm on den, we almos' there, an' it's an honor ma'am, on ma soul an honor," the woman had a strong creole accent and the sort of open-book, simple kindness in her voice that you'd expect from a Sunday school teacher or a grandmother. The woman gave an odd little half-curtsy, half-bow.

"Who are you, where am I, where are you taking me?"

Lauren's voice quaked with uncertainty.

"Only one place fern' angel," the woman winked and smiled again. "Found ye on side a'road las' night passin' through Anna. Figured on you was in some ol' bad way, peck'd y'up so's you'd be safe."

Lauren was struggling to keep up with the dialect, and as her fear subsided it left room for the soul-crushing loneliness and pain that still flooded her heart.

"Where am I?"

"Nem's Rosalina Merideaux, pleas'ta meet ya my lady. We's on' 'bout twenny miles for Mizz Caroline's. You 'gon be ok there."

She seemed satisfied with the answer and turned back ahead, leaving the door open.

Lauren nervously approached the door, the blanket still dragging along behind her. It seemed she was in the sleeper cabin of a large semi-truck.

Upon seeing Rosalina more closely, Lauren had no doubt that it was her bra she was wearing. The woman's chest was as massive as the rest of her. Rosalina motioned for Lauren to take the passenger side seat and fired the big diesel back up.

"C'mon up he'ah, if y'like. On my soul ain' nev'ah thought I's gon' live to see you return!"

Lauren moved to accept the offer, but the obnoxious feather cover wouldn't let go of her. As she wrestled with it, Rosaline began to laugh heartily.

"Neva' 'magined 'n angel have so much trouble wit'che own wings!"

Lauren's temper was worn thin already and she responded with a biting tone.

"And what the fuck should that mean."

The verbal retort that Rosaline dealt was sharp, and it knocked the sass out of Lauren, who stared in shock at the sudden transformation of the sweet old lady.

"Wat'che mouth youngin', it's the Lord's rules in my home, yes'm, Angel or not."

She made a sort of 'mhmm' noise, as if to back up her own judgment. She turned back to the road, leaving Lauren's mouth agape.

Lauren retreated back to the cabin, shutting the door behind herself.

Wings? Angels? What the hell was that supposed to mean? Lauren examined the blanket, it was big but fairly light. Lauren finally found an end, it tapered to a point. Tracing it backwards she found that it was somehow stuck to her shoulder blade. Frustrated, she yanked on it.
"Ouch!"

She jumped at the pain, flinching reflexively. The feathery appendage jerked as well.

What. The fuck.

Lauren's mind bent at the unthinkable implications of what she was seeing, feeling. It was impossible. She thought back to her last, horrifying memories of the night before. The pain, the unbearable pressure in her chest and the horrible ripping sensation in her shoulders. No way, she thought, shaking her head, more likely she still had a piece of glass stuck in there from the truck, and this stupid blanket was caught on it.

Lauren yanked again, it hurt, a lot. It felt like something was pulling at her shoulder blade, but with the kind of sharp pain you'd get from a hangnail. She examined the blanket more closely, it was warm to the touch. She dug through the feathers, looking for the fabric she knew had to be beneath them. It sent an odd, ticklish sensation down her spine.

Skin. Skin? The feathers gave way to pale, unbroken skin. Well, maybe not unbroken. The tip of each feather was embedded deeply into the skin, which seemed to be stretched tightly over long thin bones and lean, clearly defined muscles.

Maybe she had lost it, maybe she was in an asylum some-where and having some twisted, drug-induced dream, Lauren thought to herself.

As much as her mind wanted to deny it, what she had mistaken for a blanket did seem to be a pair of wings. More-over, they seemed firmly attached her back.

Resigned, but with growing excitement, Lauren experi-mented with the muscles in her back. She began by flexing and relaxing them in various combinations trying to get a reaction from the unfamiliar limbs.

They twitched and shuddered, flitting open and curling up with incredible speed. There wasn't enough room in the cramped living space, so she wound up knocking just about everything over as she practiced.

After one particularly uncontrolled motion, she knocked the portable television from its place atop the small end table. It crashed to the floor and flickered on.

"...tragic news from the small town of Anna, Illinois, this morning. A young woman was found dead after apparently committing suicide. Police there have said that there is a person of interest, I think we have a sketch, don't we Donna?" Lauren's wings drooped low as she was dragged back to reality and away from the distraction of her transformation. Erin's house was being shown with caution tape all over it, the door wide open and policemen searching the house. As she watched, an artist's rendering of her flashed up on the screen.

If the circumstances had been different she might have laughed, the girl in the sketch was far prettier than she. As it was, she barely managed not to break down again.

"...anyone with news of this young woman should report to the Anna police department..."

Dropping to her knees she picked up the device, looking for a power button. She found the button but it seemed to be broken, jammed inside the machine by its collision with the floor.

"... Police and paramedics on scene described the death as a suicide, but indicated that the young woman pictured on your

screen was a person of interest after she fled the scene..."
With increasing violence she jammed a finger into the button,
finally resorting to bashing the little television set against the
floor until the picture flickered again and died.

Lauren was no longer in the mood to experiment, she
wasn't in the mood to do anything. Remaining on the floor
she sat back and hugged her knees to her chest. Instinctively
she curled her new wings around herself, hiding her crying
face.

The truck pulled over and stopped, this time the engine
was shut off as well, leading Lauren to believe they must have
reached their destination.

Wherever that was..

Sure enough, Rosaline tapped lightly and then opened the
door.

"C'mon out he'ah child, y'oughta meet Mizz Caroline shain't
the mos' patient na."

Lauren stared stupidly at the woman, was that even
English?

Rosaline seemed to feel she'd made her point, however.
She gave another funny little bow as she backed out of view.
The cab of the truck shifted as the woman left.

The muffled sound of voices overcame Lauren's hesitation
and she crept carefully through the opening, wings tucked
tightly behind her.

The cab was cramped, but Rosaline had left the door open.
Lauren gingerly climbed down the chrome-plated ladder to
the ground.

The sun was just creeping up over a line of trees to the east,
shining cool winter light onto a large, well-maintained field.
They seemed to be near the center of that field, and about 40
feet away sat a modest, single-story white building. The building's most distinguishing feature was a quaint bell-tower,
about three times the height of the rest of the roof. A large

sign read 'Cherry Hills Reformed Church of the Immaculate Child' in big red lettering.

Rosaline was talking to a woman who couldn't have been more her opposite.

A tall, stern looking woman with ebony skin and a piercing gaze stood, arms crossed, speaking intently with the squat trucker. Rosaline seemed to be animatedly describing Lauren. At least, she was making exaggerated flapping motions with her arms.

The cold air caused Lauren to shiver, her feathers making a dry rustling noise as they rubbed together. She crossed her arms in front of herself, warding off the chill.

As she left the confines of the truck and suddenly had space again, she felt the irresistible urge to stretch.

She no sooner thought it than her muscles responded. Crackling and popping, her wings spread wide. All told they must have been ten feet or more, tip to tip. It was the deepest, most satisfying stretch she'd ever experienced.

A startled gasp brought her attention back to the pair of women now staring at her.

Lauren stood awkwardly for a moment, her borrowed pajama pants hanging scandalously low on her hips, chest exposed but for the circus tent of a bra that she wore, arms and wings spread wide.

Miss Caroline, she assumed, was the first to regain her composure. The woman dropped to her knees, raising her hands upwards to the sky and lowering her gaze to Lauren's feet.

"Holy lady, forgive me my doubts, I am Caroline Adams."

Lauren felt very out of sorts.

Who was this woman, and what on earth was she on about. Nervously she covered herself up as best she could.

"Um, hello, I mean good morning, my name is La-" she cut herself off, thinking of the television broadcast she had seen a glimpse of. She didn't know if they had given her name out, or if they knew it.

Caroline looked dutifully at Lauren's feet, her arms held wide. She seemed content to wait for a complete answer. "Could you, um, not do that?"

Lauren regretted the request immediately, as the woman reacted strongly to it.

"Yes your grace I am sorry," she bowed low to the ground. "What would you have me do?"

The woman seemed determined to keep this act up, to Lauren's irritation.

"Stop acting funny, just, just speak to me like a normal person!"

She answered a little more sharply than she intended.

Caroline looked confused, but she slowly rose to her feet. "Yes your grace, as you wish."

"Just, call me Lauren, please."

"Yes... Lauren," the woman said.

"Are you cold? We can go inside?"

Lauren was in fact quite chilled, so she nodded an affirmative.

The two parted company with Rosaline, who rumbled off in her truck before Lauren could think to thank her.

Caroline ushered Lauren into the church. "Cherry Hills" she called it, it was a small, wayside church outside of Paducah, Kentucky.

The name struck a bell. She'd traveled through this area for a class trip once, and again on vacation. Apparently Caroline lived here and looked after the rare traveler who happened through.

Lauren was grateful for the warmth of the building, but not as much for the company. She wanted to be alone. Caroline was nice enough, but Lauren was quickly growing tired of her bizarre behavior. Caroline seemed to sense her discomfort as she directed her to a small living area at the back of the building.

"Here's the shower, there's not much hot water I'm afraid, but there are towels in the cupboard."

Lauren nodded, still too shell-shocked to say much.

"When you're finished, my room is down the hall to the left. Wear anything you like, you'll find my wardrobe is modest, but you are of course welcome to it."

Another nod.

"Good, dinner is in a few hours. If you'd like to rest you can use my bed for that as well, please make yourself at home your gr-Lauren."

Their gazes met. Caroline seemed to sense the broken nature of Lauren's heart. To see the emptiness in her eyes. Lauren broke eye contact first as she turned to walk away but paused. "Thank you, Miss Adams."

The shower turned out to be more complicated than Lauren expected. Her wings made the space cramped and everything more challenging to reach and scrub thoroughly. Initially she tried to wash the wings as well, but once the feathers got soaked they were terribly heavy.

Eventually she settled on running her fingers through the feathers repeatedly while water ran over them. Drying them was considerably easier. They shed water quickly and she found she was able to fluff them up a bit if she concentrated.

Caroline's room was simply adorned. A large wooden cross hung above a surprisingly lavish bed. A series of scriptures were beautifully painted in black upon the cream colored walls. There was a small desk, a low table, a simple bookshelf, and an old box-style television. Lauren looked around for a wardrobe, but saw none. Instead, she saw a door across the room. Perhaps she had a walk-in closet?

Dread filled Lauren at the thought.

How many times had Lauren lain on Erin's bed chatting through the doorway while she changed from one black outfit to another?

For a moment, Lauren could hear Erin's voice, she was complaining because she couldn't decide what to wear. The sounds of clothes being tossed aside played out clear as day from behind the closed door of the closet.

She reached a shaking hand out, grasping the handle of the door. With a bated breath she yanked it open. A vision of her best friend stood there, in her mind at least, for the briefest instant. A single frame in the film of her life. Had she looked happy? Sad? Hurt? Lauren couldn't tell.

Behind the illusion, the closet stretched only seven or eight feet. It was filled with neatly organized dresses, shirts, and slacks. Each outfit sensible and conservative.

Erin would've hated it.

Shirts turned out to be another obstacle. After a half dozen failed attempts to creatively tuck her wings within the confines of a shirt she gave up. Instead, Lauren chose the dress with the lowest back and stepped into it.

Sliding it up she was pleased to find it left her shoulder blades, and therefore her wings, uncovered. The garment itself was a simple thing, a cool blue sundress with a bright floral pattern near the bottom. It was light and thin, made for the heat of summer more than the cold of winter, but it would have to do.

Lauren was examining herself when a soft knock at the door interrupted her.

"Lauren?"

Caroline's voice was soft, as though she were trying not to wake someone up.

Lauren strode over to the door and reached a hand out to open it but stopped. She stood there a moment, hand outstretched.

She's harmless. She probably just wants to check if I'm ok, Lauren thought to herself.

Lauren from a year ago would have answered the door. Maybe even Lauren from a few days ago.

But that Lauren was gone.

She let her hand fall and turned her back on the door, and Caroline, choosing the quiet embrace of sleep instead.

Her mind raced from one horrific nightmare to the next, repeating over and over. First Gabriel, and then Erin; both haunted her dreams, begging her to save them. They were screaming, drowning out her voice as she tried to tell them she couldn't, that she didn't know how.

She woke screaming and drenched with sweat. She didn't know what time it was, but she knew if she fell back asleep they would return.

The windows were dark, she must have slept the entire day away.

Lauren lay in the bed until her breathing returned to normal and her heart stopped pounding. All was quiet in the church, nothing but a gentle wind outside to disturb the silence of the night.

That silence grew and grew until her own heartbeat sounded like the firing of a cannon, her breath like the roar of a jet engine. Unable to bear it any longer, Lauren crept from the bed to the television set, finding a remote on top of it.

Lauren padded softly back to the bed. Wrapping herself up as best she could into a nest of blankets, she pressed the power button.

The TV came to life, sound blaring through the room. Lauren jumped and reflexively muted it. After waiting for a tense moment, listening for any sound that she had disturbed her host, Lauren turned the volume down low and pressed the mute button again.

A pair of reporters were reading the late night news as a ticker tape ran across the bottom of screen, condensing the events of the world into short, bitesize phrases.

"...which marks the nineteenth bombing in Jerusalem this year by the extremist group known as the People's Army of the Lady of Light. We'll head over to our chief political consultant in Israel, Dr. Aldridge Borowitz..."

Lauren hadn't watched much television since she disappeared from the public eye. Her parents didn't have cable in the house and Erin's news-junkie nature had never rubbed off on her. As the hours ticked by Lauren began to understand why her parents hadn't wanted her watching. Violence raged across the whole world it seemed. Groups proclaiming to fight in her name had sprung up in Europe, the Middle East, Africa, even South America. The People's Army of the Lady of Light, the Militant Order of the Christ-Child, the Army of the Divine Daughter, the list went on and on.

The relentless 24-hour news cycle fed her a steady diet of beheadings, fiery oratory, conspiracy theorists, and commentary by so-called experts. The upswing in recent violence was blamed on this year being the tenth anniversary of the 'miracle child's' disappearance.

The history channel was even running a special on her, featuring a number of interviews from people who had wildly varying theories on where she had gone.

"She's a government experiment, a test-tube baby with supernatural powers," claimed one man, a wild-haired professor of political science from a small-time university. "Her case has all the hallmarks of a CIA operation gone awry. Mark my words there will be a false flag soon, if the supposed sighting in Illinois isn't it!"

"She was a reincarnation of the Lord Jesus Christ, sent among us to determine if we were worthy yet of His salvation, and we failed his test," a representative from the Church of Latter Day Saints said.

"The wickedness of men has damned us, yet again. Only God knows when we might have another chance."

"...she's an alien, and the government is keeping her from us..."

"...It was a hoax, hysteria brought on by an abundance of media hype and too little research..."

Lauren watched with fascination, not noticing as the sun slowly crept up over the horizon.

A knock at the door startled her. She jumped, sending the remote clattering to the floor. The sudden noise broke the spell of the television and she rubbed her sore, dry eyes.

"Lauren?"

Caroline's voice came through the door again, this time with a little more urgency.

"Come in," Lauren said, feeling awkward that she had to allow the woman into her own room.

Caroline opened the door and walked in with the same mannerisms a child might have when walking into her parents' room.

"My Lady-"

"Lauren," Lauren interjected firmly.

"Um, Lauren, will you be joining me for breakfast? I don't, ah, don't know if you *need* to eat? Or wish to?"

The way she asked the question struck Lauren as funny. Why wouldn't she need to eat? Then again, she'd never really gone without either.

"Yes, please. I do need to eat. I think." Lauren's stomach growled loudly, reminding her of another time, a different place.

Lauren tried and failed to shake the memory of Erin's laughter.

"Is something troubling you, Lauren?"

The woman's concern seemed genuine, but Lauren was unwilling to share her emotional burden with a stranger.

"No, I'm ok."
Caroline turned to walk away but Lauren called out to her.
"Do you mind if I come along? To... help you cook or...?"
Caroline smiled and nodded fervently, clearly pleased, "It
would be my pleasure."
Lauren, still wearing the dress she had fallen asleep in,
followed Caroline to a humble kitchen. The pair chatted
awkwardly while Caroline cooked eggs and bacon on the old
gas stove.

Caroline seemed to believe she was an angel, the immaculate child for which this church was named. She spoke to
Lauren with reverence, and had to be reminded several times
that she didn't want to be called 'your grace' or anything
similar.

Lauren didn't know how to respond so she was mostly
quiet, preferring to let Caroline do the talking. The conversation was getting smoother as the two became more comfortable, until she asked about Lauren screaming in her sleep.
Lauren fell silent, looking out the kitchen window at the icy
dawn.

"I...I'm sorry, I shouldn't have intruded," Caroline apolo-
gized.
"No, I'm the one intruding. Here I am in your home, taking
your bed, it's a fair question. It's just not... not one I'm ready
to answer yet," Lauren replied softly.
Caroline moved to speak again, but Lauren interrupted her.
Lauren's once warm eyes locked with Caroline's, causing her
to pause.
"What if I told you I'm not an angel, and that there is no
God?"
The woman looked like someone who'd gone to sit down, only
to find there was no chair.
"A-are you telling me that? That there is no God?"

Her surprised look was quickly replaced with a stubborn half-frown.

"Because I believe I would pass that test, as the evidence of His hand is before me now."

Lauren wanted to see if her faith really was that strong, to tell her the truth. To crush this woman's hopes as her own had been destroyed. She wanted someone else to know the pain of having their world torn away.

But she couldn't do it.

"No," Lauren did her best to smile, but her eyes lacked sincerity. No god had answered her prayers for Gabriel, for her family. She turned and left the kitchen, wanting suddenly to be alone.

Chapter 8

Lauren looked out over the cold, misty field. She had been spending time each morning practicing with her wings. Stretching them. Testing the muscles. It gave her something to do and helped ease her constant worrying and self-loathing.

The morning frost glistened on the trees and sunlight sparkled across fresh snow. She could feel goosebumps on her legs and arms where the wind caressed her bare skin.

She cleared her mind as best she could
Slowly, deliberately, she spread her wings out wide. She concentrated on each muscle in turn, teaching herself as she went.

Open. Closed. Open again. Faster and faster.

She pulled the feathery limbs in tight once more and paused.

"Ok."

She closed her eyes tight and took a long, slow breath.

With an audible snap, she spread her wings as wide as they could go. She examined each tiny breeze as it rustled against her feathers.

"Don't wuss out, don't wuss out."

Lauren gave a tentative flap of her wings. Even moving slowly she was surprised by the amount of wind she generated. She could feel the powerful downdraft around her legs rustle the hemline of her dress.

Her heart fluttered with fright and curious excitement. Another downbeat, stronger this time, and she could feel herself grow light. The power she produced left her nearly weightless.

She shivered, half from the cold and half from the prospect of what she might be capable of.

Lauren steadied herself, her heart pounding. She looked self-consciously back at the church behind her, but she was alone.

"Well, there goes my excuse to bail."

Lauren moved her wings again, flapping up and down with increasing speed. Air whipped around around her and sent snow swirling away in powdery spirals.

She felt herself grow lighter until suddenly she found herself several feet above the ground. Startled, she wobbled unsteadily for a moment before losing her concentration and returning to the ground.

She landed on a patch of ice uncovered by her powerful wings and her feet slipped out from under her, sending her crashing to the ground.

Lauren scrambled to her feet, rubbing her sore behind. She didn't know which was bruised more, her pride or her tailbone. Frustrated and embarrassed, she returned to the church.

Lauren had been staying with Caroline for nearly a week. She spent most of her time inside, wrapped in blankets in front of the television, eyes glued to the train wreck of society. Rumors had started to spread surrounding the mysterious girl who had scratched and bit medics at the scene of Erin's death. Three separate people, all first-responders on the scene, had come forward saying they had been injured only to find unbroken skin where tooth marks and bruises should have been.

The media had descended on the small town within a few days, and it wasn't long before they caught her trail.

Kent Dailey was the first to corner her father. The resulting interview was looped round the clock. Daily surprised him as he was pulling into the driveway of what had been her home. "Mr. Corvidae, Mr Corvidae!"

John looked exhausted, like he hadn't slept in days. After Allison left he had picked up a second job, not because they needed the money but because it was easier than being home without her. With Lauren gone too it looked like he was avoiding sleep altogether.

"Where *is* your daughter, sir? Did she kill that girl?"

The interview was brutal. Kent barraged her dad with questions. Why had he kept her gift for himself all these years? Where was his wife? Where was he keeping Lauren? Did he know if she was involved with the death of Erin Engle?

Lauren quickly grew frustrated with the television and switched it off in search of another outlet for her restlessness.

She made her way from the bedroom to the church's small kitchen. Lauren was quite familiar with the place by now, and so she quietly began to prepare breakfast.

Caroline was a gracious host, and Lauren made sure to impose as little as possible. So far their arrangement had worked out perfectly. Lauren was left mostly to her own devices. Caroline was used to long periods of quiet and solitude, which suited her guest just fine.

As she assembled the ingredients for pancakes, she found herself humming softly.

"Amazing grace... how sweet the sound...."

"You have a lovely voice, Lauren."

Turning, Lauren saw Caroline standing in the doorway in her nightgown.

"Oh. Good morning."

"I'm sorry, I didn't mean to interrupt. Please continue?"
But Lauren was too shy. Instead, she turned on the small
television on the kitchen counter and continued cooking in
silence.

"...taken to the streets for the sixth day in a row. Officials
in New Delhi say that upwards of two-hundred thousand
celebrants are participating in what is being called the Revival
of Light. So far the largest festival marking the return of
Lauren Corvidae, it's certainly the most colorful..."
The grainy image showed thousands of people dancing
excitedly and singing in the streets amidst a riot of colorful
clothing.

"... In less comforting news, peace talks between Pakistan
and India were marred by violence early this afternoon.
Pakistan has again accused India of aiding Reformed Christian
Missionaries in their attempts to convert the largely Muslim
population of the Punjab Province..."
Caroline smiled at the news.
"You see, Lauren? The world celebrates your return."
"They don't even know what they are celebrating."
"You represent hope and certainty for so many people,
Lauren. You are a symbol. A living, breathing reminder of the
power of the Lord."
Lauren slammed the skillet she was using down onto the
stove.
"And how does that work exactly, Caroline? Christians in
Rome say I'm a messenger of God. Muslims in in Saudi Arabia
call me a demon. Israel says I am the angel Ariel. Professors
and skeptics around the world say I'm an alien, or a govern-
ment project."
"But, Lauren..."
"No, really, explain it to me," she continued angrily. "Where in
your magic book does it talk about me showing up and causing people to riot and kill each other and burn mosques and

churches and temples?"
Caroline snapped her mouth shut, looking down at her hands and avoiding Lauren's accusing eyes.
Smoke brought Lauren's anger back in check and she looked down at her now ruined pancakes.
"Damnit."
Throwing the smoking pan into the sink, she stormed out of the room. Caroline stepped obediently aside as Lauren passed, but didn't say a word.

Lauren went back outside, breathed the cold winter air and tried to clear her mind again. She too wanted the answers she demanded, unfairly, from Caroline.

What the hell am I doing here.
"Lauren?"
Caroline took her by surprise, usually when Lauren lost her temper she was left alone for a while. Lauren turned towards the door of the church to see her standing there in a thick winter parka.

"Lauren, don't you think you ought to do something?"
Lauren looked back at her vacantly.
"Like what," it was more a statement than a question.

Caroline shrugged.

"Like help. People out there need you, they are calling out for you."
Lauren rolled her eyes, turning back to the field. Let them call then, Lauren had done enough.
That night the Corvidae home was vandalized. Townsfolk calling themselves Defenders of the Faith threw bricks and molotov cocktails, demanding that Lauren be 'set free' and allowed to do God's Work. John was dragged from his bed and paraded through town by an angry mob. Cobden's tiny police force seemed unable or unwilling to step in and stop the madness.

Lauren watched the news in horror as her father was tied to a hastily erected wooden cross in the center of town, bloodied and bruised from his mistreatment.

A man calling himself Disciple grabbed a reporter's attention and spoke for the group.

"Sir, sir can you tell us what's happening? What are you doing to this person?"

"This man," he gestured to John, "stands accused of denying God's gift to the flock. He has willfully withheld an angel of Jesus Christ, an instrument of the Lord. For his sacrilege and blasphemy we, the people of God, sentence him to the same death our beloved Savior suffered."

The stunned reporter backed away from the man, disbelief in his eyes.

"You're going to kill him? You plan to... to crucify him?"

The man looked directly into the camera, his eyes ablaze with conviction.

"I am a blessed disciple of the Lady. She has spoken to me in my dreams since the day she healed me, twelve years ago. I do not question her will, I carry it out."

With that, the man turned to the hundreds-strong crowd, who roared with approval.

"He dies!"

His words broke the spell Lauren was under.

She ran from the room. Leaving the door swinging in her wake, she sprinted barefoot from the church and into the field.

As she bolted across the field, her feet impacting on the hard, frozen earth, her wings unfurled. With a terrific jump and a downward beat she took to the skies. Instincts she didn't know she had, coupled with the knowledge she'd gained from her practice sessions, helped her maintain her balance as she fumbled through the skies. Within a few hundred yards she had straightened out, and each beat of her wings was smoother and more controlled than the last.

Terror mixed with exhilaration. She felt a high unlike any other, like the rush she got from running magnified a thousand times. Her powerful wings pushed her light, streamlined body easily through the air, far outstripping her speed as a runner. She couldn't, wouldn't lose another person she loved.

Lauren pushed herself to her limit, muscles burning and back tense. Mile after mile blurred by while silently she prayed for her father's safety. Tears streamed down from her face as she flew, sprinkling the earth far below her.

For two long, gut-wrenching hours she flew, ignoring the pain, pushing through the exhaustion. Her muscles strained, tore, and repaired themselves in an endless cycle. Lauren flew directly Northwest, knowing it would put her close enough to her home to navigate.

She forced herself into the steady, mind-clearing focus she had when running long distance. Sometimes lights streamed past below her, when she followed a highway or crossed over a small town or farmstead. Other times it was dark below, silent forests and rivers the only witnesses to her passage.

Finally she found herself above what must have been Route 51.

She followed the streets of Anna, and then Cobden, as they flashed past beneath her until she could see the glow of bonfires in the distance. Dropping to a mere 30 feet above the ground, she came streaking in above the crowd gathered in the park in the middle of town.

John was there, his hands bleeding from where he had been fastened to the cross. His lips were bloody and his left eye swollen shut from the abuse of his captors. The man from the television, Disciple, was addressing the crowd, but he froze mid-sentence when he caught sight of her.

Lauren realized too late that she didn't know how to land. She beat her wings to try to slow herself, but had to settle for tucking and rolling onto the rapidly approaching ground. The crowd gasped audibly as she crashed and rolled to a halt.

Lauren could feel a great deal of pain in her shoulder and one of her wings, and she was fairly certain she'd sprained an ankle. Still,she knew her own pain was temporary where her father's was not. Not unless she could get to him in time.

Unsteadily she stood, hyper-aware of the sudden and complete silence surrounding her. The whole crowd was staring. She must have looked as wild as the wind, orange firelight flickering against the white satin of her feathers and casting long shadows across her face. As she gazed out over the crowd they started to drop to their knees, first one, then a few dozen, then the rest. A sea of faces upturned, hands reaching for the sky, enraptured by her appearance.

"Leave him alone," Lauren voice was raised in anger, her words carrying well over the hushed audience.
"The holy Lady!"
Disciple crawled towards her, his eyes cast down at the ground.
"I live to serve-"

Lauren didn't have time for zealotry, she ran to the crucifix, thankfully it was very nearly at ground level. Lauren embraced her father, holding him tightly and burying her head in his shoulder as she had when she was younger.

Instantly his wounds started to heal, his bruises lightened and disappeared, and the cuts and welts from his bonds closed, leaving only bloodstains and torn clothing as a testament to his injuries.

She tugged at the knots restraining him until they gave way and wrapped her arms around him.

Weeping, he clung to her as he regained consciousness. Her thoughts turned to the last time she had held him like this, at Gabriel's funeral. How had such a distance grown between them since then?

As John's wounds healed, a murmur rumbled through the crowd. There could be no doubt the people said, their miracle girl had returned, and grown into an angel.

"My Lady, please. Holy one tell me your will! I will spread your gospel-"

Disciple's hands clutched at the hem of her dress as he groveled before her.

"You do not speak for me!"

Lauren was screaming. Her throat hurt from the force of her words. The crowd looked as shocked as the man before her. People shifted uncomfortably beneath her angry stare. Disciple deflated, groveling prostrate on the ground before her feet.

"What's wrong with you people? Have you all lost your minds?"

As Lauren stood with her father, looking over the enraptured gathering, she realized what she had done. In choosing to save him, to reveal herself, she knew she would never be able to escape again. She'd known it since the reality of her wings set in. It was a fool's hope to think she could conceal herself now.

With her terrible realization came sudden sadness. She turned squeezed her father even tighter.

"Daddy, I don't know what to do," she whispered.

"L-Lauren, thank God you're ok. I... I've been so scared since you left."

She choked up. He had nearly died and his first words were that he was worried about her.

"Daddy," Lauren spoke softly, afraid of what she had to say. "Daddy, I have to go, I can't be near you. I hurt the people I'm near, I need to go so these people will leave you alone."

Her father only sobbed and shook his head.

"When I leave here, promise you'll leave too. Promise you'll hide. Somewhere far away."

"Lauren..."

But Lauren couldn't let him speak, she knew that anything he said would be enough to break her will. Enough to keep her from doing what she knew had to be done.

"I love you, Daddy," she squeezed him tightly, and then let go.

He didn't.

He clung to her like a terrified child, it took all her will-power to push away from his feeble grasp.

"Goodbye."

Turning to once again address the crowd, she raised her voice once more.

"You should be ashamed. Every one of you is a murderer."

People throughout the crowd paled at her accusation, and the realization of what they had nearly done.

Stepping backwards she looked to the sky. With a powerful downward beat of her wings she rocketed upward, sending sparks from the nearby bonfires shooting out over the crowd.

Chapter 9

Wind rushed past Lauren's face as she gained altitude, the cold winter air blowing her hair wildly behind her and raising goosebumps on her skin. As she rose, the smell of smoke and the noise of the crowd below dropped away.

Lauren was accustomed to running to relieve stress, to relax, to calm her frayed and battered nerves. If running was aspirin then flying was morphine. It flooded her body with adrenaline and cushioned her mind with a blanket of freedom. Even if that freedom was an illusion.

Lauren realized she had never been free, not of the burden of her power. She had ignored the world outside her carefully guarded space for too long, and because of her apathy people had suffered.

Lauren, don't you think you ought to do something?

She couldn't deny it any longer. The world seemed determined to force her hand.

She couldn't save Gabriel or Erin, but perhaps she could save someone else. Perhaps she could still redeem herself.

She clung to that hope and turned East. The nearest major city was St. Louis, and it was there she determined to begin again the work she had abandoned as a child.

It was nearly one hundred miles to the city, and Lauren was already tired from her marathon flight earlier in the night. It had only been an hour or so and already she was gliding more than flying. She knew she had to find a place to land and rest.

She hadn't been paying much attention to her surroundings, trusting that the bright lights of St. Louis would steer her when she got close. The darkness of the night obscured most of the details of the ground below her. She guessed from the lack of development that she was still over the deep, quiet expanse of the Shawnee.

Looking down she estimated she was a few hundred feet in the air. A moment of terror gripped her as the deep, animal part of her mind wrapped itself around that startling abnormality.

Security came from the knowledge that any injury she sustained would certainly be temporary, but it was still unnerving. Even with her fear suppressed she decided it was a good idea to drop lower and get a better look at her surroundings.

She tucked her wings just as she had seen red-tailed hawks do on countless occasions during the long Illinois summers of her childhood. She accelerated rapidly, and her heart pounded with the thrill of it.

I wonder what would happen if I didn't pull up, Lauren mused to herself, but as much as she was morbidly curious, she lacked the conviction. She leveled off at about five feet above the ocean of trees beneath her and started to peer around for some place to land.

Just how tall are these things? 20 feet? 50? She'd never really given any thought to assigning heights to things like trees. Words like 'tall' and 'short' had always been descriptive enough.

A bright light warned her of an oncoming billboard just in time for her to veer out of the way and avoid colliding with it.

What the hell?
Lauren pulled into a tight turn and circled back to the billboard, trying to determine where exactly she was.

The lonely billboard was parked beside a narrow, two-lane highway and proclaimed proudly that Fountain Bluff was only a few miles north, and the small friendly town of Gorham with it.

Lauren was confused, she'd been to Fountain Bluff many times as a child. Her family had gone on countless outings, exploring the waterfalls, bluffs, and other mysteries of the forest they called home.

Back when her family still took trips together.

But Fountain bluff was a forty-five minute car ride from home, even accounting for flying in a straight line, Lauren did some quick math, it had to be close to twenty miles.

Lauren was doubtful, she couldn't have been flying that fast, right? Then again, how fast does anything fly, she thought. Do birds all fly at the same speed? That seemed like a stupid question for a girl who had spent her youth in the wilderness, but she honestly had no clue.

Lauren knew that the safest bet would be to sleep in the woods, but it was far too cold outside for that. She was fairly certain she'd survive the frigid night, but it wouldn't be comfortable. Reluctantly she stopped circling the billboard and headed north up highway three, hoping to find a barn to sleep in.

Given the rural, agricultural nature of the region, it was no surprise that she came upon a farm within a few minutes. It was an older looking home, worn around the edges but in good repair. The house had a barn a few dozen yards distant and a pair of shabby looking grain silos in the back. A lonely milk cow stood in one of two fenced in pastures. Most importantly, although the windows in the house were lit, there was no one outside to see her descend.

Lauren was more careful this time, flapping rapidly to slow herself down as she dropped low to the ground. Landing at a bit of a jog, she managed to keep her feet. She congratulated herself silently on sticking the landing, but quickly ducked down into the shadow beside the barn as a figure passed in front of one of the windows in the house.

Now that she was at ground level, Lauren could see there were people sitting down to dinner inside a large dining room. Just beyond the thin glass of that not so distant window they sat together, a family.

Lauren imagined the conversations they were having. The two youngest children, both boys, looked to be school-aged. Maybe seven and nine. They were no doubt recounting their adventures at school. The eldest, a girl, looked closer to middle, or even high-school. From where Lauren stood she could see the thin, athletic frame of the girl. Perhaps she was a runner. Maybe she ran track for her school.

How different Lauren's life might have been were she born normal, without her power. Without these wings. Could she have been happy too? The cold wind rustled her feathers and chilled her sweaty skin. A far cry from the warmth of the room before her.

Lauren turned to the barn and crept inside. Without the wind the air was almost tolerable, but it was still near-freezing, and Lauren had no desire to test her power's effectiveness against frostbite.

A loud, rough snort caused her to jump with fright. Her heart pounded like a freight train, and she had to remind herself how to breathe again. Clutching her chest she peered through the darkness and into the eyes of a large brown horse.

The horse looked back at her with equal measures of curiosity and mistrust. Looking around she saw that it was one of four, each in its own stall and each staring at her with great interest.

For a moment Lauren was discouraged. Would the animals make noise and attract attention from the house? Suddenly she realized that horses meant another thing would be in this barn; blankets!

A few minutes later Lauren was laying atop a pile of hay, wrapped snugly under several heavy cotton blankets. Sleep quickly overpowered her exhausted body.

The next morning Lauren was again rudely awakened by an animal. This time an overly eager rooster announcing the rising sun.

Sitting up quickly, startled from a disturbing half-remembered dream, Lauren looked blearily around. She was still in the barn, alone but for the horses. The offending rooster called again, as if to be sure she had truly woken.

She was mulling over the events of the night before when the big barn door swung wide.

From her vantage point in the hayloft, she could see the young boys from the dining room enter.

She was trapped. She couldn't see another way out besides the door on the ground floor.

The children greeted the horses in loud, boyish fashion. Conversing with them as though they were friends rather than livestock. They set about filling water buckets and offering face rubs and ear scratches to their four-legged charges. Lauren cracked a too-rare smile as she observed them from above. They warmed her heart with their antics, at least until the oldest told his brother to stay put.

"Hang on, Ty, I'll get the hay this time."

The child started up the ladder, the very ladder that Lauren had climbed the night before in search of a bed.

Lauren panicked, looking around for some place to hide but saw nothing but stacked bales of hay and the blankets she'd brought up. Shit, the blankets alone were going to arouse suspicion.

She only had a moment, so she took a deep breath, knelt down, and tried to look as friendly as possible.

When the boy's head finally poked up over the floor of the loft, she smiled as big as she could and gave him a nervous little wave.

The kid took one look at her and furrowed his little brow. He made no attempt to hide his confusion at her unfamiliar presence, and was clearly determining what he should do.

"Are you the angel from the television?" he finally asked, his tone cautious.

"Y-yes! Yes I am!"
Great, she thought to herself, now you're lying to children and telling them you're an angel.

His expression brightened instantly.
"Tyson! Run and tell mom, the angel from the television is in the stable!"
The little boy turned excitedly and waved to his younger brother. In his enthusiasm, however, he neglected his grip on the narrow ladder and slipped backwards.
Lauren leapt after him, catching his hand by the narrowest of margins. She tucked him to her chest and wrapped him in her wings as they flew through the air, shielding him with her body from the hard, onrushing ground.

The pair slammed into the dirt with a dull thud and an audible crack. Lauren landed squarely on her back. She felt a sudden searing pain in her chest as one of her ribs forced its way into her lung. For a moment she could feel fluid filling her chest and she drew a ragged, pain-filled breath. She coughed uncontrollably, flecks of red flying from her mouth and dotting the snowy white of her feathers. A few more ragged breaths and she felt her bone slide back into place, clicking back together. Her lung repaired itself as well, re-inflating and allowing her to breathe normally.

She held the boy in her arms, could feel his breathing and hear his rapid little heartbeat.

"Are you ok there, little buddy?" she asked him, easing up on her grip and looking down into his wide-eyed expression.

He nodded silently, he seemed uninjured but somewhat in shock. Lauren saw the younger child was nearly at the house, and loudly shouting the news of her arrival. Lauren resigned herself to a morning filled with awkward conversation.

With the young man in her arms, Lauren headed for the house.

Inside herself she cherished the feeling of carrying the boy, imagining just for a moment that it was Gabriel. That he was her own little brother and not someone else's. It was a stolen moment. A treasure to be kept locked away in her heart. Irreplaceable.

She was almost across the yard when the door swung open and a tall, powerfully built man stepped out from inside the house. He held a shotgun in his hands.

Lauren pulled up short, freezing at the sight of the firearm.

The man froze as well, taking a good long look at Lauren, her wings, and his little boy cradled in her arms.

They were at an impasse, but he moved first. He set the shotgun down beside the door and ran to her, nothing but concern on his face.

With only a heartbeat of hesitation Lauren handed the boy to his father. The man's large, muscular arms easily lifting the child from her grasp.

"He um, he fell off the ladder. I think I startled him. B-but he's ok I swear," Lauren addressed the man nervously, aware that she was trespassing and had nearly caused great harm to his son.

Their eyes met. He had a piercing blue stare that made Lauren uncomfortable, like he could peer into her mind.

"Daddy she can fly!"

The little boy's words were full of childish delight, and seemed to satisfy his father's doubts.

"Yes Justin, I imagine she can with great big wings like those. Go inside and wash up, breakfast is almost ready."
He set the boy down, and with only a quick backwards glance Justin ran into the house, leaving the two of them alone.

"Tyson says you're an angel, that true?"
"No."
Lauren didn't want to lie to this man. She didn't want to lie to anyone, but she felt that this man especially, with his piercing gaze, would know if she tried.

The man nodded slowly, thoughtfully.

Lauren cast a downward look and turned to go, spreading her wings and preparing to take off when the man stopped her.
"You hungry?"
She paused, wings raised and extended to their fullest. She looked at the man. His expression hadn't changed a bit. He was unreadable, like a poker player at a high-stakes table.

"Breakfast is on the table, would you like to stay and eat?"
"Your child could have been seriously hurt. He could have died because of me."

"'Round here we don't judge people for making mistakes, not as long as they fix them. We don't put much stock in 'could haves' or 'would haves' either"

Maybe it was the man's blunt attitude. Maybe it was the curious faces pressed against the dining room window behind him. Maybe it was the crushing loneliness that Lauren felt, the hunger for normalcy and family. Whatever it was, she nodded and followed him inside.

To their great credit, Charlie and his wife Jennifer, as well as their three beautiful children, Tyson, Abigail, and Justin, took Lauren's appearance in stride. They welcomed her into their home as a guest and a friend. Jen and Lauren made small talk while the children set the table, and Lauren helped where she was able to around the kitchen.

The mouth-watering smells of biscuits and gravy filled the modest home and Lauren realized she hadn't eaten since early the previous day. Her stomach growled with embarrassing volume, causing the kids to giggle.

"Alright, alright y'all," Jennifer spoke with an endearing southern drawl. "Food's getting cold, set down and let's eat." The family gathered at the table as they had the night before, and Lauren was transported to her own childhood. This house, with its noise and laughter, warmth and closeness, was what she used to have. What she used to know.

"Justin, seeing as how you and your brother brought an angel home," Charlie smiled and winked slyly at Lauren. "You can say grace."
Justin and Tyson were quite taken with her, and they had insisted loudly that they should be allowed to sit next to her. As the family bowed their heads they reached out and joined hands. Lauren looked at the tiny hands stretched out towards her, and with a small, genuine smile she grasped them firmly.

As the young boy gave thanks for the food, his family, and for Lauren, she looked around the table. These people were good, simple, and true. They accepted her, welcomed her. She resolved to be better, to earn the kind of acceptance they had given her freely. These past few months Lauren's heart had gone cold, hardened by grief and pain and sorrow. She grew very still, committed everything to memory. A bright new candle to be held in her darkest hours.

When breakfast was over Lauren volunteered to help clean up, and after that was done she was invited to stay for coffee. Lauren was loath to leave, but she couldn't stay. They had already been more than generous, and Lauren knew too well the worldly consequences of her inaction.

Instead she said farewell, promising at their insistence to return someday if she was able. They gathered in the yard to watch her leave, and Lauren felt an awkward sort of performance anxiety. Previously she'd flown only in haste, with fear and urgency clouding her mind. Here she stood in broad daylight, a belly full of food, and with an audience looking on. Come on, she coached herself, you flew just fine yesterday, you'll be fine.

Shaking the feeling that she looked silly she spread her wings wide once more, the enchanted gasp of the children gave her renewed confidence and she whipped her wings back downwards with surety.

Powerful muscles lifted her swiftly into the skies and she did a quick circle around the yard, waving and smiling at the friendly faces below her, before heading east once more.

Lauren decided to follow Route three, the last thing she needed to do was get lost. Within a few minutes she was cruising over Gorham. The small prairie town couldn't have had more than a couple hundred residents, and it seemed to pass in the blink of an eye.

Within an hour, however, Lauren realized she had made a serious miscalculation. The first few towns she'd passed over seemed fine, a few people on the streets and in cars going about their business. But now every town had masses of people crowding the streets, faces up and cellphones out recording her passage.

The normally sparse traffic of the rural route had tripled or more, cars and trucks clogged the road and people stood crammed beside the highway, their gazes locked on her.

Shit.

Lauren had hoped to fly under the radar, at least until St. Louis.

So much for that plan.

Hoping to elude the crowds she veered farther East, leaving the highway and heading for the Mississippi, another surefire way to hit the city.

No such luck.

Lauren swore under her breath as the unmistakable form of a helicopter approached from the northeast.

By the time she reached the city she was exhausted, surrounded by news helicopters, and incredibly annoyed. The rotor wash from the helicopters made it much harder to keep her balance. They buffeted her with strong winds and caused the air currents to shift unpredictably around her. It wouldn't have been so bad if they weren't insisting on getting as close to her as they could. The vehicles circled her like hungry wolves, each network desperate to push itself to the front of the pack.

As the city rose on the horizon Lauren began to search the vast urban sprawl for the green expanse of Forest Park. She had no trouble finding it, the well-maintained greens stood out sharply against the concrete and steel below her. From above the park it was easy to spot her destination, the St. Louis Children's Hospital.

The hospital was one of the first places she could remember visiting. She would have been five or maybe six at the time. She remembered meeting children her own age who were hurt or sick, and being especially proud of making them feel better.

Lauren tried to ignore the thousands of people filling the streets. She circled a few times, looking for a place to land below. Impossible. After years of shunning physical contact the idea of landing among a crowd of people, all pressed together and groping for her slightest touch, was too intimidating. Instead she opted to land within the rooftop garden of the hospital, where she was met with the surprised faces of a few doctors and nurses, as well as their small, frail patients.

"...returned to the public eye today. Corvidae flew into the spotlight once more at the St. Louis Children's hospital. She cured all 280 of the residents, and more than 50 visiting patients as well before being escorted by police officers into a crowd of more than thirty thousand. After spending hours looking to the needs of the masses, curing everything from runny noses to cancer, we have word that she is now resting at the luxurious Fourth Season hotel... "

Kent's voice blared from the fancy flat-screen in the corner of the room. She'd tried changing the channel but his fake, plastic smile was everywhere. In the wake of her return he had soared back into the spotlight as well, being the subject of dozens of talk-show interviews regarding his initial discovery of the "Miracle Girl."

The room was one of nearly a dozen, all connected in the single most opulent suite that Lauren had ever seen, or even heard of. She'd been met by the mayor of the city, as well as the governor, in the lobby of the hospital after only an hour of visiting with and healing the children of the hospital. She was welcomed very loudly, and publicly, by both of the gentlemen. The handshakes alone lasted several minutes,with at least a dozen cameramen recording and snapping photos.

The politicians had expressed their gratitude for her visit, and told her they had policemen standing by to escort her through the crowd. Being put on the spot, and in front of live camera feeds, she had little choice but to swallow her fear and accept. The next few hours had been a horrifying combination of screaming faces and suffocating closeness.

Even now, standing in an elegant, exquisitely tiled bathroom under a rainfall shower nearly big enough for her to spread her wings all the way, she couldn't close her eyes without seeing them.

The desperate, frenzied faces. People crushing in against her and her ring of protective officers. The constant, incomprehensible yelling of thousands of voices. And always the reaching, grasping hands, tugging and clawing at anything they could touch.

She hugged herself, tears mixing with the water running down her face. She knew that if she were a normal woman, her body would be covered in bruises from their overzealous hands. She hated herself for the disgust she felt. For her desire to flee, to leave those hungry crowds far behind.

Turning the water off at last, Lauren stepped dripping from the shower. She looked longingly at the thick, monogrammed bathrobe hanging beside the bathroom door and sighed. Her gaze carried over to the long curved mirror that followed the wall above a green, polished marble counter.

Lauren examined the woman in her reflection. She was still tall, still too thin, but she had a youthful, healthy appearance. No outward sign of her exhaustion. Of the stress that held her muscles tight as guitar strings just beneath her skin.

Her hair was darker when it was wet, it looked closer to brown in the soft, recessed lighting of the room. Out of habit she gathered it in her hands, pulling it behind her head to put into a ponytail. Something caught her eye as she did so; a blemish above her left breast.

Lauren approached the mirror, leaving a trail of droplets on the tiles as she crossed the room and looked more closely. There, just below her left collar bone was the unmistakable discoloration of a long-faded scar.

Lauren reached up, stunned, and gingerly touched the area. It had a slightly puffy texture, different from the surrounding flesh. Her mind returned to the night she must have gotten it, to Erin's house. Tears came to her eyes as she wished for a moment that the dagger-like wooden shard would have actually pierced her heart. Or the alcohol would have deadened the memories. But it hadn't, and drawing a ragged breath she felt certain nothing else ever would.

She felt the scar again, remembering the brief touch of Erin's skin, and how similar it felt to hers. That only made it worse. Lauren felt in her heart she was responsible for Erin's death. If she had only spoken up, or not been so drunk.

Or told her to begin with.

But it was too late for a second chance, her own stupidity and lack of foresight had once again seen to that. Too late for Erin, too late for Gabriel, too late even for her parents.

Stop it, she told herself. She repeated it within her mind over and over again, a prayer meant to silence her inner demons. But their voices were louder than her own.

Lauren's head was pounding, she had to make it stop. She felt herself sliding down into a pit with no bottom, her heart-beat quickening with desperation. Looking up into her own eyes she was transported to another memory. Another mirror.

Lauren shook her head, trying to clear the darkness from her mind. She grabbed a towel from the rack and wrapped it around herself and headed to the kitchen. There, just where she knew it would be, was a mini-bar.

There was a seal on the mini-fridge, with a friendly notice from the hotel informing patrons that opening the bar would result in a 250-dollar surcharge.

Lauren ignored it. Snapping the thin paper she swung the door open to reveal a number of small bottles. They all had fancy names, and having never really experimented with drinking they were essentially gibberish to her. The bottles seemed designed for one or two shots, which struck her as phenomenally stupid considering the price tags. She wasted no time trying to decipher the good from the bad, grabbing the first bottle and unscrewing the cap.

Rum, vodka, gin, whiskey, Lauren opened and downed the contents of the tiny bottles as quickly as her body would let her. The combination did not sit well in her stomach, but she kept pounding drinks. Sure enough, within about 20 minutes it started to have the desired effect.

Lights began to blur in the spacious suite, and her inner demons seemed content to gorge themselves on liquor instead of her fears and doubts, at least for the moment.

Lauren decided she'd be more comfortable sitting, and after grabbing another armful of bottles she hopped up on the counter. She sent various spices, salt and pepper shakers, and other kitchen utensils flying as she both miscalculated her jump and completely disregarded her body's recent addition of wings.

Nearly slipping from her precarious perch on the edge of the gray granite, she swore loudly and dropped a pair of bottles, which skittered across the floor.

Determined and stubborn, however, she scooted farther onto the counter and tucked her wings around to the front of her as best as she could. A large crash accompanied the movement and she turned to see that she'd knocked a knife block from the counter into the sink, filling it with a dangerous array of sharp, bladed instruments.

She continued to drink, curious if and when her abilities might kick in to save her from alcohol poisoning. If her last experience was any gauge, she could hope to at least drink herself into unconsciousness.

An hour in and the room was spinning fast. A small stack of empty bottles had replaced the full ones she'd brought with her onto the counter. She knew if she wanted to keep going she would have to leave her seat.

She sighed drunkenly.

"Well fuck Lauren, you're too drunk to want to get up, and not drunk enough to get what you wanted out of drinking."

Unsurprisingly, there was no response from the room or the bottles.

She slipped, literally, from the counter, crashing to the floor with almost as much grace as a knocked over bookshelf.

Standing unstably and rubbing her bruised behind she peered once more into the mini-fridge.

Tequila.

Even with the letters swimming together she had no trouble reading the label. It was like ice-water poured into her veins. She slammed the door angrily, much too hard, and set the plates and cups rattling in the cupboards.

Denied her escape, she pounded her fists on the hard stone of the counter, raging against the sea of memory threatening to drown her. With rising anger she balled her fists and cast a wrathful gaze around the room for some other outlet.

Her eyes settled on the sink full of knives. Her mind turned to the enticing distraction she'd felt when she broke her mirror, and the words that Erin had told her long ago. Words that hadn't fully made sense to her at the time. They seemed much clearer now, in meaning and in truth.
With a trembling hand she lifted one of the blades from the basin, a smooth, stainless steel paring knife.

Bracing herself, Lauren drew the blade quickly across her forearm before she had a chance to second-guess herself further.
"Shhit!"
Gasping, she dropped the knife and clutched her wounded forearm.

The pain cut past her drunken stupor and clouded her mind, forcing the memories into a quiet, dull corner. She closed her eyes in relief, but reopened them as she felt her flesh begin to close itself.

She'd bled all over the sink, giving it a grisly appearance. She examined the cut as it closed, it was narrow but deep, deeper than she'd really intended. It stitched itself back to-gether and sealed without a trace.
She looked down at her chest, pulling open the towel and

examining the scar above her breast. It was still there. That doesn't make any sense.

Confused, drunk, and angry at the slowly returning noise of her emotions, she picked the knife back up. She ran the blade across her arm again, harder this time.

Again her mind was washed clear of everything but the pain, and she could see a flash of white for a brief instant as the knife brushed across her bone. She wondered for a moment that she had overdone it. The edges of her vision started to fade and the lights seemed to flicker inconsistently.

Sinking back to the floor and gritting her teeth, she watched as the blood pouring from the cut slowed, and then stopped. Close examination revealed her muscles and skin rapidly growing back together. This time though, a very, very faint line was left. A tiny, easily missed pink scar, no wider than a piece of thread. While it quickly faded to the same soft tan as the rest of her skin, the scar remained. Lauren hesitated for only the briefest of moments before making up her mind. From her position on the floor she reached once more for the mini-bar.

Lauren awoke to the sound of the television blaring. From the next room she could hear the sounds of screaming, shouting, and what sounded like sirens and occasional gunfire.

Dammit, that was loud. Kent's smug face must have finally been turned off and the channel must have reverted to normal programming while she was passed out.

Her head was pounding and she had no idea what time it was. She moved to stand and felt the bare skin of her legs peel off of the floor, she was sitting in a puddle of something dark red and sticky.

Looking herself over, flashes of the memory returned. Her vision was still blurry, and the room was spinning violently, so she couldn't have been out too long. The windows were dark as well, she noted, so it must still be night time. The floor, the towel, and even her hair reeked of alcohol, it made her stomach do somersaults.

She could feel her gift working, slowly, to clean the poison from her veins, but judging from the sheer quantity of bottles around her she guessed it was going to be a long, painful process.

She tried to stand, and immediately thought better of it. Her legs refused to support her, and a banged shin was the only reward she got for trying.

But the noise from the next room was relentless.

Growling under her breath she crawled hands and knees across the tacky, blood-covered floor towards the sitting room. She paused briefly, lamenting the clean, plush ivory of the carpet, but the television was drilling a hole into her skull through her ears.

Dragging her wings behind her, she crossed the floor and found herself in front of the TV at last.

The channel hadn't changed.

The news was still playing.

It was a live feed from the streets of the city. Rioters were burning cars, throwing bottles and bricks and screaming at a too-small police force that had surrounded a building with SWAT trucks and squad cars. Kent was there, bleeding from a small cut on his forehead, and providing running commentary as law enforcement clashed with the angry mob.

"...you're just now joining us, the heart of the chaos is the Fourth Season Hotel here in downtown St. Louis. Crowds have been gathering for hours, ever since Lauren Corvidae ceased her healing activities earlier today..."

Oh God, her wandering attention was pulled to the television as if on a leash. Kent's voice continued, an ongoing accusation for a crime in progress.

"...the peaceful gathering turned ugly when accusations began to surface of racial and economic bias, voiced by members of various human rights groups in the area. Corvidae's activities today were limited to the relatively wealthy Central West End and Debaliviere neighborhoods. More than fifteen people have been hospitalized with serious injuries so far during the protest and that number is expected to rise as the night continues. Police are urging citizens to remain indoors and avoid the area if at all possible. There has been no official response from from Ms. Corvidae at this time..."

The camera panned out across the ever-growing crowd. Masses of people, especially the poor and disenfranchised, as far as the eyes could see. Worst of all were the faces, they were angry, sure, but the ranks were filled with the sick. The disabled. The dying. Mothers and fathers held their crippled children up above their heads, begging for help. Her help.

And here she was. Drunk. Reeking of expensive booze and slitting her wrists to drown her own problems. She looked at her arm, a handful of faint lines crossed it now, a pitiful mockery of Erin's. A testament to her continued weakness.

Bracing herself against the coffee table she stood unsteadily and stumbled to the shower. Five minutes of icy water later and her head was a little clearer. She slipped back into the clothes she'd stripped out of a few hours ago and walked to the balcony of her suite. There below her, by the light of a hundred flashing lights, she could see the people clamoring for her.

Wings raised, she took off into the night, swooping down to the instant joyous outcries of the people. She landed about a dozen feet behind the police line. The people who saw her were driven to silence, and a hush began to spread through the crowd. It lasted only moments. Murmuring started to spread, building slowly at first and then rising to a frenzied crescendo as the onlookers made renewed efforts to reach her.

Lauren caught the eye of a nearby police officer, he couldn't have been older than 25. He looked at her, terrified, a riot shield in his hand and his knees visibly quaking. She tried to smile reassuringly at him but she knew her eyes were hollow, devoid of warmth.

Taking a tired, defeated breath she strode out to meet them.

Chapter 10

Lauren was exhausted, her mind and body had long-since gone numb. She didn't know how long she had been walking. How far she had gone. Even what day or time it was.

For what seemed like an eternity she had been moving through the crowd. Their faces blurred together and though her eyes were open she wandered unseeing from one to the next.

At last though, her outstretched arms met nothing, no one. She stopped, her inertia finally grinding to a halt. She blinked with surprise, bleary eyed from her efforts.

She was surrounded by a sea of people, all kneeling. Some had their heads bowed low, others were staring raptly at her, hands in the air. Men and women, children and the elderly. The crowd stretched around her and as far as her eye could see. She was the focal point of ten thousand stares.

She found herself once more in Forest park. Reverent, silent onlookers filled the open space. Even the helicopters circling above her sounded dull to her ears, deadened by the same thick hush that blanketed the rolling grounds.

She exhaled, overcome with relief, and her breath seemed oddly loud in the quiet. She didn't know the way back to her hotel even if she had the strength to walk back under her own power.
She hung her head, realizing that even now with her work seemingly finished, she was probably miles from a warm bed.

A man spoke from the crowd, his voice low and earnest, as though he were a child addressing a respected teacher.

"My lady, why are you crying?"

Lauren looked at the man, he appeared to be in his late thirties, maybe early forties. His short, brown hair was just starting to be flecked with gray. He looked healthy, but thin, like he may have been recovering from some long-term illness.

Her eyes must have conveyed some of the confusion she felt, because he asked again when she didn't answer. This time his words were better able to penetrate the haze of her mind.

"Y-Your grace?"
"Please, please just call me Lauren."

"Lauren, what can we do? How can we *serve* you?"
The man's genuine plea took Lauren by surprise. How could he serve *her*? The thought had literally never crossed her mind. In her stupor she allowed herself to speak frankly.
"I-I'm just. I'm so tired. I just want to sleep," she concluded, the tiniest whimper crept into her voice as she spoke.

He bowed deeply, for some reason it irritated her more than it might have if she were in her right mind.
"Stop," she said, not meaning to speak as harshly as she did. "Stop it! Quit bowing to me, get off your damn knees would you?"
She raised her voice.

"Stop! Stop bowing to me! Get up, *go home*! Every one of you has a life to live! You shouldn't be spending it following me around."

Instead of being offended, the crowd seemed even more pleased with her. They mistook her frustration for passion. Her words were filtered through made-up minds and twisted into humility by the listeners. Murmurs spread like wildfire; Lauren wanted the people to live, she didn't want to be bowed

to! Her 'instruction' was heeded, and many in the crowd began to rouse and wander away from the park, feeling blessed by her presence.
The man she was speaking to was not among them.
"Lauren, you... don't know me. But I *know* you."
The man's quiet intensity was beginning to unsettle Lauren. He stared at her with a light in his eyes and his fists clenched.
"I-I'm sorry?" she said, shaking her head and trying to clear her groggy mind.

The hairs on the back of her neck began to raise. Something about this man was familiar, yes, but also somehow... she struggled to find the word for it in her present state.

"You won't remember me, you were just a baby after all. I was younger too, of course, I-I was in hospice care at St.-"
"Ma'am, Ma'am!"

A commanding voice interrupted him, from Lauren's left. A half-dozen men in dark suits were approaching her, muscling their way through the crowd. Beyond them, a few dozen yards distant at the edge of what must have been the road, a pair of black Range Rovers with flashing red and blue lights were idling.

"Lauren," The man in front of her grabbed her attention once more, raising his voice desperately.

"You *do* remember me, don't you? Eric? I was your first! The first who felt your gift! I-I've been searching for you every day. I knew y-you wouldn't abandon us. I never doubted you, my faith was strong!"

He was on his knees again, grabbing at her hand, pulling it into his own and petting it softly.

He slid a hand up onto her forearm, rubbing her skin with his fingers. She yanked her hand away, deeply disturbed at the liberty he had taken.

She was speechless. She felt violated by his over-familiarity.

His face was heartbroken for a moment, but he turned his attention to his hands as the group of men intercepted her. As they surrounded her she noticed they were all wearing sidearms, heavy-looking black pistols in hard plastic holsters.

She gave Eric one more startled look, he was rubbing his hands to his face, smelling them deeply, before the largest of the armed men stepped in front of her view.

He was tall. Huge actually. His broad shoulders, large chest, and short, military haircut were intimidating. He was middle-aged, but in the way that a lion, at middle-age, is at the height of its supremacy. His voice, when he spoke, was matter-of-fact and just a little too serious.

"Lauren Corvidae, I'm Marshal James Dustin with the U.S. Marshal's service, we're here to escort you."

"Escort me where?" Lauren narrowed her eyes warily, she'd seen too many movies with dark vehicles and armed men to just trust them, and something about Eric had put her seriously on edge.

"I'm afraid you don't understand, Ma'am. We are your security detail for the time being, until other measures are deemed appropriate."

"Lauren, Lauren! I'll protect you I won't let these men hurt you!"

Eric tried to muscle past the Marshals. Lauren shot an alarmed look at him at took an involuntary step backwards. The Marshals took the cue immediately. Two of the men restrained Eric before he could get close to her again.

"Ms. Corvidae. If you'd like to come with us, it's very important that we speak with you..."

Lauren snapped. She was tired, confused, and growing more pissed off with every passing moment.

"Well all I want is a freaking bed!"

"Yes ma'am no need to yell."

Dustin's sober, even tone only ruffled her feathers more. She stalked past him towards the vehicles.

The men followed her from the respectful distance of about two feet. Thankfully, as she walked most of the crowd parted like water around a rock, reverent gasps followed her every footstep.

It was maddening.

As she approached the vehicles their doors opened, making Lauren jump at the unexpected movement. Two more men exited the vehicles, one each. They had their hands on their holsters. Lauren halted abruptly, causing Dustin to nearly run into her.

"It's alright ma'am they're with us."

"Um, ok, thank you, I- never-mind. Just, which car do I get in? The front one or the back one?"

Her voice was barely above a whisper, embarrassment overcoming anger. Lauren didn't really know how this worked, and she was feeling the limelight as she was put on the spot.

"Either is fine," the officer's voice was also low, for which Lauren was very grateful.

She chose the front vehicle, it was closer.

Inside, the large SUV was spacious and comfortable. She sat awkwardly in the back seat as two of the Marshals got in front, leaving her alone in the rear.

Dustin turned from the front, addressing her in a lower, but no less intimidating tone that he clearly considered his 'inside voice.'

"Ma'am, would you like to return to the Fourth Season? Or would you prefer somewhere else?"

They were going to have to work on his volume control if this was to be a long-term arrangement, Lauren thought to herself, her head was still pounding in pain.

"Whatever is fastest."

The man nodded, turning back to his driver and speaking with him quietly. The vehicle rolled off, proceeding slowly ahead as the crowds parted.

"Um, Mr. Dustin?"

He looked back.

"Thank you," Lauren knew she had been rude. Suddenly free of the crowd, her body was screaming at her. Her head hurt, her stomach was rolling, and her eyes were barely staying open.

He nodded, then returned to looking through the tinted wind-shield at the passerby.

She was asleep before they made the next block.

"Ms. Corvidae," A man's voice, soft but insistent.

"Shhhhh," she mumbled, hoping the intrusive noise would stop.

It did.

In her dazed, half-dreaming state she felt herself flying, but the wind was strong and buffeted her badly. She tried to compensate, to stretch her wings wider in the cloud-filled skies she found herself in. Her wings were restrained by an unseen force, and she could feel herself rocking, bobbing up and down in the sky uncontrollably.

She started to panic.

She looked around for the ground, but couldn't even tell which direction was down and which was up. She tried to roll, but found herself blocked once more by an invisible restraint. Her sense of direction careened wildly until she felt certain she was on her back, plummeting to the earth.

Lauren jerked awake with a short, startled scream. As she raised her body she smashed her face against a hard, dense object. Flicking her eyes open and pulling her hands to cover her badly broken nose she heard a grunt and felt herself wobbling just as she had in her dream.

Dustin was carrying her in his arms, trying to keep his balance and looking a little dazed. A red mark over his left eye gave evidence to the source of her collision.

He wobbled unsteadily a moment, a task made harder by the fact that he was currently negotiating a set of stairs sideways, and then steadied himself.

"Ahem," he cleared his throat. "Are you injured, ma'am?" Lauren's nose realigned itself with an audible pop while he spoke and she squeaked in pain, snorting a bit of blood out onto her hands.

He stood there, holding her as if she were weightless, and waited for her response.

She nodded slowly, still confused as to where she was. He correctly interpreted her startled look.

"You're in a witness protection program house that's not currently in use, still in St. Louis," he began, resuming his walk up the stairs and leaving her awkwardly sitting up in his arms.

"You said you wanted rest. We are approximately twelve blocks from Forest Park."

He seemed to think this was a satisfactory explanation and continued on in silence.

The rest of the staircase was a brief but uncomfortable ride. When they reached the top it opened into a small landing where Dustin set her down gently on her feet.

One of the other Marshals was already here, holding open a plain, unassuming wooden door labeled 139 in faded bronze numbers.

"Thanks," Lauren said quietly, uncomfortable with the number and size of her escorts and unsure how to conduct herself.

She saw the mark above Dustin's eye again and reached out to heal him, but he moved away, avoiding her touch.

"I'm fine."

They seemed to be waiting on her, so she crossed the threshold first. Inside was a simple apartment, a variety of old but comfortable looking furniture filled the rooms and the walls were painted in soft, neutral colors. The floor was worn wood that, combined with the decor, reminded her of Erin's house; it was small, but cozy.

Wandering through the apartment, with a little more room to separate herself from the men, her confidence increased.

"Why were you carrying me," she called across the dining room as she examined a muted painting of a gazelle racing through tall grass.

"You were asleep and..." he paused.

"Uncooperative."

"Uncooperative?"

"You told me to shush, and then swore at me when I tried to wake you up. It would have caused a scene to continue, and you seemed very tired."

Caused a scene? So that's a concern now? She smiled at her inner monologue, thinking that if he intended to avoid "scenes" he had definitely made the wrong assignment.

She moved to the kitchen, it had a small window with dark green curtains covering it. Curious of the time, she strode over and pulled them wide open.

What she saw below was a street scene like any other; Cars lined the small, residential road and iced-over puddles sparkled in the December sun. Something struck her as odd, though she couldn't put a finger on it.

"What time is it?"

"9:27."

Well, isn't he just a talkative fellow, she thought to herself.

"9:30 what," she tried to remember the day. "M-Tuesday?"

"Wednesday."

"That can't be right," she was certain she had gotten to the hotel Monday evening. "I came down late-"

"Monday evening. At approximately 1:30 a.m. Tuesday, actually. You then proceeded to, ah..." he seemed to be looking for a word or phrase.

"Help people?" she offered.

"Help people," he agreed. "For the next thirty hours, leaving us at 9:28 a.m. Wednesday."

Thirty hours, no wonder I'm exhausted, she thought to herself. She tried to remember the past day, but it was a blur. The haze of alcohol had been replaced by the crushing numbness of exhaustion, leaving her little room for thought.

Suddenly it hit her.

"Where is everyone?"

Silence.

"H-hello?" She looked around the corner into the next room, Dustin was watching her.

"Everyone who?" he asked evenly.

"All the *people*, are they... are they gone?"

"No ma'am. They've been ordered back behind a police security perimeter for the time being, for their protection."

Lauren was confused, again. She was beginning to think it was a new default setting she had discovered.

"Why?"

He paused, allowing the silence to lengthen and hang in the air before continuing.

"One of the... individuals became violent when we removed you from the scene. As soon as the crowd realized you were gone others followed suit. For your protection, and the safety of police forces we ordered a temporary restriction on organized meetings in certain public areas."

Lauren was too smart for her own good, it seemed; she knew he was covering for something.

"And everybody just up and left, peacefully, just like that?"

Whether it was her tone, or his general honesty, he chose to tell her the truth.

"No. As with most large gatherings, there were a small number of troublemakers."

"Trouble makers?"

"A few protesters disagreed with your leaving."

"But why? I'm fine..."

"They interpreted you being accompanied by law enforcement officials as you being taken into custody against your will."

"Oh..."

Lauren furrowed her brow.

"Was... Is everyone ok though?"

"A police officer was injured, not severely, as were several protesters."

Lauren mulled over the news, uncomfortable with the idea that more people were hurt because of her.

Noise blared suddenly from the living room as one of Dustin's companions turned on an old television.

"... coming to you live from outside the security fence put up by the police here in St. Louis. Lauren Corvidae, miracle healer, has been taken by federal agents from the scene of a peaceful rally. Law enforcement officers were seen in this exclusive cell-phone video clip carrying what appeared to be her unconscious body into a house on Brine Street. Corvidae, of childhood fame, reappeared in the public eye less than 96 hours ago and has already been taken into custody in what some are calling a government kidnapping. This on the heels of a 28-hour marathon of selfless..."

"Turn it off," Lauren's rage-filled shout drowned out Kent Dailey's voice as a waterfall drowns out a stream.

Dustin, in his first visible show of emotion, recoiled from her sudden change in volume and body language. His hand drifted to his holster but he threw out a hand in the direction of his partner and repeated her instruction.

"Dan, cut it!"

The TV, and the house, fell silent. Dan looked confused, an expression of innocence on his face like he was being framed for a crime.

"What?"

"Don't ever turn that man on again in my presence. He is a liar, a fraud, and a bastard."

Lauren's anger glowed beneath her cheeks, lending her skin a reddish glow as she spoke through gritted teeth.

"Calm down, ma'am," Dustin began to speak with all the mannerisms of a seasoned hostage negotiator.

"I will not calm down! That man, that man destroyed my family!"

"Ok, Lauren, Ok, we understa-"

"Swear it!"

"Ok. I swear it."

Dustin's willingness to give his word took her off guard and her anger lost some of its steam.

"I just need you to calm down ok? How 'bout something to eat?"

Oh hell no. Was he implying she was being unreasonable because she needed to eat?

"What because I'm being a bitch?" The question was no less loaded, and no less dangerous, than the Glock he had on his hip.

Her tone was softer, but her posture threatened violence. Her shoulders were squared, her head low, and even her wings were poised as if to strike.

"No ma'am," he said, unafraid. "But I could sure go for a snack."

"Well I'm going to bed."

She pronounced her will and promptly stormed off into the bedroom she had seen earlier, slamming the door behind her in a fit of childish anger.

She immediately regretted it, feeling overly hostile and knowing the man hadn't meant to offend her.

Worse, she was starving.

The bedroom was small. It held a low dresser, a simple, utilitarian bed with an ancient-looking floral bedspread, and a night-stand with a short lamp on it. The only other feature of the room was a small window, offset from the bed a ways and covered in another thick curtain like the others in the apartment.

Lauren's stomach growled angrily. She had nothing to silence it with, and too much pride to ask. Instead, she pulled off the heavy bedspread. The thick layer of dust made her sneeze, and she promptly dropped the blanket to the floor. Thankfully, there was another comforter beneath the first, and a pair of decent sheets below that. She had just crawled beneath the covers, building a nest for herself and settling into it, when a soft knock came at the door.

"Come in," she grumbled. Still sour, but feeling foolish for her outburst earlier.

It was Dustin.

"I brought you a sandwich. It's peanut butter and jelly." He stayed in the doorway. She could imagine his massive frame filling it comically, but, determined to uphold her pride she didn't look.

"I said I wasn't hungry," she lied defiantly. Her stomach gurgled again in protest, and she hoped the thick covers masked the sound.

"Well," he said in a tone that suggested he was smiling. "Just in case you change your mind I will leave it here on the bed-side table."

His loud footsteps thumped across the room and he set down a plate with a huge, mouth-watering sandwich on it.

He stood over her for a moment, as if he wished to say more, and then turned to leave.

"Thank you," she whispered, if only to satisfy the manners her parents had taught her.

He paused, but pretended not to notice and kept walking out.

No sooner did the door shut than she sat upright and devoured the sandwich like a wild animal. It was divine; and he had made it just the way she liked. Loads of peanut butter and only the faintest accent of jelly.

She chuckled to herself around a mouthful of peanut butter, her dad hated "unbalanced" sandwiches like this one. At least this guy knew what was up. Thinking of her parents put her back on edge. She hoped they were ok. She worried about her father. Had he made it somewhere safe? Should she try contact him? Could she?

Laying back down she contemplated the changes in her life, to include this latest development. It felt surreal, like a television drama.

In her tired mind, blacked out vehicles and dark sunglasses mixed and mashed with bonfires, thick primeval forest, and crowded city streets, only to be replaced with thoughts of the looming presence of her new guardian.

Still, though, she thought as she drifted off, maybe he's not all that bad.

Lauren was jogging barefoot through the Shawnee, her feet impacting lightly on the packed earth and springy moss. She wore a simple tank top and a pair of yoga capris, perfect for the cool, late summer weather.

She knew this trail, though she couldn't remember exactly where it let out of the forest. Her pace was leisurely, and she took in the familiar sights and smells of the deep woods.

The citrus smell of crushed pine needles beneath her feet combined with wildflowers, filling her heart with peace as she breathed deeply.

"Lauren," a familiar voice called from just ahead, around a soft, slow bend in the trail.

She quickened her pace. Who was that? Why did that voice tug so strongly on her heartstrings?

A little of the warmth left the air with a cool breeze from behind her. It raised goosebumps on her skin and brought with it the faintest smell of rain.

"Lauren!" This time there was no doubt in her mind, it was Erin.

Lauren broke into a sprint, tearing off down the trail and calling for her friend.

Strong gusts of wind picked up, turning the trees beside her into wildly dancing columns of green and brown. The first fat drops of a summer squall struck her back, stinging from the force of the gales.

The curve in the trail seemed to extend further, a never ending spiral that wound tighter and tighter. Her feet thumped hard on the dirt of the path, kicking up bits of stick and moss in her wake.

The voice continued. It called to her for help, and despite her break-neck speed it seemed to be getting fainter and fainter.

"Erin!" she tried to scream, but her throat was tight and the word lacked the volume she needed to overcome the cyclonic winds.

The rain fell like bullets now, and her footfalls were splashes in an infinite puddle of mud and tangling tree roots.

With another shout she burst through the last of the trees. The forest ended abruptly at the edge of a huge cornfield. The dry stalks were well past harvest-time, looking like a forest of dull tan sticks a few feet high. In the center of the field, only a hundred yards distant, was a large, two-story farmhouse. It was old, with faded white paint and large bay windows at each corner of its front. An old, decrepit wrap-around porch sheltered a massive wood door.

Erin was nowhere to be seen.

The door slammed shut in the distance, propelled by the howling, still fierce wind.

"Erin!"

Her voice was a snowflake in a blizzard, impossible to distinguish from the storm around her. If anything, the winds howled louder in response.

She resumed her sprint, legs aching and lungs burning. As she strode among the cornstalks they brushed and scratched her legs, rattling like the exposed bones of autumn.

Ozone filled her nostrils, and lightning flashed around her as she crossed the last few dozen feet to the porch. Taking the stairs three at a time she slammed into the door, gripping the handle and trying to pry it open.

The wind was pressing so strongly against the door that she struggled to even separate it from the frame. She clawed at it, finally managing to slip her fingers into the crack around the door jam, and pulled it open. Her scraped, bloodied fingers left bright red streaks on the chipped paint.
She forced herself inside, the door pushing her a few feet into the room as it slammed shut against her back.

The noise of the wind was quieted, but only just. The inside of the room was comfortable and well furnished. Warm natural wood accented neutral earth-tone walls and a dark, deep-grained wood floor. Bookshelves lined every wall of the massive sitting room, each filled to the brim with books.
"Erin?" Lauren called out loudly. Her voice had returned, and without the storm to drown her out her voice carried well.

Only silence answered her.

Lauren felt the oppressive emptiness of the house as a growing weight on her shoulders. Driving her posture downward until she was creeping from room to room like a field mouse in a library.

She began to examine the first floor. There was a large, well-lit kitchen with massive storm windows and cabinets full of every kind of cereal she could imagine. Further exploration was halted by a noise from upstairs. The sound of running feet and a slamming door.

"Erin? Erin!"

She searched desperately for, and finally found, a tall winding wooden staircase. She climbed the stairs as fast as she could, coming out on a landing with only a single door at the top. The door had faded brass numbers on it, and an all too familiar handle.

Her sense of uneasiness grew.

The howling of the wind outside took on a long and mournful character, altering in pitch and intensity as she listened.

"Lauren!"

The voice, which came from beyond the door, startled Lauren so badly she squeaked in momentary terror.

"Lauren help me, please," the voice sounded afraid, like Erin was hurt and crying.

Fear was replaced by urgency and Lauren grabbed the handle. It was locked. She beat on the door, screaming Erin's name until her fists were bruised and her throat was hoarse.

She sank to her knees, looking at her hands. The bruises deepened in color, turning purple and then a blackish color tinged with green. Her nails were still broken and her fingertips bloody from the door downstairs. Her shins still bore the scrapes and scratches of the cornfield. Even her feet were bruised and battered.

A loud click dragged her from her horrified inspection of her growing injuries. With a look of disbelief she stared at the handle of the door as it slowly turned. The door popped loose, a tiny crack appearing next to the frame.

Lauren pushed her pain aside and yanked the door open.

Lauren rushed inside, lost her footing on the wet floor and fell, jarring her wrist painfully. Her hands slipped on the slick floor as she tried to stand and she stared horrified and the flood of crimson covering the tile. She couldn't see Erin right away, from her vantage point she could only see her pale arm hanging over the side of a deep, cast iron bathtub. Her wrist was laid open as far Lauren could see.

No, not again, Lauren thought to herself. Her mind started to shut down. She had been here before, seen this before.

She stared, entranced, at Erin's arm, too afraid to look over the edge of the tub at what she knew she would find. There was a rushing in her ears, like the roar of a waterfall. Her heart pounded in her head and felt like it would beat out of her chest.

As she watched, thick red blood began to spill over the edge of the tub as if someone had left the faucet on and the drain plugged.

She scrambled backward, banging against the now closed door. She turned to face the door, which now locked from the other side. Her running clothes were gone, replaced by an unforgettable garment. Her slinky, light brown dress smeared blood across the floor as she struggled to stand.

She grasped at the door as the crimson tide slowly rose. One inch, two.

Splits began to appear on Lauren's arms, her own blood springing forth amidst a burning pain.

Tearing at the door she finally managed to get it open. Blood rushed out of the room as she retreated to the landing and slammed the door behind her.

Turning, she pushed against the door. She was painfully aware of the slow trickle from beneath the seal.

Lauren backed away, unable to comprehend what was happening. She tore off down the stairs, stumbling as she did and nearly falling twice.

When she reached the living room, Lauren made a beeline for the front door, throwing it open with a crash. A gust of wind nearly knocked her backwards, and it tugged painfully at her wings. Even so, she had to get out.
She ran across the porch, then out into the yard, fighting the storm. The winds were so fierce they ripped some of her feathers out, sending dark shadowy shapes out into the howling fury.

Above the howl of the wind came another, more animal noise.

The howls of wolves filled the darkened skies, at least a dozen separate animals.

Lauren froze, rain battering her like hailstones and the wind throwing her hair and feathers around chaotically.

A flash of lightning illuminated the cornfields. She could clearly see the dark, sleek shapes of the wolves. They were coming from every direction.
"Lauren," the voice was even closer, whispering in her ear.

Lauren awoke, screaming. Her eyes were wide with terror, she clawed at the now-suffocating embrace of the blankets and sheets covering her.

It was dark, and for a moment she didn't know where she was. So absolute was her terror that she simply sat weeping and tried to remember how to breathe as her heart threatened to explode.

"Lauren," the voice wasn't Erin's, but it still startled the hell out of her.
"It's ok, it's just me."
Dustin.

He was sitting quietly in the total darkness, he had pulled up a chair at the foot of the bed.

"W-what are you doing in here, why are you here."

It was impossible to read the man's tone, and the darkness hid his face and masked his body language.

"You were screaming. I'm sorry. I can go if you would prefer, I didn't mean to disturb you, I just ..."

Lauren waited, but no further words seemed forthcoming.

"No," she finally said. Deep down, it was comforting to not be alone. The nightmare had felt far too real.

"Ok."

The pair sat quietly as the silence lengthened. Finally Lauren could take it no longer.

"I'm sorry," she said softly.

"Why would you be sorry?"

"I worried you," she continued, feeling guilty for keeping him awake. "I'll be ok, I think. I've had these nightmares almost every night since..."

A lump formed in her throat and her half-dried cheeks were wet once again with tears.

"Since Gabriel d-died. Now Erin's gone too and I just, I don't understand. What did I do wrong? I miss them so much..."

Dustin was silent, but not in a judgmental way. He was a patient stranger, a vigilant statue with an open ear.

"Since Erin, it's gotten even worse. I see her every night."

Dustin shifted slightly, and she knew his dark blue eyes were looking at her, she could feel his gaze.

"There was nothing you could have done for your little brother, or for your... friend."

"That's not true," she was becoming hysterical, her voice high and tears forcing her to stutter. "A-at least n-not for Erin. I could have stayed, I should have been there. I betrayed her." The guilt in her voice was palpable, and it filled the room.

Dustin seemed to choose his words carefully.

"I... do not envy you, but you should not blame yourself. You could not have saved your brother, you yourself said it doesn't work on your family members except for John."
"My dad, except my dad's side," Lauren interrupted softly, but turning her thoughts to him she became even more distraught. She might never see him again.
"Yes, ah, your dad. As for Ms. Engle, I... can't speak to-"
"Stop," her voice cracked on the simple word. "Please stop. Can we not talk about her please."
He nodded, stopping mid-sentence at her pleading.

"What do I *do*?" Lauren asked him finally, leaving it to him to interpret what exactly she was asking for help with.
He sat quietly a moment before answering.

"About the nightmares? Or about your abilities?"
"Either. Both, maybe."

Chapter 11

The sun creeping over the horizon found Lauren standing on her hotel balcony. She was looking down at the streets of Sarajevo. The faded scars of past war dotted the growing city, tiny reminders in a sea of optimism and peace.

She clutched a mug of hot tea in her cold hands. Steam carried the scents of warm peppermint and chamomile to her nose and calmed her frayed nerves and worried mind.

She relished the silence and the stillness. The rest of her entourage must still be asleep. She thought about her new companions. Since St. Louis she'd been accompanied by a small army of handlers "provided" by the State Department. Security officers, public relations managers, official press representatives, even a liaison from the United Nations.

It was a circus.

At least Dustin is still with me, she reminded herself.
A cool breeze floated over the red-tiled roofs of the still sleeping city. It encircled her and sent a shiver through her body. She'd had to modify her wardrobe, favoring strapless dresses and warm leggings these days due to her... unusual requirements. She sighed, unfortunately dresses and leggings were not ideal winter wear.

She pulled her warm, woolen Shahmina tighter around her shoulders, grateful once more to Selimah, the woman she'd met in Pakistan just a few short weeks ago.

They'd been visiting Azad Kashmir, just to the west of the capitol, Islamabad. Tensions had been mounting between several of the larger religious groups in the region. With riots and violence rising, Dustin had suggested that visiting the Middle East might be way to help stop the bloodshed. Her crew loved the idea, and in no time she found herself on a plane headed around the world.

"Show the world your gifts are for everyone, that they come without bias. Maybe they'll stop trying to tear each other apart."

He didn't have to add that most of these groups were fighting over her.

It was Lauren's first trip abroad. It should have been a magical, enlightening experience for her. Like it would have been for any other 18-year-old. Instead she was met with the same throngs of frenzied people as she'd contended with in the States. She knew nothing of the language, or of the culture, but she saw plenty of people in need when she arrived.

Selimah though. She stuck out.

Lauren thought back to Selimah's face, to the stark reminder of what people could do to one another. She couldn't have been more than twenty, tall and bronze-skinned with ebony hair. Her most striking feature, however, were the horrible burns across her face. Badly scarred, she was missing most of her lips, and was blind in one eye. She was so caught off guard by the woman, Lauren almost didn't notice the child Selimah was holding. Her oldest son, Fatihm. He was six. The boy had a badly maimed leg, the product of a roadside bomb a few years before.

Lauren wasted no time healing the boy, giving him a reassuring smile and a pat on the head, but she couldn't tear her eyes away from the woman. Selimah had dropped to her knees, planting her face against the dirty, trash-covered street in gratitude for Lauren's gift.

"She is praying, giving thanks to Allah for his mercy and for your kindness," her translator told her.

"How did she become injured?"

The translator conveyed Lauren's question. Selimah's face was difficult to read, but she seemed ashamed when she answered.

"She says it is a punishment for her dishonoring her husband. Another man grew attracted to her because she did not keep her beauty hidden."

Lauren felt certain that Selimah would have lived the rest of her life with that horrible scarring. That it would have never crossed her mind to ask for Lauren's gift herself.

Lauren couldn't understand.

"Why? Why would someone do that to another person?" she had asked Dustin.

"Well... it's complicated. Culture takes many forms, Lauren. Art. Music," he paused. "Even Justice."

"This is justice?"

She was appalled.

"Lauren... it's a different way of life."

He'd explained that women's rights weren't the same everywhere. That women in that part of the world might find themselves subject to having their features disfigured with acid for a variety of reasons.

Lauren grew more horrified the more he explained. She dropped to her knees and wrapped the woman in her arms. Selimah raised her head to look at her, and Lauren was awed by her restored beauty. She had bottomless, forest-green eyes that reminded her of Erin's, and a face that belonged in a museum amongst great works of art.

But she didn't look grateful, she looked terrified.

Selimah had held out her the shawl then, insisted that she take it.

"T-tell her I don't accept payment," she nudged her translator.

"She says you must take it, ma'am."
Lauren had finally been forced to accept it for fear of insulting the woman.

Immediately she had taken her son and disappeared back into the crowd.
"Why was she so upset? She'll be ok, right?" she'd asked. Dustin's silence that day still weighed heavy on her mind.

A shiver brought Lauren back to the present. The thick wool on her shoulders could only warm her body, not her heart. She sipped her too-hot tea, tasting the heavy dose of medovina she'd poured into it before it burned her tongue.

The hotel attendant hardly spoke any English, but she'd eventually managed to convey to him both her desire for liquor and for discretion. She enjoyed the sweet liquid, relishing its warmth spreading through her as her thoughts returned to the past few weeks.

The whirlwind tour that had brought her here was a blur. Ethiopia, Somalia, Moldova, Afghanistan, and now, Bosnia.

She'd barely slept.

Each city was the same. Each country. Each continent. Always the crying, screaming faces pressing in around her and the outstretched hands reaching and grabbing at her.

She shivered again, but not from the cold this time.

"You should still be asleep," Dustin's voice startled her, causing her to splash some of the scalding liquid from her cup onto her hand. It burned for a moment, and she stared dispassionately as an angry red welt raised itself and then immediately faded from sight again.

Some things never change, she thought ruefully.

Her eyes settled on a hair-thin scar that the fading burn brought back to light.

Others do.

"Lauren, you need to rest."
Dustin's paternal concern irked Lauren.

"Even when I sleep I don't rest, Dustin, you know that. Don't pretend you can't hear the screaming."
Silence.

Her bitter words weren't meant to cut so deeply, but it was true. The nightmares hadn't gotten better. If anything they were worse. The details changed, but the dream itself mostly stayed the same. Some nights it was Gabriel she was chasing, others it was Erin. But it was always to the house in the woods, always the wolves pursuing her.

She'd discovered that alcohol would help to deaden the impact, even help her sleep if she could get enough of it. But it was next to impossible to find her fix under the watchful gaze of her escorts.

Especially Dustin.

He'd nearly caught her twice, and she didn't want to con-sider what might happen if he did.

"Where are we going today?" She tried to change the subject, to lighten the mood somehow.

"There's a cathedral here, Katedrala Srca Isusova. It means Sacred Heart," his response was businesslike, brusque.

She hated when he did that.

"Why?"
"You're having dinner with a representative from the Vatican, they're the ones that paid for most of this leg of the trip."
Lauren thought of her self-imposed penance.

"I don't want to visit priests and politicians. I'm supposed to be helping people."

He took a long slow breath, in through his nose and out through his mouth.
"And you're doing that from a balcony? By stewing in your own bitterness? You're doing that by denying yourself basic needs like real meals and rest?"

Turned out his words were sharper than hers.
"Shut up, Dustin," her tone could have melted steel, and the

look she shot him over her mug could have brought down a building.

She moved to storm past him, upset at his insight, but his hand shot out and grabbed her arm.

"What's in the cup," It wasn't a question so much as a statement.

"T-t-tea," she stammered in startled surprise.

"Lauren," his scolding tone inflamed her anger.

"Let me go," she snapped, yanking her arms from his grasp. "If I say its tea, it's fucking tea."

His hand lashed out, quick as a viper, and he grabbed the mug. He held it briefly to his nose and then, scowling, poured it out onto the balcony floor.

"Lauren you are a teenager, and in an unstable emotional state. The last thing you need is a depressant in your system." Lauren was floored, beyond offended.

"I'm unstable? I'm fucking unstable now?"

Her wings twitched and flicked, and her fist clenched tightly, cues to her impending explosion.

"Honestly?"

Exhaustion and stress found an outlet through anger and she swung wildly at him. Her fist impacted futilely on the steely muscles of his arm. He hadn't even bothered to flinch.

"Lauren," he started again, his tone still maddeningly even.

"How *dare* you. How dare you judge me," her tone was caustic.

"I hate you."

The spirit of her anger danced when it seemed, just for a moment, that his eyes truly registered pain at those three little words. Deep inside she knew she was burning a bridge that might never be repaired, but she didn't care.

To her dismay he simply nodded, replying in his usual businesslike manner.

"Ok."

Lauren was beyond words. Speechless with anger she stormed away from the balcony, retreating across the suite to her bedroom and slamming the door shut as hard as she could. Expensive paintings rattled on the pristine, midnight blue walls of her bedroom. She locked the door behind her, knowing it would irritate Dustin.

Bastard, what the hell did he know.

Lauren threw herself onto the large feather-bed that was the centerpiece of the room. She stared dejectedly out of her large, four-paned window as the sun crept higher into the sky.

It was too bright, too cheery to suit her current mood so she walked over and dragged closed the thick, floor-length curtains, plunging the room into darkness.

Returning to the bed she chewed over Dustin's words. Her relentless, never-ending exhaustion eventually overcame her anger, and she slipped fitfully to sleep.

Lauren was jogging barefoot through the Shawnee.

A powerful storm was building and already fat raindrops had started to pelt the ground, stinging her skin. She knew this trail, though she couldn't remember exactly where it let out of the forest. Her pace was brisk, and she felt an ominous foreboding as she ran ahead of the storm.

The citrus smell of crushed pine needles beneath her feet combined with midnight rain, roses, and... something else. Some sickly sweet scent she couldn't place.

"Lauren," a familiar voice called from just ahead. Just around a soft, slow bend in the trail. She knew the voice, but couldn't put a name or face to it.

Lightning ripped across the sky, accompanied by peals of thunder that shook the ground as she emerged out into a cornfield.

She paused, her neck hairs raised and a sudden and ominous sense of deja vu filled her with dread.

A long and lonesome howl rose from the woods behind her, joined quickly by many others.

A large white house sat in the middle of the cornfield ahead, could she make it in time? For some reason even the prospect of safety in the home ahead of her filled her with fear.

Faced with the fury of the storm and the threat of the wolves, Lauren had no choice. She tore across the field, the beasts still howling behind her. She could hear their tireless, panting breaths by the time she reached the yard. She crossed the yard and porch in seconds, propelled by the gusting winds. Even so, she barely made it before the first of the wolves cleared the steps. She managed to slam the door in its face, but she could hear it clawing at the wood.

She moved to lean against the door, to hold the tide back, but wings suddenly blocked her way. These wings were different, they weren't white but covered in menacing, jet-black feathers instead.

Desperate, she looked around. She was in a large, dimly lit living room with four doors, one for each wall.

Lauren ran to the closest and went to open it, but she noticed a trickle of blood from underneath. Mortified, she checked another. It was the same. All four of the doors were pooling blood into the room, staining the dark wood of the floor-boards.

The front door creaked and buckled, the beasts outside growled and snarled through ever-growing cracks.

At last, Lauren yanked open a door at random.

It was a staircase.

Unquestioning, terrified, she ran up the stairs. She climbed and climbed, not pausing even when she heard the sounds of breaking wood and knew they had gotten in. The sounds of pursuit grew closer and closer, she could feel the hot, fetid breath of the animals on her neck.

Higher and higher she ran, the hallway narrowing as she went until she was barely able to squeeze through with her wings. A sharp, piercing pain in her left wing told her she was caught.

She was dragged forcefully backwards until the mouthful of feathers was ripped out. Wasting no time, she sprang back to her feet and continued her running. The wolves were distracted for a moment and she gained a little ground.

Lauren finally burst out of the tightening tunnel and onto the top of a windswept bell-tower.

Looking around for an escape Lauren saw none, only the tumultuous, lightning-scarred skies.

She ran to the edge of the tower and stepped up on the low ledge. Looking down, she realized she was at least fifty feet in the air.

The clicking of paws alerted her that the predators were here, spreading out behind her and preparing to pounce.

She leapt.

For a brief moment she believed she was free, but as she flapped her wings she felt the iron-strong jaw of one of the wolves clamp down on her leg. Razor-sharp teeth dug into her calf and the animal began to drag her back to the platform.

She started to scream, knowing no one could hear her, as the wolf pulled her down and the rest of the pack descended upon her.

Lauren woke still screaming.

Dustin was pounding on the bedroom door, calling out to her.

Lauren curled up and hugging her knees to her chest as she wept. She sobbed, begging the empty room for it to go away, for the nightmares to stop. She wished desperately for an escape, for a return to normalcy, for a normal to return to.

"Lauren, open the goddamn door!"

She registered his voice, but her mind was a tangled mess of fear. She couldn't yet bring herself to move.

Dustin threw his weight against the door. The wood buckled and cracked, just as the wolves did every time she closed her eyes.

Lauren covered her ears with her hands. She couldn't listen to the breaking wood. It felt too much like the dream was bleeding over into reality. Seeping through the cracks like blood under a door.

Lauren screamed for him to stop, but her words were garbled.

Dustin was relentless, he was making quick work of the door and Lauren couldn't take it any longer.

She ran to the window, tearing curtains open she was blinded for a moment by the full afternoon sunlight. Not waiting for her eyes to clear she pushed open the window and climbed unsteadily to the sill.

Shapes were beginning to form against the blinding brightness when Lauren leapt. The sound of her powerful wingbeats competed with crunching wood as Dustin finally kicked in what was left of the door.

But he was too late.

Lauren climbed rapidly, shooting up into the sky like a firework with sun glinting off her snowy wings.

The cold wind roaring past her face nipped at her nose, but it also helped wash away her terror. Here, in the sky, she felt truly untouchable. Her pulse slowed and her breathing stuttered back to normal as she rose.

Her eyes finally adjusted fully to the sunlight and Lauren looked around. She was freezing cold, and much higher than she'd ever flown before. The cars below her were tiny swarming ants running along narrowly defined tracks through a maze of tiny boxes and blurs.

Lauren realized she had no idea what their hotel looked like from up here, or even a really clear concept of where it was in the city. Dustin should be furious with her, but she knew he would instead show more of his endless patience.

Which would in turn make her feel worse.

The wind at this height was arctic, and cut through her clothing like a knife. Besides, she was going to have to drop lower if she wanted any chance of finding the hotel.
She swooped low, paying little attention to the gathering crowds of people who marked her passage. By now she was used to seeing swarms gather around her as she traveled.
From up here in the air they weren't so bad. Still intimidating certainly, but also humbling. Even a little flattering.

But from within, when the sky seemed miles away and the press of flesh crowded her from every side, it was a living nightmare.

Soaring a few dozen feet over the rooftops she attracted considerable attention. Camera flashes and shouts followed her and before long people were gathered in waiting at every turn, anticipating her arrival.

Dammit, all the freaking buildings look the same.

She kicked herself for her rash decision making.

A loud pop, like a firecracker, caught her attention from below. Lauren instinctively pulled into a tight, fast turn to circle back.

A man was laying on the ground, he had on a thick, bulky winter jacket and worn, faded blue jeans. A growing pool of red stained the street below him and the crowd there was yelling and forming a circle around him.

Alarmed, she dropped quickly from the sky, landing a few feet from the man. The down draft from her widespread wings blew across the crowd, eliciting awed gasps.

He was a young man, early twenties perhaps. He had a pale complexion and was wearing mostly threadbare clothing. His jacket was the exception, it was a puffy, nearly new winter coat. There was a large hole in it by his shoulder, nearly an inch wide, where the white polyester stuffing was spilling out. As Lauren watched, it was slowly turning red, soaking up blood from some unseen wound beneath. Lauren began to unzip the bulky garment, trying to better see the wound so she could reach it and heal the man.

As soon as her fingers grasped his zipper, however, the man reached up and grabbed her arms. He gripped her forcefully, pulling her close to him. She pushed past the discomfort, used to desperation from the people she helped. She could see his chest rising and falling with more surety as he healed swiftly. But he didn't let go.

Instead, he growled something at her in a language she couldn't understand. The words were harsh, guttural, menacing.

Lauren pushed at him, trying to pull herself away, but he was too strong. As she shoved at his chest she felt something hard and block-like under his thick jacket. Something hidden beneath it. She fought harder, her wild eyes searching the crowd looking for help.

Everyone watching seemed as frightened and confused as she was. Finally, realizing what was happening, a pair of men stepped forward. They joined her in prying the man away. The man below her was chanting something, his eyes closed and his face calm despite the increasingly violent actions of the men trying to rescue her. One of the men, a tall, broad-shouldered fellow with thick leather boots gave the man a solid kick, catching him in the temple. The hands holding her went limp for a moment as a deep gash appeared across the man's head, and she jerked her arms back as her second savior pulled off of her attacker.

Everyone was shouting by now, yelling angrily. They seemed outraged at her treatment, pointing at her as well as the man.

The man on the ground lurched suddenly upwards, his wound healed from those last few moments of contact with her. He tried to grab her arm but she dodged him, his hand landing on her left wing instead. As she crawled backwards to escape him, assisted by one of her rescuers, his fingers caught a handful of her feathers and tore them out, sending a light spray of blood across the pavement.

It was excruciating, as though someone had ripped her fingernails out. She stumbled and fell to the ground, crying out. The man's hungry, hateful expression mirrored the wolves of her nightmares perfectly.

The crowd turned violent, Lauren's visible pain leading them to take action. They turned on the man, who had already dropped the feathers and was digging in his jacket for something. The crowd thrust forward, shoving Lauren to the side and blocking her view.

The man who had pulled her away stepped in front of her as she lay upon the ground, his young face full of concern. He had a dark tan, middle-eastern complexion, black hair, and the most startling blue eyes.

He was speaking to her in a familiar language. She didn't understand him, but it sounded the same as the woman from Pakistan. He was pointing at himself, and then at her shawl, and then away from the growing masses. He kept looking over his shoulder at the mob surrounding the man on the ground, and he grew increasingly distraught.

After only a few seconds he grabbed Lauren's arm and tried to drag her to her feet. He was yelling now as he pointed away from the gathering crowd.

Lauren knew he was desperate to communicate *something* to her, but she was so shell-shocked, and in such horrible agony that she couldn't figure it out. She simply shook her head, trying to see through her watery eyes and clutching her injured wing.

A strangled yell from her would be attacker rose above the crowd in front of her, and suddenly people started screaming and shoving each other to get away from him.

A strange look crossed her savior's face and he knelt before her, wrapping his arms around her. They were eye to eye now, only inches apart. The look on his face was that of grief.

Lauren didn't understand.

The explosion ripped through the crowd like a hurricane. Lauren's vision filled with blinding light as the very world shook beneath her.

She felt a wave of pressure hit her like a freight train, felt her ears crack, pop, and then fall silent. The air was torn from her lungs and she felt several of her bones crack from the impact of the ground behind her as she slammed into it.

Reeling, she tried to stand but couldn't find her balance. Instead she crawled in dizzy circles, trying to make sense of what had happened. Her vision was swimming, everything was hazy and spinning violently. Her ears were still silent but she could feel something, a liquid of some kind, dripping from them. Slowly, her gift began to repair her body.

Her vision was the first of her senses to return fully.

Bodies were everywhere. Pieces of people strewn about like the leftover toys from a child's tantrum. Smoke and cracked stones littered the street. And the blood, blood was every-where.

On the ground beneath her, between her scraped, dirt-smeared hands, was the blue-eyed face of her rescuer,.The man who had put his body in front of her just before the bomb went off. His eyes were frozen, wide open but unseeing. His body was badly broken, and Lauren could see he was al-ready gone.

Her hearing returned with the sharp, thundering staccato cracks of gunfire. She ducked her head instinctively, hearing bullets zip past and impact on the stone faces of the surrounding buildings.

The screams and moans of agony from the injured and dying were all around her, a chorus of misery.

She didn't know who was shooting, or why, or even at what. A smaller, secondary explosion erupted a few blocks away, rattling her teeth and shaking the pavement below her. A group of men in dark masks and fatigues were piling out of an old van a few dozen feet away. They were well armed, and fired into the crowd of onlookers.

Her wing still burned with pain, but it was a dull throbbing now, she didn't bother to look at it. Instead, she crawled among the fallen, trying to find people who she could still save.

She proceeded with laser-like focus, trying to push out the sirens, the screams, the sounds of the madness raging around her.

Pushing aside some rocks she saw a child, he couldn't have been more than four. He had curly, jet-black hair. Lauren pulled up short, stopped by her baby brother's dust and dirt covered face.

"Gabriel!"

Lauren screamed, shaking the boy and blinking back tears. He wasn't moving. Lauren sat back, wiping her eyes. Gabriel's face was gone, replaced by the ruddy features of the unfamiliar child before her. She shook her head, it was still ringing so badly, and tried to process the carnage around her. She'd made a mistake by losing her focus, by pulling back. Looking around she was frozen in shock and dismay at the bloodshed and violence erupting around her.

Police had arrived and pushed back the gunmen. Several nearby buildings were burning, and distant explosions echoed across the city as the scars of a long-buried war tore violently open.

"Lauren!"

Dustin's voice.

He was nearby. Lauren stood unsteadily, turning in a slow circle and searching for him like a storm-bound ship seeks a lighthouse.

There.

Dustin and two of his fellow agents were running towards her, guns drawn, long black coats flapping in the wind as they came. The other two were covering the vehicle amidst the chaos, twenty feet distant.

She was safe.

Relief flooded her, freeing her momentarily from her paralyzing anxiety. She ran towards them, her wings tucked tightly behind her and her head down.

When Dustin and his companions reached her, he scooped her up in his arms and spun nimbly, carrying her body back toward the vehicle's flashing lights. As soon as the doors slammed shut the tires spun on the slick, dirty ground and they were off like a rocket.

"Lauren, are you injured?"

His tone was serious, filled with concern, and as he spoke he looked her over for damage.

She knew he'd asked a question, but a strange sort of paralysis was coming over her. Her mind was slowing down, senses and sensations dulling as the ramifications of what had happened started to sink in.

All those people had died because she was there.

That man, and his bomb, were meant for *her*. She had landed among innocent men, women, and children. She had condemned them. Committed them to the grave as surely as if she had set the trap herself.

"Lauren!"

He was shouting, only a few inches from her face. She felt her heart rate spiking and dropping erratically and her breathing becoming more rapid, more shallow. Her body's betrayal only served to further her anxiety and she started to shiver uncontrollably.

"Multiple... throughout the city... well-coordinated... need to re-route to the..."

Dustin's voice was fading in and out and she felt suddenly tired, completely drained of energy.

His lips were still working, still moving, but his voice was jumbled like a poorly tuned radio station. She felt her head start to dip forward as darkness overcame her.

Lauren woke with a start to the dull roar of aircraft engines. For a moment she stared upwards at the curved ceiling and tried simply to calm herself.

Her nightmares had taken on new horrors; the faces of the wolves changed and shifted now. They morphed into the victims of her latest failure and then returned to savage, toothy maws. Her face and pillow were wet and she knew she'd been crying.

What have I done, she murmured softly to herself, blinking away visions of the broken bodies she'd left behind in Sarajevo.

As she lay there, she noticed a shadow on her left wing. Stretching it out she looked more closely. A patch of her feathers, those that had been ripped out, seemed to have grown back in pure ebony.

They were so dark they seemed almost to absorb light. A patch of night amidst the bright white of her wings. Reminded uncomfortably of her nightmares, she looked around for something to distract herself.

Dustin was asleep, his back against the door at the foot of the bed and a pistol in his hand. His chin was tucked to his chest, resting on a thick, bulletproof vest he wore outside his customary button-up shirt.

Her throat was terribly dry, and she knew she must have screamed herself hoarse several times while unconscious, as she did every night.

A bottle of water and a pair of large cough-drops in a cup were waiting for her on the bedside table with a note that simply had a large arrow pointing to the medicine and the letter "D" scribbled on it.

Thoughtful as ever. Despite her aggression, her irresponsibility, her emotional outbursts. He had yet to truly lose his temper with her. On the contrary, he had been a vigilant caretaker despite her best efforts.

She tried to move quietly, but her rustling wings woke him. Unlike Lauren, Dustin woke up like some kind of large, apex feline. His eyes snapped open to full alertness and his muscles coiled, ready to respond to any situation.
"Lauren."
With this single word her stoic friend spoke volumes.

"I'm... ok," she managed a weak smile, but knew he wasn't fooled. He never was.

"Are you, ok? Do you have any ringing in your ears, headache, nausea?"
Physically she felt fine, certainly still a little nauseous, but only when she thought about the consequences of her unscheduled tour of the city.

She nodded, sniffling and tearing up again at the thought of all those people.

He shifted awkwardly on the floor, her tears always made him uncomfortable.

"Drink some water," he motioned to the bottle. "And take those drops, they'll help."
She did, silently following his instructions.

"How did you find me?"
She knew the answer. It would have been hard to miss the explosion. She felt stupid for asking as soon as the words left

her lips. Her face must have shown it because he didn't answer aloud, he only nodded.

"I'm sorry, Lauren."

His words took her by surprise. What did he have to be sorry for?

"I'm sorry I lectured you. You are, in fact, an adult. Capable of making decisions for yourself."

He seemed relieved to have gotten the words off his chest, and lapsed back into silence. She couldn't convince herself he was right.

"My decisions got people killed. Again."

She stated it matter-of-factly, they both knew it was true.

"I chose this assignment you know. Volunteered for it."

Again he surprised her with an unexpected confession.

"Would you like to know why?"

She nodded again, looking at him with great interest, trying in vain to interpret his unreadable face.

"I believe very *strongly*, in you."

He looked like he was ready to continue, to say more, but a soft tap on the door stopped him. He froze and put a finger to his lips, indicating silence.

Turning quietly and rising, He tapped back an odd pattern. A whispered word made it through the door, though not to Lauren's ears, and he relaxed. Holstering his weapon he cracked the door inward. Lauren couldn't see who was on the other side of the door at first, but after a brief conversation an elderly priest and a young, sharply dressed man in a suit were allowed to enter.

The men moved past Dustin to the foot of the bed. The door was promptly shut, and Dustin again put his back against it. Lauren gave him a confused, inquiring look. His only response was a small but reassuring nod.

The priest, an older man, bowed deeply to Lauren and held this posture long enough for Lauren to become uncomfortable.

"Please, sir, you don't have to do that."

The younger man, who had also bowed, though not as deeply, said something to his elder which prompted them both to rise. The language was lyrical, Italian maybe?

Flushed in the cheeks she stared at her visitors until the old man spoke. It was the same language that the young man used, and she realized he must be a translator. Sure enough, the old man's flowery Italian speech was converted to English, albeit with a thick accent.

"Your Grace, it is with great honor that we meet with you in the name of his holiness the Pope."

What?

"Um, you're welcome. I mean thank you. Uh, the pleasure is mine."

Lauren was unsure how to respond. She hated these awkward, overly eager sorts of conversations. She preferred to visit among the people, help as many as she could, and then retreat to the peace of her solitude. Entertaining strangers with a language barrier while sitting unkempt in bed was definitely not her idea of a good time.

"We would like to invite you to the Vatican City, to meet his Holiness and discuss a way forward together in faith."

"I'm sorry, I don't understand. A way forward? What does that mean?"

The old man seemed confused at her misunderstanding. He had a quick, untranslated conversation with the younger man, who shrugged and gestured at her.

"We would like you to meet to discuss God's will. His Holiness has many questions and wishes to speak to you about the coming days."

Lauren balked, now she was supposed to give spiritual advice to the Pope?

"Absolutely not," she blurted out without thinking.

The young man looked surprised, but dutifully translated for his partner. The priest was stunned.

Dustin gave a slow head-shake from behind the men, eyes wide. He was definitely in disagreement with her word choice.

"I, um. I mean that I am very, uh, taxed from the events of the day. I cannot meet him right now, I need to rest."

Her words rang true, as the men could both clearly see she was tired.

"Yes, of course your Grace. It is still several hours until we reach Rome. We will leave you to your privacy until then. Please allow us to fulfill any needs you may have. May peace be with you."

The men seemed to be waiting for something.

"Um, yes, thank you," she said, unsure what they were looking for. Dustin was giving her a funny look, almost like he wanted to smile.

"Your Grace," the men said again.

They bowed low before exiting the room, chatting rapidly in their native tongue once more.

As soon as the door clicked Dustin cracked a huge smile.

"You definitely weren't raised Catholic."

Lauren threw a pillow at him.

"What's that supposed to mean? Who the heck are those guys, and why did you let them in here! I looked like a moron!"

Lauren was hissing loudly at him, trying to whisper and shout at the same time.

He easily caught the pillow as it flew through the air, and responded in his typical, deadpan fashion.

"When they said may peace be with you, you were *supposed* to say and also with you," at this Lauren buried her face in her hands, cheeks red with embarrassment.

"They are Cardinal Giordano Bruno, and his translator, Mr. Restrepo, representatives from the Vatican. Since this is their plane, I thought it wise to let them in," Dustin continued.

"*Why* are we on the Vatican's plane!"

Dustin was quiet.

"Dustin?" she pressed with increasing concern. "Why aren't we on the plane we arrived in?"

"I... couldn't be sure it was still safe. The conditions in the city were such that we needed to get you out as quickly as possible."

Lauren fell quiet as well, wondering just how bad it had gotten.

"How many-" she began, but he interrupted her.

"Don't."

A lot, then.

Chapter 12

Lauren spent the remainder of the plane ride watching the news. Lauren's crew was substantially reduced, many of the "non-essential" personnel had either been recalled by the department or had been unable to make it to the plane in time. Sarajevo had turned into a warzone as decades of tensions between the major religious groups in the city ignited.

Reporters speculated about the man who had detonated the vest. Pundit after pundit crossed the television screen, each arguing over who was at fault for the horrific incident.

Within an hour an extremist group known as the Armiya Sveta, "Warriors of Light," had claimed responsibility. The group, a militant organization in southern Chechnya, had been implicated in a variety of terrorist activities over the past decade. They had become famous for their unusual zealotry, believing that Lauren was a *qarin*, an evil jinn sent to tempt men away from God.

A solemn British journalist was reading the latest developments for the BBC in London.

"... We'll go ahead and play the video, released to us just about thirty minutes ago..."

A swarthy, full-bearded man appeared on a grainy video clip. His speech was thickly accented, and had been subtitled in English..

"... Lauren Corvidae. To follow this woman is Bid'ah, it is forbidden. All true followers of Allah and of the prophet will seek to destroy her. In Bid'ah there is only damnation..."
The video continued in similar vein for another minute or so before turning to a group of captive men and women. As she watched, a number of heavily armed men forced the group up against a wall and the video cut out.
"... as you can see, it is a very, very disturbing video. Our sources in Washington have indicated that the large number of individuals you saw there were executed on suspicion of believing in what the group calls 'the false messenger,' Lauren Corvidae. The name refers to the deeply held Islamic belief that Muhammad was the last and final messenger, or prophet, of God. During the next hour we will be speaking with Mr. Qadir Ibn Hazm al-Hajar, a leading Sunni scholar on the subject of jinn and their place in the Muslim faith..."
Other news channels were playing similar programming, with some variation depending on the source. On American news, politicians debated whether or not an attack on Lauren constituted an attack on Christianity at large, and what the political implications were.
"... is clearly an Angel and an instrument of Jesus Christ and the Holy Father. Any attempt to harm her should be taken by the Christian community as an act of persecution..."
One of the men, a representative from Kentucky, argued.
"... to assign a particular extant religion to this woman is absurd. She would have certainly been more proactive in spreading 'the Word' if she was truly an instrument of the Christian God, any god for that matter. Maybe she *is* god. If she is, then she acts by her own divine right and we should not be deciding a course of action when She has yet to speak on Her own behalf..." argued his counterpart, a Chicago politician who was recently re-elected on his support of a non-

specific religious interpretation. He favored the idea that she was a divine being worthy of following on her own.

A physicist, and self-professed atheist was even being interviewed on one channel about how likely it was that she was in fact an extraterrestrial, stranded here and simply taking the form of a creature from ancient human mythology as a matter of protection.

By the time the aircraft started to slow down Lauren was nearly hyperventilating.

The body count in Sarajevo, according to various news agencies, was already nearing one thousand as extremist organizations from every major religion flooded the city with violence.

Dustin was characteristically quiet, her silent guardian once more. She found herself wishing, not for the first time, that he would talk to her.

"Dustin... I need your help."

She had his attention instantly.

"What's wrong, are you ok?"

"Yes. No. Well, I'm ok but I'm worried about my dad."

He nodded soberly.

"I've already made an inquiry. There are people from the department looking for your parents."

"And?"

"And it's going to take time. I haven't been able to learn anything regarding your father, and I lost track of your mother about a month after she... left."

"You saw my mother?"

What the hell! Why hadn't he told her before?

"She was seen in Chicago. You should get ready, Lauren, we will be disembarking very shortly."

Lauren opened her mouth to question him further, but Dustin's tone allowed for no argument.

"I'm going to check with the pilot, but I expect we'll be on the ground within thirty minutes. We need to be ready to move as soon as we land."

The aircraft was met on the runway by a convoy of armored vehicles. Beside each vehicle stood a number of men in subdued blue uniforms, all carrying compact machine-guns and wearing thick body armor. Also present were two men in bright crimson robes. They bowed deeply as Lauren walked down the stairs to the tarmac.

"Greetings, Your Grace, I am Cardinal Roberto Fafoglia, and this is my friend and fellow Cardinal, Eugene Figlio de Sangue. I apologize on his behalf - he does not speak English very well."

Lauren felt awkward and shy before these two men, each easily double her age, if not triple. They spoke to her with reverence and respect, unwilling to meet her gaze even indirectly. She wasn't sure what to say, but she thought back to her conversation on the plane.

"Th-thank you, may peace be with you," she said, stumbling a little over the unfamiliar phrase.

The men were overjoyed, and Dustin gave her the slightest nod from the corner of her eye.

"And also with you, Your Grace."

Giordano and Mr. Restrepo joined the conversation and were greeted warmly by the two cardinals. While they spoke, Lauren took the chance to whisper quietly with Dustin.

"Who are these soldiers with guns?"

"They're the Swiss Guard. The bodyguards of the papacy. They are here for your protection."

Lauren shot him a startled look.

"Do we really need thirty people with machine-guns?"

He was silent for a moment, and she thought back to Sarajevo and shivered.

"I don't know."

It was hardly the reassuring answer she had hoped for. She

found herself scanning the horizon compulsively for signs of danger.

"...Grace... Your Grace?"

Shit, he had been talking to her.

Lauren blinked at Figlio like a deer in headlights. She knew he had asked her a question from the way he was waiting patiently, but she had been so absorbed in her own mind that she hadn't the faintest idea what it was.

Opting for a non-committal answer, just to be safe, she nodded slightly and smiled.

He returned her smile, and her nod.

Crap.

"Thank you, Sir. As Lauren's head of security, I would also prefer she not ride in the first vehicle. I agree with you that we should be in the third, and we would love to accept your invitation for an early dinner."

Dustin spoke up, rescuing her and simultaneously filling her in on what she had missed. She let out her tensely held breath in relief and followed him as he stepped off towards the third SUV in the column.

"Thank you," she whispered.

He didn't respond, but she knew he had heard her.

As the pair approached their vehicle, the cardinals split off towards the vehicle directly behind it.

A man about her age opened the door for them as they approached. It was massive, at least four inches thicker than any car door she'd ever seen.

After they had settled themselves inside, never an easy feat with her cumbersome wings, he climbed into the passenger seat.

"Your Grace, I am named Wachtmeister Kaspar von Sile-nen. I will be, ah, protection for you while you visit here. Please, if you need a thing to ask me."

He smiled broadly at her, unabashedly staring at her wings

and clearly mesmerized. He had a funny accent. It was like nothing Lauren had ever heard before, she assumed it must be Swiss. His accent aside, his English was decent and his meaning clear.

"Thank you, Mr. Wachtmeister-"

Dustin nudged her gently with his elbow, whispering so low that only she could hear him.

"Wachtmeister isn't his name, it's a rank, a position. It's something like sergeant."

Lauren glared at Dustin, her cheeks red once more with embarrassment, and started again.

"I, uh. That is, thank you very much, Mr. um, Kaspar."

The last part of her sentence rose almost high enough to be considered a question.

Dustin nodded again. Good, she thought.

Kaspar seemed enthusiastic about her informal address, and took it upon himself to point out various highlights of the city as they cruised past. Within the vehicle all outside sounds were eliminated. It was like being in a coffin, silent but for the company she had.

From her seat she saw the faces of hundreds of unconcerned, unknowing people. Each passerby living a normal day in a normal life, oblivious to her presence.

She was invisible again.

Unfortunately, she was unable to fully enjoy the sights around her. She couldn't let herself relax, couldn't let herself soak in the beauty. On every passing face she saw the lifeless expressions of the people she had failed to save that morning. The streets and sights of Rome flashed past, a blur to her thousand-yard stare, all accompanied by the cheerful and informative ramblings of Kaspar.

Eventually though, he fell silent. Perhaps recognizing that she was heeding little if any of what he said.

The ride took nearly an hour, even with vehicles moving out of the convoy's way.

Eventually they pulled up to a large gate, guarded by more of the Swiss Guard. These men had colorful outfits of bright gold and deep purple, like something out of a Renaissance fair.

The garish outfits snapped Lauren from her dark contemplation. As they passed through the gates onto empty streets winding between towering, beautifully carved stone structures she found herself in awe of the magnificence that was Vatican City.

When the vehicle finally stopped, it was in front of a short, three-story stone structure. The building itself was rather plain, rust-red brick with symmetrical, white-trimmed windows. The sun shed a fiery orange glow over the entire area as it set on the city, casting beams of light between the buildings.

A small greeting party was waiting outside, a half dozen or so men in various religious garments, a woman in a nun's habit, and another pair of Swiss Guards as well.

"You ready, Lauren?"

Dustin's question mirrored her own thoughts.

I hope so, she thought to herself.

Kaspar left the vehicle first, rushing to get to Lauren's door before she opened it. Thankfully, she saw him moving and resisted the urge to get the door herself. She waited patiently, thanking him when he took care of the door for her.

The group all bowed low as she stepped from the SUV, leaving her awkwardly taller than everyone but the guards.

"Please stand, you don't need to bow," she said quickly.

An elbow from Dustin reminded her of her manners.

"B-but thank you, very much."

When Roberto and the other cardinals joined them, she was ushered into a large, beautiful foyer.

Lauren was awestruck. For all its simplicity on the outside, the building was a museum of priceless, beautiful treasures inside. Paintings and frescoes from the hallowed halls of history decorated every wall. Gilt crosses and shrines to the various Saints and archangels dotted small alcoves, and votive candles burned before small altars.

The guards remained outside, reducing the size of the party considerably, and making Lauren feel far less claustrophobic.

"It's so beautiful," Lauren marveled aloud. It took her breath away and stifled her worry and stress for a brief moment as she lost herself entirely in the splendor.

"These are the papal apartments, Your Grace. The earthly home for his Holiness," explained Fafoglia. The group wandered through hallways and down corridors lined with immaculate, priceless art before finding themselves at a large staircase.

"His Holiness lives on the third floor, in a modest suite. We will be dining with him there, Your Grace."

Lauren was too busy admiring the artwork to be bothered by all of the 'Your Grace' business. For once she was just a young woman swept away by the beauty of timeless art.

"If it please Your Grace, we will leave you to get settled before dinner."

Again they bowed, waiting for Lauren to reply. But she was enchanted, soaking up the beauty around her, and their words fell on deaf ears.

Dustin nudged her foot with his own.

"We're very grateful for your hospitality. We look forward to seeing you at dinner, right, Lauren?"

"Yes! Yes, thank you so much. Cardinals I- *we* look forward to dinner."

She blushed furiously as the men left. Within moments she was mesmerized again by her surroundings.

A huge fresco topped the archway before her. It showed an

angelic figure rescuing a man from a jail cell. As she studied the piece she could see that it was divided into three distinct sections. In the first, a man lay in a cell guarded by soldiers. The second scene had an angel beside the imprisoned man, and the guards were asleep. In the final portion the man and the angel were nowhere to be seen, leaving only the confused guards. It was like nothing Lauren had ever seen before. She was spellbound by the subtle details of the piece, at its classic beauty.

"It's the Deliverance of St. Peter."

Dustin's voice was hushed, reverent.

"Do you know the story?"

Lauren could only shake her head no.

"St. Peter was imprisoned by a King named Herod. The night before his trial an angel came to him and led him safely from captivity."

"Excuse me, Your Grace," a nun broke into the silence. She spoke softly and with a delicate French accent.

"In case you would like to refresh yourself before dinner, we have prepared a selection of clothing and a warm bath for you."

Lauren's heart almost skipped a beat with excitement at the prospect of a hot bath, but the reality of her massive wingspan had her immediately doubting the reliability of such an offer. Still, she felt grimy and sweaty. Besides, any delay in dinner seemed preferable to facing one of the most powerful men in the world and telling him he had it all wrong.

"God yes, I'm dying to clean up," she said emphatically, realizing a little too late that that was probably a poor choice of phrase.

To her great credit, the nun kept her facial expression neutral and simply gestured for Lauren to follow her. Working their way through the maze of hallways, they quickly found themselves in front a a large wooden door.

"Here we are, Your Grace."

Dustin turned to face his charge.

"I'll be back before dinner. Don't leave this suite with anyone but me, alright?"

Dustin's face may have been calm, but Lauren could tell he was worried.

"I won't."

With that, he turned on his heels and headed down the hallway. The nun waited expectantly for Lauren to enter the large, well-appointed guest suite.

Lauren was awed by the decorations here, as well. Everywhere she looked she found priceless murals and unparalleled tiling on the walls and floors of a moderately sized living room.

The suite was, frankly, opulent. It's only sacrifice was the generally smaller room sizes. Lauren didn't mind at all. It lacked the hollow, empty feeling of the embassies and hotels she'd been sleeping in recently.

"A bath has been drawn for you, Your Grace," the nun informed her softly.

"I am Sister Johanna. Myself or Sister Renee will be at your service while you are here. If you require anything, if you have need of us, please ring the bell."

At this she gestured to an intercom system on the wall, hidden amongst the antiquities.

"Will there be anything else, Your Grace?"

Lauren shook her head, trying to convey her gratitude through more than just her words.

"No, I'm ok. Thank you very much, Sister Johanna."

"Of course, Your Grace. Dinner will be in an hour and we will send someone to guide you."

With that the nun left Lauren to her own devices, the door softly clicking closed behind her.

Lauren let out a long, tired breath.

Alone, finally.

She let her shoulders droop and her head hang low. Sarajevo was a maddening contradiction in her mind. It felt like a lifetime ago that she had been there, on that street. At the same time, the faces of the dead were still raw in her mind. As though her eyes were closed, and if she just opened them their faces would be right in front of her.

She tried to clear her head, shaking off the building pressure in her chest and trying to turn her anxiety away with distractions.

She wandered through the suite, taking stock of her accommodations until she eventually found the bathroom. True to her word, sister Johanna had in fact drawn a bath. Steam was rising from a large porcelain tub that looked at least a hundred years old, and with it came the scents of essential oils. The bath screamed at her to get in, to enjoy the soak she so desperately craved. Lauren knew she wouldn't fit, and sighed disappointedly before turning on the shower instead. She slipped out of her grungy clothes and stepped into the steaming water.

The water washed loose dirt and gravel from her hair and feathers. Worse, the water was streaked with dull, rust red. Lauren tried shutting her eyes, wishing she hadn't seen it. Wishing she could forget that she was still covered in the blood of innocent people. That those people were now dead because of her.

Her anxiety spiked again, her breathing turning shallow and rapid. The now familiar feeling of a panic attack was building in her chest.

Lauren turned the water as hot as it would go. She scrubbed and scrubbed herself in the scalding water, wearing away at her skin until it was pink, raw, and painful. Still she could feel them, feel their deaths clinging to her like dirt under her fingernails.

Unable to rid herself of the horrors of the morning, she buried her face in her hands. Bitter tears mixed with the water running down her cheeks as she finally let herself grieve. She sobbed quietly, shoulders shaking, for a long, long time.

The water began to cool, drawing Lauren back to the real world. Back to problems she couldn't put off any longer. She stepped out onto the deep green tiles of the bathroom and pulled a pair of fluffy towels from a nearby rack. Wrapping herself in soft cotton she dried off, pausing a moment to linger on the faint remnants of scars on her arm and on her chest. Her thoughts turned to Erin, wishing for the thousandth time to see her again.

She would know what to do.

But thinking of Erin was still too painful, she couldn't face it. Not yet. Maybe not ever. She shook her head clear of broken dreams and continued exploring the apartment, coming next to a spacious bedroom.

The bedroom was subdued, at least compared to the rest of the rooms. It had a large, burgundy covered bed, a bookshelf, and a small vestibule for candles and praying, as well as the usual amenities.

Lauren's eyes were focused mainly on the bed, however, where four of the most elegant evening gowns that she had ever seen were lying. A ball gown, a sheath dress, a mermaid, and a flute. As a girl accustomed to leggings, shorts, or jeans, they were breathtaking to Lauren's eyes.

They looked like something a queen or a princess might wear. Mountains of tool, brocade, and perfectly tailored silk, all in stunning ivories and creams. Erin would have teased her mercilessly for wearing any one of them. But, Lauren thought to herself sadly, as soon as she'd picked one Erin would have been the first to tell her she looked beautiful, too. Lauren was a bit overwhelmed by the ball gown and the mermaid, they looked like they would require assistance to lift, let alone wear. The other two dresses were harder to choose between.

Apparently doomed to dwell on thoughts of her friend, she tried to put herself in Erin's mind, to think as she would have. Comfort above style. She smiled thinly, remembering a certain pair of too-small boy-shorts. She finally opted for the flute at the foot of the bed. It had delicate beadwork around its calf-length hem, and a low-cut back that would allow her to wear it comfortably with her wings.

Pulling it up over her hips she marveled at its fit. It was as though it was made specifically for her. Although, to be fair it probably was. She thought guiltily about the hours of work that had no doubt gone into tailoring each of these gowns. She felt like a little girl trying on her mother's clothes. Though it fit like a glove, she didn't belong in this dress built for models.

Each dress had come with a pair of shoes, perfectly matched to the gown. Lauren looked them over. She despised high heels. They made her feel like a newborn giraffe, clumsy and loud. She decided to go for the lowest pair that they'd brought, before turning to look at herself in an ornate, gold framed mirror on the wall. The reflection looking back at her was unfamiliar, foreign to her.

"You look like a doll. Overdressed and fake," she criticized herself.

She was just starting to unzip the gown, feeling foolish and embarrassed, when a soft knock at the bedroom door caused her to turn. She'd been so absorbed with the clothes that she failed to notice a young woman waiting.

"I'm sorry to interrupt, Your Grace, I came to see if you needed any assistance, I'm Renee."

This girl was Lauren's age. She was staring wide-eyed at the pearly expanse of Lauren's wings in awe. Lauren felt even more like an impostor; this girl was visibly moved by what she thought Lauren was. By what she looked like.

Lauren knew it was a lie. A lie she lived every day. A slight scowl clouded her features, unnoticed by its host.

"Y-Your Grace?"

The girl seemed unsure, as though she was afraid she might offend Lauren and be made to leave. In her hands she held a small, ornately carved wooden box.

"I'm sorry," Lauren reassured her quickly. "I'm alright, thank you"

The girl bowed slightly and started to leave before remembering the box in her hands.

"Oh, Your Grace, his Holiness asked that we provide you with these, in case you wanted to wear them," she held the box out before her, clearly afraid to approach uninvited.

This is exhausting, thought Lauren, her irritation growing.

"Please stop calling me 'Your Grace,'" Lauren emphasized. "Just Lauren is fine."

"Yes your G-, um, Lauren," another confused look from Renee. "I'll just leave this here!"

She took a big step, set the box on the end of the bed and rushed from the room.

Damn, you're *terrible* at this stuff.

Lauren swore under her breath as she approached the box.

Opening the lid she saw it was stuffed full of jewelry. Not regular buy-at-a-department-store jewelry, but massive diamonds woven into necklaces, marble-sized pearl earrings, gem-encrusted crucifixes, and the like. Each piece was a unique treasure, a crown jewel worthy of royalty.

Lauren's jaw dropped.

Once the initial shock of seeing a pirate-like chest full of gold, silver, and jewels wore off, Lauren snapped the lid back closed. Not only did she rarely wear jewelry, the last thing she needed to do was lose Mother Teresa's favorite pearls, or break some saint's treasured rosary.

Looking around wistfully, Lauren left the bedroom and walked delicately into the living room, trying to get used to the heels before she had company to worry about.

As she passed the threshold she met the gazes of the last people she expected to be there; her mother and father.

Lauren misstepped, stumbling in surprise. She managed to recover before toppling over, barely.

"Dad? M-mom?"

Lauren's voice was high with surprise. She was dumbfounded, how could they possibly be here?

"Lolo," her dad broke out into tears, stepping across the room and gripping her in a bear hug.

Lauren couldn't help but cry as well. Finally she was safe and warm. She felt sheltered like she hadn't for weeks now. The waves of anxiety, anger, and grief that constantly threatened to overwhelm her abated in the safe harbor of her father's arms.

Allison's welcome was more standoffish. Lauren was still torn between hating her for abandoning them when they needed her most, when Gabriel had died, and missing her like only a daughter can miss her mother.

Allison was holding a glass of deep red wine in one hand, with the bottle and an empty glass in the other. In the end it seemed like the drink won out over her daughter, because she smiled weakly and took a large swallow, refusing to meet Lauren's steady, accusing gaze.

"Mom," her single, pleading word broke the spell for a moment, and they locked eyes.

Allison approached at last, holding her arms out and giving Lauren a quick, superficial embrace.

Lauren felt her mother pulling away. The move had a feeling of finality. Inside, Lauren felt the cold seed of betrayal, planted in her heart months ago, grow into icy anger. Lauren's frustration began to creep across her face once more. Her brow furrowed and a frown replaced her smile.

Allison looked around for something to placate her, to calm the storm she saw brewing.

"Have a glass?"

"Allie...," John said uncertainly, his voice soft and defeated.

"John, for God's sake it's *Europe*," Allison's tone towards her father only deepened Lauren's frown.

Lauren glared at her a moment longer, but the temptation to dull her heartache was greater than her pride. Besides, maybe a stiff drink would drown some of this awkwardness. She reached out and took the offered glass, allowing her mother to fill it for her.

She took a bold sip. Not having had wine before, she was surprised by the dry, woody flavor of the liquid. It wasn't at all what she expected, and her face must have shown it because her mother let slip a tinkling laugh. Some of the tension started to clear between the two women.

Allison was clearly several glasses ahead of Lauren, and she wasn't slowing down. The trio sat down on a pair of small couches with a low marble coffee table between them serving as a resting place for the quickly emptying wine bottle.

"How did you get here," she finally blurted out.

"I went looking for Allie, for your mom," John began. "I went back to Galesburg. When no one had seen her there, I tried to get in touch with your grandmother in Chicago. She said Allie had stopped by, that she had talked about going back to the City."

He gave Allison a strange look, which she pointedly ignored in favor of her wine glass.

"She reached out to... an old friend of ours. He put her in touch with the diocese. He tried to get her some... help."

Allison snorted, briefly interrupting his tale.

Lauren nodded slowly, surprised that her mother had gone to

the church. She didn't expect that her mother had wanted any help.

Especially if it meant sobering up.

"John is exaggerating, obviously," Allison slurred drunkenly.

"I visited your grandmother and then went into the city to meet an old friend, yes. We went to dinner, he suggested I go to rehab, I told him to fuck off. So, he said I should go to confession and 'straighten out' instead. The end."

Allison rolled her eyes at this last piece and fell silent again, giving John a moment to pick the story back up.

"Yes, well. At any rate she got in touch with the bishop there and he apparently contacted the Vatican."

As John spoke, Lauren finally saw the toll the that the past few months had taken. How *old* he suddenly looked. Where once there were laugh-lines, now a slight, ever-present frown had taken up residence.

"I was contacted by the diocese there through your grand-mother about a week ago. I've been here ever since," he shrugged.

"They said you were coming, that you'd be here. We saw you on the news every day! God Lauren we've been so wor-ried. A-and then, this morning..."

His voice trailed off, and he cast her a helpless, frightened look.

"I'm so, so sorry Lolo. I never wanted this for you."

"Daddy, please don't be sorry. This isn't your fault."

Lauren hated to see her once-proud father cry. He was a broken man now, small and unsure.

Allison snorted derisively again, casting a hateful, jealous look at the two of them.

"John's not your father, Lauren," she said spitefully, downing the last half of her glass of wine and rising to her feet.

"Allison," John yelled with unbridled anger.

"What, John?" she continued, snapping at him and pouring herself another deep glass of wine.

"She's not an idiot, she has to have figured out by now that's why she can heal you."

The silence in the room was absolute.

"What the *fuck*," the words slipped from Lauren's mouth before she could stop them. Her hand tightened so hard on her wine glass that the bulb shattered and her hand was showered with broken glass and Cabernet.

Lauren grasped her wrist, hissing in pain as her hand was sliced open, spattering the marble tabletop with wine and blood. Glass tinkled to the floor as her hand stitched itself closed. She was stupefied, her other troubles forgotten in the wake of Allison's words.

A firm knock at the door caused all three to jump, and the intercom clicked audibly.

"Your Grace, we've sent someone to fetch you and escort you to the dining room."

Lauren couldn't be sure, but it sounded like Johanna's voice.

"H-hello, um can we have a minute? I'm uh, not ready just yet," Lauren stammered.

"Yes, ah... yes Your Grace. As you wish."

The intercom clicked off again as the knock at the door repeated.

The three looked silently at each other, no one seemed to want to move first.

At the third knock Lauren stood unsteadily and rushed to the door.

"I'm coming, sorry!"

She opened the door to see Dustin. He was wearing a dark gray suit and a pair of slick black dockers.

"Lau-" he sniffed the air, "Dammit have you been drinking? Are you *kidding* me!"

"Dustin I-"

"Lauren do have any idea how that *looks*? You're going to what, stumble drunkenly through dinner with the goddamn pope?"

"Dustin!"

He was fuming, a vein throbbing in his forehead as he whispered furiously at her. He stepped past her into the room and froze. His eyes fell on her parents, who were in the midst of their own whisper-quiet shouting match.

"Are you out of your damn mind, woman?"

Allison had an ugly look on her face, she was unused to being on the receiving end of verbal abuse. Lauren had never heard her father take that tone with her before, it usually went the other way around.

"Excuse me? Don't take that tone with me, *John*, it's about damn time she found out. I'm surprised the whole goddamn world doesn't know about it at this point!"

"Mr. and Mrs. Corvidae-" Dustin tried to interject.

The two ceased their squabbling.

Allison had a surprised look on her face and quickly emptied another glass of wine. John, on the other hand, approached the doorway and turned even redder.

"Back off, Jim," John jabbed at Dustin with his outstretched finger, poking him hard in the chest as he spoke.

John's words only furthered Lauren's angry confusion. "Jim?"

Another low but firm knock came to the door, cutting the argument short. Lauren looked helplessly from John to Dustin and back again. Finally Dustin reached out and grabbed the door handle, opening it a little too roughly.

Kaspar was there, bowing low.

"Your Grace, it is my honor to escort you to dinner. I was told you needed a little more time. Is there anything I can..."

Seeing the small crowd in the apartment his words trailed off in confusion.

"Thank you, Lauren was just finishing something up, we're ready now," Dustin interjected before anyone else could speak.

Kaspar took it in stride and beamed at Lauren, unaware of the minefield he had walked into.

Turning on his heel he motioned with his arm that they should follow him, and stepped off down the hallway. As she walked behind him she cast an angry look at Dustin, he wasn't going to squirm out of this.

With every step they took, however, her worry turned to the coming meal. What do you say to a Pope? How do I tell him I'm not God's chosen anything, let alone His instrument of divine power?

Her thoughts ran in circles, tiring her already burdened mind. Her feet felt like they were made of lead, and she had long since fallen into a brooding silence by the time they reached the third floor landing.

The group came to a large door, which Kaspar reached first. He held it open, allowing her to pass before him.

Lauren entered the room, keenly aware of the stares of the other occupants.

They can totally tell. Dammit Lauren what the hell were you thinking? She covered her worries with a small, nervous smile.

A delicate cough from the head of the table caught Lauren's attention in the otherwise silent room. An aged man in large, ceremonial robes was standing there, looking her over with a mix of amusement and interest on his face.

"Welcome, please come in."

""H-hello sir," Lauren started, unsure of how to address the man.

They were saved an uncomfortable silence by cardinal Fafoglia, who slid seamlessly into the conversation and tried to diffuse the awkwardness.

"Your Holiness, let us present to you Lauren Corvidae." The group filed in behind her and she caught Dustin's eyes. His look begged her to behave. She managed another weak smile as she approached an empty chair.

"Your Grace, it is my pleasure to meet you."

The pope didn't bow, but he did nod to her as he spoke.

"L-likewise," she managed.

Besides her group, the only other guests at dinner were the cardinals she'd met before. Everyone else was standing behind the chair marking their place at the table, so she moved to do the same.

"Let us pray."

The pope spoke, and the group all bowed their heads as he recited solemnly in Latin. Lauren snuck a peak around the table, seeing that only Dustin still had his head raised. As she watched he looked at her out of the corner of his eye and, catching her gaze, he winked at her.

Lauren had to choke back nervous laughter. Her waning confidence rose a little, she trusted him to get her through this.

"...and finally Heavenly father," the Pope said, switching to English.

"Let us give special thanks to your messenger. Our guest here in these humble surroundings. Your Seraphim, the instrument of your will, amen."

With his prayer complete the pope sat down, and the cardinals followed suit afterwards.

Lauren's eyes widened at the pontiff's words. She didn't know which of the two titles was less appropriate.

Her mouth popped open and closed like a fish as she tried to sort out the introduction she'd been given. She shot Dustin a startled look, but he only said a soft amen and took his seat nodding to her and indicating she should do the same.

Lauren mumbled a quiet amen as well and reached for her wineglass as she sat down, taking a deep gulp of the chilled white wine that filled it.

Dinner was anything but comfortable and stuffy silence was the mainstay during the meal. The guests exchanged small talk, but no one addressed the herd of elephants in the room.
Sarajevo.

How her parents had gotten here.

Lauren's divinity, or lack thereof.

These and other serious subjects were avoided like the plague, replaced instead with trivialities like the weather and the food.

Lauren calmed her nerves with the wine. By dinner's end she'd had three glasses, only slightly behind her mother. She pointedly ignored Dustin's stern gaze and the concerned looks from her father.

Eventually the meal wound down, and as footmen came in to clear the dishes and bring coffee the pope finally broached a more delicate subject.
"Your Grace, I imagine you have questions," he intoned. "I assure you I do as well."
Lauren fidgeted with her hands below the table. She felt a strong buzz now, and it was making it hard to organize her thoughts.

"Yes sir," she said, her voice weak.

"Please, allow me to answer any questions you might have first."
She looked around the table, her cheeks flushed from the wine and from being the uncontested focus of everyone present. The wine made her bold, and she decided to speak her mind.

"With all due respect sir, why am I here?"

Dustin coughed loudly, nearly choking on his coffee. He cleared his throat and kicked Lauren beneath the table.

The question hung for a moment before the pontiff cleared his throat delicately, commanding the attention of the group. "Your... Grace, perhaps we should speak further on that *particular* subject in private," his tone was serious, almost menacing.

Her neck hairs prickled, a warning that her wine-fogged mind ignored.

"I'm sorry sir, I'm just trying to understand. I don't know what it is that you want from me."

The pope pondered her words for a moment, looking at each member of the dinner party in turn before answering carefully.

"God often speaks to me through His Word. As his mouthpiece on Earth it is my duty to relay His Will to the people. As a living testament to that will, I'm asking for your help to bring the message of our God to the people. Starting tomorrow. We've made arrangements for you to lead the people of Rome in prayer."

"But I'm not a living testament to anything! I don't know anything about 'His will.' He has never spoken to me."

Lauren knew immediately that she'd messed up. The guests at the table were staring slack-jawed at her. Dustin, the exception, was stiff as a board and tense as a tightly coiled spring.

"Excuse me?"

The pope was the first to recover from her words, and his eyes narrowed as he spoke.

"I'm not sure I understand."

"I-I'm not God's chosen messenger. I can't tell people what he wants because *I don't know* what he wants."

"I see," the pope's tone was quiet, serious.

"You know, young lady, that even Jesus Christ himself had doubts? We know this from Scripture."
His words were not unkind, and his tone was even, but Lauren felt her unease growing.
"I have great faith in you, in your ability to aid our cause and to champion the Word to the people of the world. I am certain you will find your calling among us."

His words were more than mere suggestion to her ears, and she began to see the dangerous ledge she walked upon.

"I understand, sir. I certainly mean no harm to you or to the Church. I think the work you do is noble and good-"
"You are correct, Lauren," he interrupted her softly.

"We do *God's* work. It is through His will that you were granted these powers. Powers to spread His message to the world. Imagine for a moment what would happen if people lost faith? Do you want hateful, violent religions like that of the man who attacked you this morning to overpower the one *true* Church of God?"

"Well, no sir, but-"
"Men acting out in violence can be a very destructive thing. You alone may have the power to overcome such enemies of God. To bring light to the darkness of the world. Don't you want to be that beacon? To light the way?"

Lauren was fighting a losing battle. He was backing her into a corner and she couldn't see a way out. The other diners were carefully avoiding eye contact with Lauren, as well as each other.

"I can't... I can't just tell people something I don't believe. If there is a God, He has been nothing but cruel to me."

Her conviction strengthened as she thought about the injustices of her past.
The tension in the room grew, building like an offshore storm that threatened to crash down and sweep away the diners at any moment.

"Lauren," the pope spoke softly.

He seemed ready to say something, then visibly changed his mind. Instead he gave her a short nod and looked curiously at her feathers.

"I noticed the spot, on your wing there."
The words were spoken like a question, but it didn't sound like he wanted an answer.

"I-I'm sorry sir, to have wasted your time. I'm just not who you want me to be."

Lauren tried in vain to fill the void of silence, desperate to redirect the threatening energy of the room.

"We should perhaps call it an early night tonight," Dustin said, following on the heels of her words.

"Thank you so much for your hospitality, your Holiness. I think Lauren will likely wish to speak with her family privately for a moment and then get some rest. She's had a very long day."
Without waiting for a reply he pushed his chair back and stood, looking down at Lauren. She followed his cue and did the same.

"Kaspar and I will walk you to your rooms," Fafoglia chimed in as he stood quickly, joining them.
"Thank you so much for your hospitality and for dinner, your Holiness. I'm so sorry I disappointed you."
John and Allison followed suit and the group walked out of the room and into the hallway. Lauren could feel the stares of the others boring into the back of her head as she walked.

As soon as the door had clicked shut behind them, Fafoglia turned to address Kaspar in Italian. Kaspar nodded and took off down the stairs at a jog.

"Your Grace," he said in a worried tone. "It is perhaps best if you follow me right now."
Dustin didn't give Lauren a chance to respond, he placed a hand on her back and propelled her ahead of him, following in

the guard's footsteps.

"Hey, get back here with my daughter!"

John protested in a loud whisper, but Dustin turned and towered over him like a giant; Goliath to his David.

"Lauren's safety is my only concern, John, do not get in the way of it."

"I'm not going anywhere, Dustin," Lauren said, irate that he had shoved her.

"Yes, you are."

Dustin's voice was unlike she'd ever heard it. Steely and cold. She took an astonished step back from him.

"John, I suggest you and Allison come with us," Dustin continued, his voice low and menacing.

Her father stood his ground a moment longer before breaking eye contact reluctantly.

"Alright."

"Like hell," Allison argued drunkenly. "I'm staying right here."

"Fine," Dustin's one word response was utterly remorseless. He moved immediately to follow the cardinal. Lauren felt a little ashamed as they left her mother standing there alone in the corridor.

The group made their way swiftly through a winding series of halls and stairways. The art that had seemed so mesmerizing just a few hours before was suddenly much more intimidating Lauren thought to herself, her concern building. Priceless statues meant to inspire now loomed ominously, keeping silent judgment as they passed.

They moved quickly but quietly. Though they weren't running, it felt just as frantic and the mood in the group was tense.

At last the group stopped. Kaspar was there, standing beside a small side door.

Fafoglia turned to Lauren, a sadness in his eyes.

"I am sorry, I cannot take you any further. They will become suspicious if I don't return, I wish you luck."

The Cardinal bowed deeply to Lauren and turned back down the way they had come.

Dustin nodded silently at Kaspar, the pair exchanging a meaningful look that Lauren didn't fully understand.

Kaspar met Lauren's gaze before dropping to one knee and looking down at the tiled floor.

"I have never questioned my faith before meeting you, Your Grace. If you say you have not spoken to God, I believe you. More than that, I believe *in* you. I wish that I could be a better servant, but this is the only way I know to help you."

He stood, turned on his heel, and took off back down the hallway before she could stammer a response. She moved to go after him but was stopped by a hand on her shoulder.

Dustin shook his head no. He had a grim, determined look on his face and in his eyes. He drew his sidearm and cautiously opened the door to reveal a dark alley. There was a jet-black sedan idling there quietly with its lights off.

Dustin looked up and down the alley before carefully approaching the car. Opening the door he revealed it to be empty. Lauren let out the breath she didn't realize she'd been holding.

"Dustin," she whispered. "What the hell are we doing?"

"Get in," he said simply. His expression softened a little at the hurt look on her face and he elaborated. "We can talk in the car, please get in."

Lauren nodded, compliant from fear, and hurried into the backseat.

"Just a minute now Jim. Just, just *wait* a second," John was trying to gather his thoughts, clearly still torn at leaving Allison behind.

"Certainly you're over-reacting. We have perfectly comfortable beds in there to sleep this off. We can just sort this all out in the morning, can't we?"

Dustin was unswayed.

"John, listen to me, please. Set our personal issues aside and think."

Dustin's tone had an almost pleading quality to it. He was desperate and it put Lauren even more on edge. This display of weakness, of fear, was unprecedented.

"Your daughter just told one of the most powerful men in the world that she's batting for a different team. He's the pope. He *is* the Catholic Church. He sure as hell can't have the only angel that anyone's ever seen running around saying his God doesn't exist."

Comprehension dawned on John's face.

"I'm not saying she's in danger. Maybe you're right and this will all blow over by morning. I do know that guard was worried enough to arrange us a getaway, and at who knows what cost. I'm not willing to bet her safety on his good graces, are you?"

"No, I'm not. Just... give me five minutes. I have to get Allison, I have to try."

"John..."

"Just promise me you'll wait, okay? I have to go back. She's still my wife."

Lauren watched the two from the car, wondering what the hell was taking them so long. As she watched, John ran back into the building. Dustin paused a moment and then turned and slowly walked to the car and opened the driver's door, stepping into the vehicle.

"Hey what the fuck? What's dad doing I thought we had to go!"

Only the click of the door lock answered her.

The car sped away into the night, Lauren screaming at Dustin to turnaround and tearing wildly at the door handle.

Chapter 13

Lauren hadn't spoken in nearly two days.

Not a single, solitary word had crossed her lips since they'd arrived at the U.S. Embassy in Rome. She was under constant guard, right up to the minute they loaded her into a different black car, this one with diplomatic plates, and drove her to a private hangar at the airport. Only her silent tears had protested boarding the plush private jet chartered to return her to the States.

Nevertheless, Dustin continued to carry on the same conversations they normally shared, albeit only his side. His trademark one-liners, curt remarks, and brief explanations of the processes they went through may as well have been addressed to the boots on her feet for all the good it did him.

It wasn't until they were airborne, when a large TV in front of their seats flickered to life with the morning news, that she made a sound.

"Dad!"

Her voice broke on the single word as she searched frantically for the volume control.

Sure enough the TV in front of her was showing local Italian news. A reporter was describing a riot from the day before while clips played of a scene around Vatican City. The pope was addressing a huge crowd. John and Allison were standing on the balcony beside him as he spoke to thousands of onlookers. Allison had a sloppy, intoxicated smile on her face whereas John was more subdued. At least they both looked healthy and unharmed.

"...had pressing matters to attend to. She regrets being unable to lead us all in prayer today but has instructed me to lead in her stead. Her mother and father stand here beside me, testament to her good will, and to her commitment to the one true church of God. Let us give praise for their guidance. For the tenderness and sanctity of their daughter. Let us thank them for God's blessing, which they helped usher into this world..."

His words placated many of the people in the crowd, but others were angry. Most of the assembled people were not content without the savior they had been promised. Within the space of about ten minutes, the police were breaking up fights inside the audience and removing people from the premises.

The scene degenerated further, looking more like a bar-room brawl than a Catholic mass. Eventually the police were forced to call for backup and had to use tear gas and riot gear to restore law and order. Lauren stared at the screen holding the remote with a white-knuckled grip.

Dustin shifted uncomfortably.

"They're going to be ok, Lauren. The State Department is already working on getting them back home."

Her gaze slowly, excruciatingly, turned to him. Her eyes screamed murder.

"The *State* Department? The State Department is 'working' on it," she managed to say through clenched teeth, her anger barely held in check.

"Lauren, you didn't have a choice. You needed to-"

"You think you have to tell me that I didn't have a choice? I know I didn't have a choice!"
She threw the remote at him, catching him off guard and hitting him square in the mouth. Blood sprang from his newly split lip and he flinched at the unexpected blow.

"Dammit Lauren," He put a finger to his lip and held it out, finding that he was bleeding.

"I would do it again! I would do it a thousand times if it meant you were safe a thousand times!"

"Well just what exactly is going to hurt me, Dustin, hmm? It's not like *literally* anything could happen to me for god's sake!"

"That's not the point, you're my responsibility and it's my job to make sure you're-"

"Shut up."

Lauren caught herself reliving an argument she'd heard from her parents. She never thought she'd be playing the part of her mother. Her mind drifted to other vices they shared, besides a loose-cannon temper.

"I hate you."

She muttered softly to Dustin, but in her heart she didn't know if she was talking to him, to her mother, or to herself.

"I can live with that," he muttered, turning off the television. Dustin put in a pair of earbuds and leaned back in his seat, content to ignore his troublesome charge.

Lauren sulked in her anger a while longer, but eventually she got up to explore the aircraft. She was determined to out-run the thought that haunted her; that her father had *chosen* to stay behind.

The plane was huge, but nearly empty. In fact, they appeared to be the only passengers besides the crew. Dustin had said it was generally used to shuttle around dignitaries.

Little wonder it was so... over-done.

No expense had been spared. The plane had plush couches, comfortable chairs, even several small meeting rooms. There were a half-dozen expensive televisions throughout the cabin area alone.

As she wandered past the meeting rooms, she saw they were split down the middle. The two sections were divided by a galley of sorts.

This small, intimate dining area was empty of crew. Hardly surprising considering it was still quite early. She paused mid-step, catching sight of a small but expensive looking mini-bar. Her better judgment wrestled with her anger and anxiety.

It was no contest.

I'll just look, she thought to herself, checking to see if anyone was watching her before walking over.

She deluded herself. Told herself she was just examining the fine crystal glasses and the stainless mixing instruments, tumblers, and measuring devices. Her eyes scanned the long row of expensive looking liquor bottles arranged neatly on the shelves. Licking her lips dryly, the temptation to have a quick sip was hard to resist.

The devil in her mind nudged her. Why not?

It made her think of her mother.

"No, I'm *nothing* like her."

Her mind wandered down the well-trodden path of her insecurities. Now she knew at last, Allison *had* abandoned them. When she'd left that night, months ago, Lauren had allowed a slight hope that maybe she would return. Now she knew she wouldn't. She had left Lauren and her dad with no intention of ever coming back.

Dad? John? Dad.

Now we've both abandoned him, she thought grimly. Or did he abandon me? The thought crept back into her mind, and she could not force it out again.

The small bar filled up quickly, not with people but with the ghosts of her past. Trapped within the confines of this plane she had nowhere to run, no escape.

Well. *Almost* no escape, anyway.

She ducked behind the waist-high counter of the bar and selected a glass bottle of amber liquid at random from the shelf, along with a small glass.

"Don't mind if I do..."

Sliding to the floor, she sat cross-legged behind the bar, her wings tucked close. She'd be invisible to any casual passerby at least. She took stock of her stolen prize; the bottle she'd nipped had fancy gold lettering on it, but all of the words were written in French. Scanning the bottle she finally found what she was looking for; written in small lettering near the base were the numbers "60%."

Good, Lauren thought to herself, pulling out the cork top and taking a hesitant sniff of the bottle.

Oh god, that's awful. She crinkled her nose at the pungent smell, like smoke and wood chips mixed with fruit. Plums maybe?

It doesn't have to taste good, it just has to be strong.

She took a long swig from the bottle, ignoring the tumbler she'd gotten for herself.

The taste wasn't as bad as the smell. It tasted like wood and plums alright, but had a smooth, silky texture that coated her mouth and took a bit of her breath away.

"So *this* is a good idea then?"

Dustin's words crossed the room like bullets. Lauren flinched, splashing expensive alcohol all over herself. She froze, but he clearly knew she was there.

She stood defiantly, looking across the bar at him. He was standing by the door, arms crossed over his powerful chest and a deep scowl on his face.

"Shut up."

A moment passed in silence. The ten feet between them could have been a thousand miles.

"Lauren..."

"How do you know my parents?"

Her blunt question gave him pause.

"We're... old friends."

"Bullshit."

"We went to college together, a long, long time ago."

"Well ain't it a small world."

She scowled, he was hiding something.

"Why doesn't my dad like you?"

She took a deep pull from the bottle in her hand.

"He and I... had a fairly substantial falling out."

"Oh thank you, that clears everything up. You know what? Forget it. I don't care. I never want to speak to you again."

"Lauren, I did what I had to do. I'm not going to apologize for it."

"Why? Why did you have to do it!"

She was screaming at the top of her lungs, no doubt everyone on board could hear them.

"You are my *responsibility*, Lauren!"

"Well you're fucking fired! I want my parents, not some self-righteous asshole who thinks he knows what is best for me!"

"Lauren..."

"Just leave! The minute we touch down. Nothing is keeping you here, I don't *want* you here, you understand me? I. Don't. Want. You. Here."

His mouth snapped shut and he remained speechless for a long moment. She could see pain in his eyes as he finally bowed his head in defeat and left the room.

After a few minutes she took another long swig, and then another after that. Her anger grew as she waited impatiently for her mind to cloud. The press of memories pushed in around her and she felt hot, angry tears streaming down her face.

She thought back to Sarajevo. To Erin. To Gabriel. She thought about the riots that had broken out across the world. The trouble she had caused in the Vatican. About the mob that nearly killed her father. Had she *ever* really helped any-one?

Or was she a monster?

How could she be anything else, considering all the suffering and death she was responsible for?

Her thoughts turned to the people she had let down. The family she'd met in Gorham, the Cardinal and the guardsman in Rome, Caroline and Rosaline. Was she worthy of the faith they placed in her? Was it even possible for her to be the person they needed her to be?

Lauren took another pull, her thoughts hounding her relentlessly. She closed her eyes and sobbed, the bottle in her hands her only safe port in the storm. Eventually the numbness she was so desperately seeking started to sink in, and the crashing waves inside her receded.

Lauren raised the bottle to her lips once more, but only a few drops wet her lips. She stared at the bottle in frustration.

"Stupid thing," she slurred to herself, struggling to stand. Her legs seemed to have fallen asleep at some point. Cursing under her breath she steadied herself against the counter.

She selected another bottle at random, yanking it from the shelf amidst the loud clinking of glass.

"Shh," she whispered.

She caught sight of a television remote behind the counter and grabbed it, looking around for the TV in the room. She saw it now, smaller than most of the others on the plane. It was settled against the backsplash of the bar behind the counter.

Taking her new prize around the bar with her, she settled herself on one of the bar stools bolted to the floor. She pulled on the top of the bottle for a moment before realizing it was a screw cap.

"You're an idiot," she muttered, chuckling darkly at herself.

Her bottle now open, she fumbled with the power button on the remote.

She took a drink as the device powered up to reveal a fierce soccer match taking place.

"Boo," she said loudly, jamming the channel button down, her clouded mind causing her to raise her voice again.

She drank as she flipped through children's programming, a pair of movies, a nature documentary of some kind, even some live music. A few channels later she hit the news.

The remote fell to the counter, slipping from numb fingers as Lauren stared horrified at the screen. A news anchor who had clearly been crying was speaking in front of several live feeds from around the world.

In one, Jerusalem was burning, the streets rife with gunfire and piles of bodies. Soldiers moved street by street exchanging bullets with armed, violent mobs.

Another feed showed a village on the Pakistan-India border. Men in biohazard suits were walking among piles of dead civilians, their skin bluish and blood dripping from their open mouths and noses, victims of some undetermined nerve agent.

The video switched to show large trucks in formations, thick white streaks of smoke streaking across the skies as the trucks unleashed flurries of rockets into the distance.

A quarter million dead, the bottom of the screen read.

Video after video, news feed after news feed. Villages burned in Sudan, a ritual suicide in Moscow, riots across the Bible Belt in America, the carnage was endless.

And then, the Vatican.

An angry mob, tens of thousands strong, had marched on the Vatican *demanding* Lauren. Some clamored for an explanation, a solution to the atrocities across the globe. Others came demanding guidance and salvation.

Many had come armed.

The reporter on the screen was speaking, but Lauren's mind couldn't process what he was saying. The words were disjointed and warped to her ears.

"...on the Vatican earlier yesterday evening, overpowering the largely ceremonial Swiss Guard and damaging many of the structures on the grounds. Preliminary reports suggest that at least four guardsmen were killed with more than a dozen others seriously injured..."

The video skipped ahead, showing the pope addressing a loud, angry crowd in the courtyard of the Vatican.

"... appears to have been a major split within the Church following the unofficial announcement that the Vatican will be denouncing Lauren Corvidae. Unconfirmed reports are that the College of Cardinals has divided itself into two camps. The majority of the church seems to support the papacy. A second group, which has considerable strength outside of Rome, supports Lauren Corvidae's status as a 'Divine agent' and disputes the decision by the papacy to declare her anathema..."

Wheels spun in Lauren's mind as the report continued.

"...Theologists are already calling this the second Great Schism. This second group is reportedly being spearheaded by a rogue Cardinal, Roberto Fafoglia, who has fled the holy city along with his supporters amidst a series of violent clashes between police, citizens, and the Swiss Guard. We've obtained video that appears to show the cardinal cautioning Catholics against the pontiff's condemnation of Corvidae..."

Again the video shifted, this time to a shaky video of Cardinal Fafoglia. He was bleeding from a small cut on his cheek but he spoke with fire, an impassioned plea to viewers. "... instead let us turn to our hearts to God, for only through him can we find Truth. The Word holds many mysteries, even to those who have served it for a lifetime. I have met this woman, her grace and her kindness are indisputable. Look how she has come among the people of the world to heal wounded hearts and bodies..."

The familiar face of Kaspar entered the frame and he whispered something into the Cardinal's ear. Roberto nodded, but continued speaking to the camera.

"...Can we be so swift to disavow her, as our forefathers condemned The Son of God to death upon the Cross? To condemn her actions because they do not fit our flawed and human understanding of God? Consider Saint Joseph and the Virgin Mary, who were visited by the angel Gabriel. Gabriel spoke to them and prophesied a Savior, our own Lord Jesus. What dire consequence had they not heeded his edicts..."

The reporter returned, cutting the previous video short. He stammered out an apology at cutting the video short..

"I-I apologize, we're going to take you live to Vatican City where the Pope is addressing the people in what official representatives have announced as a 'call to action for all true believers.' We want to warn our viewers this *is* a live feed and given the events of the past 24 hours in particular, strong discretion is advised."

An aerial shot of the Vatican took over the screen. More than a hundred guardsman, all wearing thick body armor and carrying assault rifles, lined the courtyard of the Vatican. Scores of similarly armed police forces were scattered throughout a crowd that seemed endless.

The mass of people roared as the pope walked out onto a balcony of St. Peter's Basilica, though with approval or anger it was hard to tell. The pope raised his hands and the crowd quieted. There was a deep, zealous energy that Lauren could feel through the screen.

"Brethren in Christ, We stand before you as a humble servant of God."

As he spoke, a squadron of guards hauled a man forward from within St. Peter's Basilica. The man was wearing torn and dirtied clothing and had a cloth bag over his head.

"Let it be known that we have consulted the Word of God and

the Holy Spirit and the Lord has spoken. Our very world is threatened. We live now in an age of marked tribulation, prophesied in Revelations. Thus, by the authority of our Lord Jesus Christ, of the Blessed Apostles Peter and Paul, and by our own authority, we pronounce, declare, and define it to be a divinely revealed dogma: Lauren Corvidae is *not* a faithful servant of our God the father."

The crowd grew restless, rumblings of anger rolling through them in a wave.

"Rather she is a fallen angel, of the host of Lucifer! Never has the Lord spoken through his Word that such a being would come to us. No. This creature is a foul trick by the Devil. She is a tempter of men. Indeed she did deceive even us, that most faithful mouthpiece of God, made infallible by the trust of Jesus Christ..."

The pope paused in his address, taking a moment to let his confession sink in to the onlooking crowd before he continued.

"But, through divine providence, we have seen the mark of the Beast upon her! See too that her once-pure wing is blemished with darkness. She revealed not as seraph, but as the whore of Babylon."

The violent, ugly mood of the crowd deepened and darkened. The soldiers and policemen looked nervously around, their hands visibly tightening on their weapons in the face of the horde.

"More than that, we denounce her supporters as idolaters. As anathema. Foreign to God and irredeemable. The Catholic Church is alone in keeping the true worship. This is the fount of truth, this the house of Faith, this the temple of God: if any man enter not here, or if any man go forth from it, he is a stranger to the hope of life and salvation."

The crowd was frothing with emotion at the pontiff's stirring words. Latent aggression visible throughout the crowd. Lauren paled at the fury of the people. The pope raised his hands,

again seeking silence from the assembly, but they were
beyond reason.
"It is the duty of the Church to root out wickedness, to be the
salvation of the whole of mankind. In this duty we bring forth
Jonathan Scott Corvidae."
Lauren's heart stopped.

The raggedy man in the square was shoved roughly to his
knees, and the bag ripped from his head. There, blinking in
the sun, was her father. Again the crowd roared, louder this
time. Their shouts and cries nearly drowned the voice of the
pope as he spoke.

"Jonathan Corvidae, you stand guilty of heresy, of witch-
craft, of devil worship, of bearing false witness, and of tempt-
ing the hearts of good men. Witness the infinite patience and
forgiveness of the Lord. Will you repent, cast down the false
prophet, and confess before the body of Christ?"

The pope gestured widely to the gathered masses, but John
was steady before the accusing shouts of the people. Though
tears streamed down his face he was unbowed. Unashamedly
he held his head high and spoke as loudly as he could.

"I can confess to many sins, but loving my daughter is not
one of them. I am just a man, but I believe more truly in my
Lauren than in any God that would allow-"
His words were cut off as a stone thrown from the audience
struck him across the forehead, visibly dazing him and leaving
a nasty gash. The guards surrounding her father tightened
their ranks, and police rushed to secure the man who had
thrown the rock.

Lauren felt dizzy, her breath short as she held the wood of
the bar with a death-grip. The single, violent action threatened
to send the crowd into an uncontrolled frenzy. The pontiff had
a grim look on his face as answered John's words.
"Then let it be witnessed; as shepherd of the flock of God, and
an agent of Christ, we will cast down this wickedness to the

Pit. For it is ever the charge of Good Men to fight the agents of Evil."

Lauren screamed, her hands flying to cover her mouth as the crowd surged forward and engulfed her father. The guard surrounding him held their ground for only a brief moment before being driven back by the lethal crush. Police tried to get to him, and many officers were dragged into the press and disappeared from sight as the pope prayed.

"St. Michael the Archangel, defend us in battle. Be our defense against the wickedness and snares of the Devil. May God rebuke him, we humbly pray, and do thou, O Prince of the Heavenly Hosts, by the power of God, thrust into hell Satan, and all the evil spirits, who prowl about the world seeking the ruin of souls. Amen."

The coverage cut swiftly back to a horrified reporter, who stared open-mouthed at something off camera.

"I... we're very..."

Lauren threw the bottle in her hand, unwilling to believe. The bottle exploded into a thousand pieces as it impacted the TV, destroying it in a shower of glass and shattered LCD crystals.

She raged like a hurricane.

Lauren ripped through the delicate glassware hanging above the bar, casting shards tinkling off of the walls of the small room. She ripped an expensive looking painting from the wall beside her and smashed it against the bar, gouging the wood and shredding the canvas. She pulled the television from the back-splash and dashed it to the ground, as though it were somehow responsible for her father's death.

Bottle after bottle crashed against the walls, expensive liquor staining the plush carpet of the floor and the pristine walls.

She was wanton in her destruction, her rage-filled screams echoing throughout the plane.

Seconds after her rampage began, a steward burst through the door, confusion apparent on his face. He narrowly dodged a bottle as it impacted the door inches from his head, showering his face with brandy and glass fragments. He retreated, as quickly as he'd entered.

In his haste to leave he ran into Dustin, who shoved roughly past him, slamming him against the wall of the aircraft.

Dustin burst into the bar-room, weapon drawn. Lauren was a living maelstrom of violence; unbridled, righteous anger of such magnitude that for a moment even Dustin was afraid.

Her wide but unseeing eyes cast a baleful gaze upon him and he knew her fury was such that she didn't even recognize him. Screaming and incoherent, she stripped one of the barstools from the screws that held it to the floor and launched it across the room at him.

Dustin ducked back behind the door, which shook with the impact of the blow.

"No one is to enter this room without my express permission."

He left the steward cowering on the floor as he walked past and pulled out his phone.

The staff of the aircraft cast furtive, terrified looks towards the closed door of the bar as the flight drug on. Lauren had raged for nearly four hours before the room had fallen eerily silent.

Lauren was sitting amid the splintered remains of the once-proud bar.

Lauren stared blankly at the mountains of shattered glass, jagged scraps of wood, and battered walls that surrounded her. Her fingers and hands were only now healing fully. They were covered in glass, in liquor, and in thick ragged cuts and bruises.

Even the pain of the fractures in her knuckles and fingers were like light scratches against the devastating pain in her heart.

She felt like a ship, tossed by storms in an ocean of despair. She sought desperately for a sign, a light in the darkness.

She could feel herself sinking when she finally saw them; two anchors in the storm. Two cracked but unbroken bottles offering salvation.

Lauren crawled to them, pulling herself through the wreckage to the only way out that she could see. She didn't bother to read the labels, not even to see how strong they were. She only hoped they were strong enough. She tore open the cap of the first and drank as fast as she could, moving to the second as soon as it was emptied.

She begged the harsh, clear liquid to bring her darkness.

When Dustin finally braved the room once more, after nearly an hour of silence, he found her among the remains of her tirade.

Lauren lay there, breathing shallowly in a pile of rubble, shattered glass, and vomit.

The room reeked of alcohol and despair.

Reaching down, he gently picked her up and carried her from the room. He paid no mind to the mess, cradling her gently like a child and taking her to the washroom of the plane.

Dustin cleaned her up as best he could. He wiped her face, hands, and arms down with a clean, damp cloth before brushing the dirt and debris from her hair and feathers. Dissatisfied, but unable to do any more, he carried her back to their section of seating.

Dustin placed her softly into a reclined chair and covered her with a blanket, then took his own seat. He brooded silently beside her, watching the news with the volume muted and subtitles on.

Lauren woke to the turbulent rocking of the airplane. She kept her eyes closed at first, wishing that she wasn't *really* awake. Wishing that she wouldn't *ever* have to be awake again. But her steady heartbeat and clear, hangover-free head reminded her of the curse of her invulnerability though.

Would she ever be free?

Lauren couldn't help but tear up, her soft cries slowly building in intensity. She felt a warm hand on her back and stiffened for a moment before she realizing it must be Dustin. It was amazing how that simple gesture calmed her soul. Dustin wordlessly rubbed her back between her shoulders, and she silently thanked him.

"Lauren, I want you to know this won't go unanswered. Not even the pope can murder an American citizen without retribution."

So he was definitely dead. Her gentle crying became deep, shuddering sobs.

"I promise you. I *swear* to you I'll keep you safe."

They sat in silence a while before he spoke again.

"Lauren, we're rerouting from JFK to Chicago, alright?"

She was silent, so he continued speaking.

"The weather's a little rougher, but we think we can avoid most of the more... active crowds. You'll have a home-field advantage, there's still a lot of support for you out there, especially in the Midwest."

What else was there to lose, Lauren thought bitterly to herself as she buried her head deep in her arms.

"I know it seems bad right now, and I won't lie to you and say I have a magic fix to make it go away.

She offered no response.

"My... my dad always used to tell me something. Picture life as a stream, right? Sometimes a boulder gets tossed in the stream, and it seems like it's going to block the way forever. But life trickles on, and eventually, eventually that rock wears down. Life will take that jagged rock that seems impossible to move past, and before long it'll just be more sand on the river bank."

Lauren sniffled, half smiling despite her sorrow.

"You're *awful* at analogies," she mumbled softly.

"Well, my dad was anyway," he corrected her gently. "But I'm not much better."

After a long pause Lauren spoke again, her voice barely above a whisper.

"I don't hate you."

"I know."

Chapter 14

The rest of the flight was uneventful. Lauren drifted fitfully in and out of sleep, haunted by storms in her nightmares every bit as real as the one raging outside the plane.

Finally giving up the pretense of sleep when the plane began its descent, Lauren turned her red, tired eyes to her caretaker.

He looked worried.

"What happens when we land?"

"Honestly, I'm not sure."

He chewed his lip.

"There will be other Marshals there, local police as well. Don't be surprised if there are crowds. Things like this rarely stay as secret as we'd like..."

Her pulse quickened, the press of crowds seemed so much more menacing in the wake of Rome. As if to underscore her concern the plane lurched wildly, dropping a few hundred feet as it hit a dead spot in the air.

She looked out the window. The aircraft was swimming through a rough sea of dark thunderclouds. Lightning flashes illuminated the wings and heavy rain pounded the thin aluminum of the hull.

As she watched, they broke through the low cloud-cover and the city opened up below her. Towering skyscrapers dotted a bleak, concrete wasteland far removed from the open country she called home.

Lauren's thoughts turned to the Shawnee, to the only place that seemed to hold comfort for her anymore. But those thoughts were tainted, too, poisoned by the nightmares that haunted her. The forest had been a dream as well, perhaps. A misguided illusion that she could somehow live apart from all the madness of the world.

A loud peal of thunder dragged her back to the present. It shook the skies and she gripped the armrests of her seat as the plane rocked and swayed in the sky.

I wonder if I'd die if we crashed.

She tried to shake the morbid thought, but it stuck stubbornly in her mind. Looking at Dustin she realized that to find out he would certainly perish as well.
The thought of it was terrifying.

He was her only remaining tether to sanity. Lauren made a pact with herself, she wouldn't let harm come to him. She had failed too many times before to protect the ones she loved.

She would be his guardian, she needed to be.

"Wheels down in five."

A steward, clearly still frightened by Lauren, poked his head into the cabin to deliver the news.

Dustin said nothing, simply nodding his understanding. The plane tore through the sky, buildings and streets whipping past as they descended into the heart of the city. The dimly lit streets below were fairly empty, for Chicago. The weather, it seemed, was keeping most drivers at home. As they neared the airport, however, traffic picked up. Lauren was left with a frightened, sinking feeling that word had gotten out of her arrival.

The last few minutes of flight were harrowing, the aircraft bounced and bucked through the high winds like a stallion. At

last the tires hit the runway with a screech and the plane
slowed.

Dustin's phone rang immediately.
"Yes... how many?"

Lauren tried to read his tone, his body language, but he was
back to his poker-faced self. He motioned wordlessly for her
to stand as the plane neared the terminal.
"Got it. Understood."
He ended the call abruptly, dropping the phone into his
pocket and looking over his shoulder at Lauren. She examined
him, his proud chest and wide shoulders. His face was so
much more expressive than Lauren had first thought. She had
learned to notice the differences in his eyes, the way he held
his chin. Her eyes were drawn to his split lip, it was still puffy
and red.

"You should let me fix your face," she said, tactless as ever.

"And what *exactly* is wrong with my face," he actually
smiled a little.

"You know what I meant."
"I do, but I like it. Reminds me not to mess with you," he
winked warmly at her.
He's never this... open, she thought darkly to herself. He must
be worried.

"Lauren, no matter what happens you need to stick with
me. We'll get you through this, ok?"
She nodded.

A pair of marshals met them at the door to the plane, they
had stopped short of the terminal and the staircase had been
lowered to the rain-slick asphalt.
"Ma'am, for your safety we need you to remain behind us at
all times, do you understand?"
Lauren nodded again. Beyond the officers was a ring of armed
police, they had surrounded the aircraft in the moments since
it landed.

Her eyes widened with fright as she gazed upon a massive, ever-growing crowd pressed against barricades that had been erected at the edge of the tarmac.

The people were rendered inhuman by the weather. Their motions made jerky and strange in the eerie, intermittent flashes of lightning that illuminated the darkness. The airport's floodlights battled the crushing blackness of the stormy skies and the torrential downpour soaked Lauren to the bone and obscured her vision.

"Why aren't the vehicles here on the tarmac," Dustin questioned the officers angrily, shouting to overcome the volume of the thundering rain.
"There was no way to keep-"
"I don't have time for excuses. We need to get her inside a vehicle and moving right now."

The policeman chafed at Dustin's tone, but he nodded curtly. He turned back down the stairs, starting down them with one hand on the rail and the other on his sidearm.

Lightning flashed, setting half of Dustin's face in deep shadows as he turned once more to Lauren.
"Remember. Stick with me, no matter what."

Together they hurried down the stairs, the rain coming down with such force that it stung Lauren's skin. The closer they got to the crowd of onlookers the slower Lauren walked, and the wilder the people became. More than a hundred officers in riot gear were holding the crowd back when Lauren and her entourage reached the perimeter.

The crowd lulled briefly, like a deep breath before a plunge. Dustin cast Lauren a grim look, then turned back to the crowd. He pulled his sidearm and put his off-hand hand on the back of the officer in front of him, taking firm grasp of his bullet proof vest and helping him push into the crowd.

The riot police folded in around them, a dense bubble of security that forced it way into the madness.

Lauren swiftly lost all sense of direction, the crowd seemed to tower over them, pressing the group tighter and tighter. The frenzied faces of the masses were dark and shadowed, lit only briefly by brilliant flashes of lightning. Their drenched hands reached past the officers, clawing at the air to reach her.

Dustin was yelling something over his shoulder to her, but the roar of the people was too loud. She couldn't make it out. The only sound that could compete with the din of the crowd was the earthshaking blasts of thunder that tore through the sky.

Lauren tried to focus on Dustin's back. She tamped down the fear in her heart, sealing it off with grim determination and total faith in his leadership. He alone seemed taller than the crowds. He was a mountain in the sea, a lighthouse taking her to safety.

Another flash lit the crowd, this one less bright but much closer. The voices surrounding her took on a different tone; an angry buzz like ten thousand hornets. The flash was repeated three more times in rapid succession and Lauren knew it wasn't lightning.

She watched with terror as officers at the edge of the group were dragged into the crowd, flashes of light and the reports of gunfire flickering out into the crowd before being extinguished like candles in the wind. Their group picked up the pace, muzzle flashes breaking apart the thickest part of the crowd before them. They were just shy of a sprint as they pressed forward to some unknown destination.

Lauren could see flashing lights ahead, she could see fire trucks with high pressure hoses blasting into the crowds, knocking people off their feet and sending them tumbling across the asphalt head over heels. They were only a few dozen feet away when the crowd surged once more, a crashing wave desperate to reach her. They pushed in from every direction, undeterred by the threat of violence and fighting to reach her.

Suddenly, strangers were among them, three and four people per officer, dragging them violently to the ground while others made their way in closer to her innermost guardians.

A man loomed in front of Lauren from her left. His familiar face was illuminated in bizarre flashing red and blue. He was wiry, middle-aged, and his salt and pepper brown hair was buzzed into a sort military cut.

He grabbed her roughly by the shoulders, his eyes wide and manic and his voice shrill with passion.

"Your Grace, it's me!"

He shook her like a ragdoll, so hard she couldn't speak.

"It's me, your disciple, Eric! I found a way to save you from this, from these people! I'm going to set you free, so you can return to heaven and leave us who are unworthy of your gifts!"

He had a terrifying, cheek-splitting smile plastered on his face. The hairs on Lauren's neck stood straight out, and she had goosebumps completely independent of the freezing rain. She finally overcame her speechlessness, letting out a piercing scream.

Dustin appeared, wading through the chaos untouched. He grabbed Eric from behind, clamping his arms to his sides and lifting him bodily from the ground. Grunting, he threw Eric to the pavement where he impacted with a dull thud.

"Lauren!"

She could feel herself drawing inward. The faces of the crowd were shifting back and forth between their own violent human visages and the grinning, psychotic wolves of her nightmares. She shut her eyes to their slobbering, gnashing, razor-sharp teeth as they tore their way through her defenders.

"Lauren, we have to move right now."

She shook her head, still screaming. She could feel herself getting short of breath, but she couldn't seem to stop, an endless wail of terror left her lips as the world crashed in around her.

"Lauren," he lowered his voice, no longer shouting. "Lauren you have to trust-"

Three loud bangs interrupted him, he was backlit briefly by three close-range flashes of light and blood sprayed out from his chest onto her stunned face.

A confused look crossed his face as he slumped to the ground, revealing Eric on the ground with a stolen handgun and an even more maniacal grin.

Eric was bleeding from a nasty cut on his forehead and one of his wrists was bent at an odd angle, but he seemed immune to the pain. His wide, bloodshot eyes were trained on Lauren.

"*See*? See! I'm going to protect you, Your Grace!"

He rose unsteadily, blood pouring into his eye and giving him a demonic appearance. He lifted the handgun, pointing it shakily at Lauren's chest.

"I'm going to send you *home*, Your Grace. I owe you this, for the gift you gave me! *This* is the mission you saved me for!"

He pulled the trigger twice, still smiling.

Lauren felt the rounds punch through her frail chest. She felt a visceral tearing, then a white hot heat followed swiftly by an icy chill that worked its way through her body. Numbness was spreading quickly from the bullet wounds. She tasted copper in her mouth, and shuddered, not knowing if it was Dustin's blood or her own. She fell to her knees, clutching her shattered chest and taking gasping, gurgling breaths through unbearable pain.

"I'll be there, waiting for you, Your Grace."

Eric put the gun to the side of his head and closed his eyes in obvious ecstasy.

"Thank you."

He pulled the trigger again, the flash of light illuminated a spray of brain matter and bone fragments from the opposite side of his head.

Lauren flinched as hot blood showered her face, but her mind immediately returned to Dustin. The rest of the world seemed to dull, and her vision swam as she crawled past Eric to Dustin, who was lying on his back. She could see his chest rising and falling, albeit shallowly.

She still had a chance.

"Dustin, Dustin," she croaked weakly, pulling herself up to him.

He didn't respond, his eyes were clenched shut, his breaths short and quick. Blood was draining slowly from his mouth. She could see clearly the three ragged holes where Eric's bullets had torn through. Every breath he took seemed to rattle and gurgle, much like her own. She could see a bloody foam bubbling up from one of his gunshots every time he took a breath.

Lauren struggled to rip open his ballistic vest. From such close range it had proved ineffective against the powerful handgun.

With every passing second she could feel her strength returning, so she fought through the excruciating pain.

"Lau-" Dustin sputtered, unable to complete even a single word for the blood in his throat. He weakly reached a hand up. Lauren gripped his outstretched hand with all her might, willing her power to work and rescue him from the pain she could see written on his face.

He blinked away the rain pouring down on them, mouthing silently at her. His eyes had the saddest expression she had ever seen. His body shuddered, and he winced as he was clearly wracked with pain.

Lauren was confused. Her own wounds were healing as well as ever but nothing seemed to be happening to Dustin. His breaths were getting shallower, his pulse weaker, even the strength in his grip was fading. He reached a shaky hand up, brushing a wet strand of hair from her face and tucking it behind her ear, unintentionally smearing blood across her face as he did.

He opened his eyes wide, drawing a strained, raspy breath.

Revelation hit her like one of the bolts of lightning crashing down around her.

She could hear his voice tugging at her memory, tearing her heart to shreds.

"I chose this assignment you know. Volunteered for it, would you like to know why?"

She placed a hand on either side of his face, begging for her power to work, unwilling to believe that she would fail again. But he was already gone, his wide, vacant stare a hideous reminder of the treasure she'd lost without knowing she had.

"Dustin... Dustin!"

Screaming, she pounded her fists on his chest. The storm inside her rivaled and surpassed the one raging outside as she vented her anger.

"Why didn't you tell me!"

She was still there, oblivious to the carnage around her, shouting her rage to the heavens and trying to drag him back from the clutches of death, when a group of men grabbed her and started to pull her to the police vehicles in the distance.

She fought them with all her might, clinging to him, unable to let go. When at last they pried her desperate fingers from his clothes she went limp.

She was a silent, impotent prisoner in her own mind as they carried her body to the safety of the vehicles. Her heart felt like lead in her chest, or else a burning coal. A white hot searing pain that burned her mind clear of everything but the darkness overtaking her.

What else do I have to lose, she had asked herself.
Now she had an answer.

The next few minutes were a dull blur, like the still-playing soundtrack to a movie on a screen gone black. The passage of time was meaningless to her, as was the world.

She was loaded into a black SUV, one of a dozen, and driven at breakneck speeds away from the airport. Each of the SUVs had split off, no doubt an attempt to divert would-be pursuers.

Lauren had been whisked away from the riot by a group of men in neat black suits who silently conducted her about the city. After a half dozen vehicle transfers in settings that varied from an underground parking garage to an alley between two homes, she had been loaded at last into a sleek silver sedan with tinted windows and driven to the heart of Chicago.

They'd checked her quietly into a luxurious, high-rise hotel. She was taken in the back of the building and walked through conspicuously empty hallways until she reached an elevator that she took to the very top floor. The men left without intro-ducing themselves, replaced, they told her, by anonymous, 'plain clothes agents'.

She was free to come and go as she pleased, they said, but she was instructed not to try to slip her escort if she left the suite.

In other words: Don't try to avoid anyone suspiciously following you around after being attacked by strangers, because there's a chance it's the good guys who, while also anonymous strangers, will be there to protect you at all times.

As soon as the men left she drifted through the empty rooms like a ghost, stopping only when she found the bed-room and fell into the deep embrace of her nightmares.

She hadn't left the hotel since.

To her crushing disappointment, Lauren woke up again. It was the third day of her isolation. She felt cold and alone, laying in the center of a huge king sized bed. The rich, cream colored blankets were thick and the dark ebony sheets were soft as silk, but they felt wrong. They felt hollow, like this vast, immaculate suite.

She had two bedrooms, two bathrooms, a full-sized kitchen, even a sitting room, all decked out in sleek ivory and black.

But no one to share it with.

She was an empty vessel, a husk of her former self. Heartless, dead, trapped in a prison of youthful vigor.

For two days she had stewed in her emotions, not once leaving the suite, or even fully exploring it. They'd brought her a few boxes of clothes, and someone had ordered her room service a few times, but she'd only pecked at the food and left most of it uneaten.

She had no appetite.

The phone beside her bed rang, as it had a number of times since she'd arrived. She ignored it. Removing her head from under the covers she glared through the bright morning light. The message light on the phone was still blinking. She wondered absentmindedly just how many messages she had.

Reluctantly Lauren crawled from her bed, the hardwood floor was smooth on her bare feet as she made her way to the bathroom. She still had the sheet wrapped around her, it dragged behind like the train of a mournful funeral dress as she traversed the massive room. The master bathroom was huge, it had a bathtub set into the smooth, tiled floor as well as a walk-in shower. Lauren desperately wanted to soak in a hot bath, but her wings had made it impossible to figure out, at least so far. Instead, she slipped out of the sheet and stepped into the shower.

The hot shower did wonders for her worn, tired body, but nothing for her shattered psyche. As she scrubbed herself she dwelt on the fresh new scars from Eric's gunshots. So much for escape, she thought bitterly to herself, wishing the bullets had claimed her life, instead of her soul.

But even the relief of her aching joints was temporary. The moment she stepped from the shower the storm-clouds of worry and doubt brewing in her mind pulled her muscles taught with anxiety.

Her sluggish thoughts were interrupted by a loud, clear knock on the door. She paused, the suite was silent. She had just convinced herself she had imagined it when the knock came again, longer, louder, and more insistent.

Lauren forced herself to care just enough to seek out the source of the noise. She padded silently to the living room her wings dragging across the floor behind her. Lauren stood there dripping, gazing with flat, dull eyes at the door. As she watched, the handle turned and clicked, and the door started to open. She cocked her head to the side.

"Ms. Corvidae, are you there? I'm special agent Grant with the secret service," a woman's voice, clear and strong, called out from behind the cracked door.

Lauren, and the suite, were silent as a tomb.

"We just want to make sure you're ok, no one is going to hurt you... ma'am?"

The intruder pushed the door slowly, it opened with a whisper to reveal the sharp eyes of a thirty-something Latina with a stark black, no-nonsense ponytail and a finely tailored suit. She held a handgun. It looked just like Dustin's had.

Lauren was surprised, not at the dull ache in her heart when she noticed the similarity, but that it didn't hurt worse. Could it?

No.

The woman stood there, unsure of how to respond to Lauren's passive, unclothed form in front of her.

"Ma'am... a-are you ok?"

While Grant averted her eyes awkwardly, Lauren took stock of the woman in front of her. She was pretty, but not beautiful. She had laugh lines, but a furrowed brow. She whispered something into her coat sleeve and returned her weapon to the holster on her hip.

Lauren moved her lips to respond, but her voice didn't work. She cleared her throat, hoarse from screaming for hours on end each night.

"M'fine," she mumbled unconvincingly.

"I-is, is there... anything you need?"

Grant was looking at her now, at least, but she still seemed supremely uncomfortable.

Lauren didn't care.

Of course these people were going to check on her if she never answered the door or her phone. She should have expected them to intrude once more on the only solace she had left. Silence and solitude. At least alone she wasn't hurting anyone.

She knew that was a lie. She pondered for a moment the death toll that night at the airport. It felt like a lifetime ago, but she could picture with perfect clarity the bloodstained brass of the shell casings littering the tarmac. The fallen officers, dead in her name. The desperate, wretched men and women who had given their lives to reach her as well. Her burdened soul, already buckling, couldn't hold any more grief. Instead, it added just another layer of ice to her frozen heart.

"How many people have died because of me?"

She asked the question aloud, but didn't really know to whom. Nor did she expect an answer.

"In Chicago, ma'am?"

The fact that she'd had to clarify told Lauren everything she needed to know. She was still staring vacantly, and it was clearly unnerving her guest.

"We're um, we're working on a solution, ma'am." Something in the woman's words stirred Lauren's mind.

Solution.

But she remained silent, and the woman slowly retreated back to the door of the suite.

Before she left, she took one more concerned and confused look at Lauren.

"It's um, not your fault. Some of us still believe in you." With that, she bowed her head and took her leave. As the door clicked shut Lauren turned to face the floor to ceiling windows that lined one wall of the living room. They were clear glass overlooking the city.

Lauren knew the woman was wrong, as many others had been about her.

She turned to the boxes of clothes sitting on one of the couches. Each had a designer label on it, and probably cost as much as her old truck had. Absentmindedly she picked through the boxes, now nearly dry.

She uncovered a dress. Black and strapless, it reminded her of the last night she had seen Erin alive. She wanted to smile, or cry, but couldn't find the will to do either. Instead, she slipped into the garment. It was a close fit. By now she was used to people knowing intimate details about her like her dress size, it didn't even faze her.

She returned to the bathroom and pulled a hairbrush from the counter, analyzing herself in the mirror as she teased the knots and tangles from her long blonde locks.

Erin would have said she was beautiful. Before, that is.

She could almost see her speechless face, smell her perfume. She closed her eyes and treasured the brief stirring of warmth within her before it was replaced by icy despair once more.

She thought about her father. The man who had raised her despite the infidelity of her mother, despite the difficulties that he could have by rights walked away from.

She thought of his blood staining the time-worn stones of a thousand year old cathedral.

Her hair brushed to a luxurious shine, Lauren returned once more to the living room. She stared out the window at the city below.

She thought about Selimah, the woman who had been so frightened when she removed the scars of acid from her face.

She's probably dead too, Lauren thought, accused of witch-craft or disfigured again for someone else's slighted honor.

Looking around for something heavy, Lauren spied a dense marble statue on an end table. The smooth stone depicted a man and a woman locked in a lover's embrace. She lifted it, it was beautifully carved, flawless.

She thought about Gabriel, her beautiful brother. He had relied on her, and she had let him die. Her own invincibility had distracted her from his ailments. She should have been more careful, she accused herself mercilessly.

Spinning violently, she hurled the statue at the cool glass of the window, shattering it into a thousand jagged blades that blew out into the air like leaves in the wind. Strong gusts blew freezing air into the suite, swirling around the room and raising goosebumps on Lauren's arms and legs.

She thought about the boys in the horse barn. They had joyously told their parents she was an angel. Their family had invited her, a murderer, into their home.

"Round here we don't judge people for making mistakes, not as long as they fix them," Charlie had said to her that morning not long ago.

Well she couldn't.

She knew that now. She couldn't fix her mistakes, but maybe she could pay for them.

She stepped to the ledge of the window, taking a moment to observe the vast urban sprawl before her. She stepped through the hole in the glass, her wings coming open. Her dress clung to her in the wind, the hem blowing wildly as she rose higher and higher, passing the highest point of the high-rise.

As she climbed, straining ever harder as the air thinned, her thoughts turned to Erin.

Lauren's wings missed a beat as Erin's unbroken face came to her mind's eye. She nearly wept. She'd been haunted by her pallid, dead countenance for months, unable to recall her this way. Full of life and love and passion.

The dull drone of helicopters and sirens in the distance fell on deaf ears as the sleepy city took notice of her rising, shining figure in the sky.
She thought of the love that could have been, should have been. Of the journey cut short by her own stupidity.

Lauren hovered a moment, her wings wide, cupping the air as she held herself a thousand feet above the cruel streets below. Already she saw crowds gathering.

Yes, an angel these people had called her, and perhaps they were right. An angel of death, a harbinger of destruction, an embodiment of the cruel irony of good intentions. A dark beacon of the tragedy of power; that she alone should possess the ability to heal any wound, to bring someone back from the brink of death, and be powerless to stop the wanton destruction and shameless loss of life that followed her like a specter.

"I miss you. It ebbs and flows, but I'm never free of it. I'm drowning."

Whispering her confession to the empty air around her, she leaned back and folded her wings tightly.

For an instant she hung there, suspended by her last wing-beat like a feather in a strong breeze. But gravity tightened its grip on her and she began to fall.

Lauren closed her eyes, wondering as she plummeted from the sky if she would feel anything, or if she would finally be free.

Epilogue

Weyland looked out over the bustling roofs and busy streets of one of his favorite cities; Athens. People filled the streets, flowing like the current from some massive, sluggish river.

From his place upon the plateau all the sounds, sights, and smells of the city were diluted, reduced to a soft hum nearly 500 feet below.

He closed his eyes, soaking in the warm summer sun. The shining rays warmed his deep brown skin and filled him with peace. He breathed deeply of the salt air blowing in from the coast.

A deep thump sounded in the depths of his mind and a tremor flickered through the ground. Startled by the unfamiliar sound, Weyland opened his eyes.

The people below didn't seem to have noticed.

His brow furrowed. Certainly if he had felt it then the masses before him should have. He looked around, trying to find something, anything out of order. But the gulls drifting in the sea breezes kept their lazy course. The waves on the distant shores kept their steady beat. The hustle and bustle of the city went on undisturbed.

The soft sound of rustling feathers drew him from his contemplation, making him turn.

She was as radiant as he had ever seen her. The woman standing there was tall, lean, and tan. Her golden hair was sunshine brought to earth, her eyes were honey flecked with bronze. A cream-colored silk dress accented her most noticeable feature; A pair of snow-white wings, covered in broad, sleek feathers.

She flashed him a dazzling smile from across the courtyard.

The sight of his beloved against the backdrop of the massive marble columns of their estate cleared all worry from his mind. Truly, she was a goddess, and a worthy companion for his own station.

He stepped towards her, his own face breaking into a smile from her infectious grin.

Thump.

This time the sound hit him like a fist in the gut. He stumbled from the blow and shook his head to clear the ringing it had left in his ears. Worried, he looked back up at his bride.

She looked... different. The smile on her face seemed more forced, less warm. The Grecian morning lost a bit of its heat as the sun paled for a moment.

But she was there, still waiting for him.

He struggled towards her, his legs growing heavier with every step. His temper flared, and he shook himself. His powerful muscles flexed and suddenly he was free of the unseen burden upon him. The sun was once again warm and bright, and he could move just as easily as he ever had.

The sweat dotting his brow and his heavy breathing were the only physical side effects of the unknown weakness he'd experienced.

He looked down at himself. Everything appeared normal. His towering, seven-foot physique was as muscled and strong as it ought to be, his dark skin tight over sculpted flesh.

He recoiled when he again laid eyes upon his wife. Her shining golden hair had been replaced with wild, lightly curling darkness. Her eyes matched her new hair, as did her wings. The snowy feathers that he was used to looked like they were freshly dipped in the deepest black he had ever seen.

Her smile was a faint, cruel curl at the edge of her lips. Her arms were outspread, waiting for him, but he felt no welcome there. He took an involuntary step backwards.

As he did so, she spoke.

"Weyland *please*, I need you."

Her familiar voice was like velvet to his ears, enticing him.

"Weyland."

As she spoke, she returned to the form he was used to. His shining maiden once again. She sounded desperate.

A mere twenty feet separated them.

He sprinted towards her, driven by a sense of urgency he couldn't explain. His strong legs propelled him at inhuman speeds but the distance between them seemed only to grow.

Frustrated, he pushed himself, running harder and harder. She was speaking, but the wind rushing past his ears drowned out her words.

Thump.

www.ingramcontent.com/pod-product-compliance
Lightning Source LLC
Chambersburg PA
CBHW060437310726
48977CB00001B/231